# The Man
## The Past

## James Dodwell

*First Printing: 2017*

*James Dodwell Publishing*

*40 Percy Road*

*Isleworth*

*TW7 7HB*

*www.themanyfacesofthepast.com*

Twitter @tmfotp

*This edition is published as*

**ISBN** 978-1-9997299-0-5

# Chapter List

## Forty Four Years before the event...

The room sits shrouded in a dense haze. Cigarettes glow brightly, then wane. Smoke circles carelessly, joining an ever-growing swirl of smog. Within the small, ill-lit basement the effect is stifling. The place is a bustling mass of chattering bodies. Laughter rebounds off the walls and drowns out the background music. It is a tiny venue, but always rammed with more people than they should safely squeeze in.

There is a raucous atmosphere within the club, yet four men sit apart, their expressions sombre and detached. They are nestled within a partially hidden snug at the very rear of the building. The room thrums with life, but the group is stuck within their own reflections. They exchange wary glances and speak in deliberately hushed tones. They have been seated here for nearly an hour - plotting and arranging.

'This part of the plan must never go beyond the four of us. What we are talking of here, is a cataclysm.'

A rotund man, several years older than the first, waves his hand absently. 'We, my friend, are only doing what our Governments should have done. But they are neutered. They pander to the whims of the ignorant masses, while also being bullied by the chattering elite. It has therefore been left to us to enact this divine proclamation. *We* must correct the errors of our time. *We* must go beyond blinkered political interests. *We* must act, for the wider good!'

The man's speech draws nods of approval from around the table. They are already well on their way to setting their plan in motion, but they still appreciate hearing his rallying call. This will be their last meeting. From here, they must each individually face the enormity of what they are about to enact.

'Do you have the formula here?' The rotund man asks of a small, delicate looking person sitting opposite.

Soft fingers pass him a hand written set of numbers.

'It is possible that each of us may be picked off as we each strive, in our own ways, to bring this to fruition.' He takes back the note and pushes it into safety of his inner jacket pocket. 'If any of us should fall or fail in our own part of the wider task, someone else must step forward to fill that void. But whatever happens, we must carry on. We must somehow succeed.'

The small man stands and offers his hand to each of the others in turn. 'I wish you all the best of luck. God speed. May - *He* - forgive us for what we are about to do.' He then turns and paces from the room.

The remaining three sit and ponder in silence; about his leaving, their own departures, and what the future may bring.

'Shall I order another round? Or are you two off too?' The question is posed by an expensively dressed man. He exudes cold corporate calm. The others nod acceptance of a further drink, and with a determined swagger the City-man slips from his seat and sidles to the distant bar.

As soon as he is beyond earshot one of the men expresses his concerns. 'I don't trust him Dr Halesham?

The rotund man smiles to placate him. 'I don't *like* him Maximillian, but I do *trust* him. In truth, we are all now bound to each other in a way that exceeds and outstrips such feelings. For what we must do, we require more than trust. We must *believe*. This mission must take us beyond the small mindedness and petty squabbles that so beset and stifle daily life. I long ago realised that I need not *like* this man. But *we will* work with him. He has something very specific to offer our venture, and we could probably not make this work without him freeing up adequate finance.'

The younger man nods understanding. Although uncomfortable at the prospect of having to rely on someone that he does not like, he is completely convinced by their wider purpose.

'I have recommended you for a position at the Broxston Institute.' The large man states. 'You will be running their Symbiosis projects. It will be a Professorship Max. It is no more than you would have deserved anyway...eventually...but these things take far too long to unfold. So I had them fast-track the promotion. Your placement there will serve our purposes perfectly.' He offers a hand to his friend. 'Congratulations are in order.'

The spectacled man beams. He had not expected this, and is overcome with both pride and appreciation.

Looking over his mentors shoulders, his grin is cut short. He notices a commotion in the cramped confines of the doorway. Someone is struggling to get through the door. There is fighting. Alarm grips the entire room. The outburst of unexpected violence elicits a stunned reaction. The crowd are caught, transfixed by the aggression. A murmur hangs mingling within the dense blue smoke. There is uncertainty and anticipation on every set of lips.

The rotund man signals to his corporate colleague, who then slips as subtly as possible from the serving area.

'We must leave. Now!'

They had already propped the rear Fire Door ajar, and now use it to make good their escape.

The front door finally smashes open. The club offers a

collective gasp. Battered and bleeding, a delicate little man is manhandled into the bar area by burly security-type individuals. No-one in the bar recognises this bruised little man. The three men who would have known him have already exited the premises. They had foreseen what was about to unfold and are now mounting the rear staircase. They can hear screams and shouts accompanying a manic eruption of panic in the bar below. They know that this chaos will slow their pursuers, but they still hold desperate fears. For all of their bold words and meticulous planning, not one of them had really expected to be caught. They would not waste time now thinking of what would befall their captured colleague. But an ingrained terror chills their blood and speeds there exit. None of them wants to find out what it will feel like to be strapped to a chair in a dark room, and forced to tell all that you know. They are certain that their colleague can't be connected to any of them directly - even when put under the harshest of duress. But knowing what sort of persuasion

At the top of the stairs they find the way barred. Some busy-body member of staff must have found the door open and thought it their duty to close and lock it. That this was supposed to be an emergency exit, had obviously escaped their attention. The three men are now trapped fast.

There is a rasping ring as a gun fires below, which only serves to increases the volume of the clamouring people trying to escape the bar. It also serves to stress the urgency with which the three men must get through the barred exit. But after several kicks and shoulder barges

9

it is obvious that the door will never give.

'I will need to pick the lock.' The spectacled man states. Panic rings his words.

'There isn't time. They will soon reach the rear exit.'

'It is the only option!'

The corporate face acknowledges the truth of this. The rotund man turns away and starts to descend.

'Where are you going sir?'

'You need time. I will hold them off. You two must get away. You must set events in motion.' His forced smile cannot hide his expected fate. 'Get that lock undone. I'll do what I can to stop them. You may though, need to fulfil my own part of this process. I fear I will now be unable to do it myself!'

He is gone before Max can protest. The reality of the situation forces back his tears and speeds him to the lock. It gives way surprisingly easily. The suited man pushes out, and with a nod he is off into the darkness beyond. The academic is torn. Should he return to try to save his friend and benefactor. There must, he feels, still be a chance that he can? He can't just leave him! He must at least try - for his own peace of mind, if nothing else.

The decision is actually taken from him. He can hear a scuffle at the bottom of the stairs. A shot echoes up from below. There is a scream by an unknown voice 'Aghh my leg...'

There is then a volley of shots - this time accompanied by a very familiar voice. At first the old man screeches out in pain, but it soon turns to a groan, and then there is the thud as he hits the floor. His mentor has been shot. The enemy is now very much at the gate. He no longer has a choice but to flee.

The cold darkness wraps around him as he stumbles through the doorway. He has paced this route a dozen times in preparation for this day. He had never thought that this *worst case scenario* would possibly happen for real. Yet know that he actually has to do this, he is relieved at the intricate planning they had undertaken. Left. Left. Right. Straight for two minutes or so... Even in the pitch black of the alleyways between the decrepit old buildings he is confident he knows the way out. The route is clear in his mind and he speeds forward. Behind him he can hear the calls and shouts of his pursuers as they exit the Fire Door. The dark shroud at the back of the buildings is all encompassing. Without knowledge of this maze like alley system, you would easily get lost here. They are now way behind him, and he is nearly at the park. Once within the cover of the trees and bushes, he should free of them for good.

As he finally turns the last alleyway-corner he tumbles out onto a busy commercial street. In the far distance he sees the shape of a smart suited man disappearing from view. Though he has absolutely no care for the man, he can't help but be relieved that he has also managed to escape. His thoughts fly back to his friend that hasn't. He can only hope that the gunshot killed him straight out. He can't bear to think of him having to endure the abuse that would inevitably accompany being caught alive. He feels sick at wishing a close friend dead, yet knows too that it would be merciful.

As he jumps and clambers over the fence and into the park, the trees seem to close in to protect him. He jogs on feeling safer already. This will be the first day proper of their mission. Tomorrow he will take up the pre-arranged Professorship. From there - he will set his part of the events in motion - as agreed.

# Part One - Now…As it soon shall be.

## Chapter 1 - The Body

The lab is alive with activity. Assistants move to-and-fro, their white coats swishing in tandem to their movements. Sterilised instruments lay gleaming on pristine surfaces, all relentlessly scoured by face-masked minions who sweep like ghosts from room to room. The air is tepid. A smell of chlorine is just determinable at a point high in the nostrils.

Ben stands in the centre of the throng, as a rock in a stream. The attendants ignore and work around him. He walks over to the new *patient*, leans over him and stares intently. He wonders what it was that this particular person has seen that is of such importance. It must have been something very significant, as it has cost a considerable amount of time and money to get him here.

The *patient* is being held in limbo, at the very limits between here and gone. He is neither dead, nor alive, but instead lies within a nether zone. He will remain trapped within this artificial purgatory until his mind has been accessed and his memories plundered. He has been linked to the machines through every orifice. Many additional probes, tubes and cable-ways have been specially cut into various vital access points. Ben looks down at him and tries to imagine him *alive*. But all he can now see is a distorted husk, being temporarily suspended in an induced state. The man's fate now is akin to teetering on a narrow ledge. One slip, and there will be an inevitable fall towards death. At present though, his mind is still accessible and so he is a valuable resource - which the Company will tap for everything they can possibly take.

Ben wanders around the room. He is not needed at this stage of the procedure, but he still routinely comes in to the lab to see how things are progressing. He is always keen to see who he will converge with. He also enjoys watching the reaction of the staff when each new body is brought in. No matter how hardened and professional the attendants are, they always show signs of fear and disgust. Ben believes that what the staff actually see is their own mortality - a realisation that they too will one day be robbed of essence and being. It is a disturbing image, and one that any normal person would avoid. Yet here, they are all faced with that chilling notion every single day - for that is the very nature of their work.

Ben spots a nurse approaching the prostrate patient. Her job is to *administer general medical care*. He knows this, because he is using his implant to blink-read her Staff Profile. Such information is technically strictly confidential, but Ben has somehow managed to break the firewall. The Company is very particular about who gets into its labs. It does not flinch at breaching any number of international laws in order

14

to fully ascertain what the staff are 'up to' in their daily lives. Ben was aware of their illegal activities from the moment the Company had forcibly taken control of his research project. The more effort they put into keeping their files hidden, the more interesting they became to him. He had long ago hacked a Trojan into their core system - so that nothing that they do is ever really a secret to him at all. Ben stops scrolling through the nurse's file and switches his attention to focus upon her face instead. He leans on one of the lab walls and ghoulishly registers her involuntary recoil as she works around the prone figure. 'Mortality; writ large'. He voices quietly to no one but himself, and smiles devilishly as he continues to observe her discomfort.

Eventually growing bored of the spectacle, Ben returns to again look at the man he must read. Flicking back to his implant, he looks through the accompanying research file, in an attempt to understand the person whose mind he will soon experience. *Mr William G Montgomery* - his notes read - mid-level executive. Middle age, mid height, mid weight, mid income.

'Bloody hell! Middle bloody everything.'

He is tempted to stop reading about what he now considers a tedious little man - but also knows that he really must try and find a way to assess what it is that Montgomery holds. Ben has been through this procedure so many times it has become a ritual. His routine is important, and could well be the difference between a good or bad result. He is all too well aware that he *must* try to get a wider handle on this man, and to tie down the general details of his life. If he can get a clear grasp of who Montgomery was, it will not be such a shock to his own mind when he experiences him through the machine. Despite knowing all this Ben really can't help but wonder why The Company is keeping Montgomery alive. He appears to be of no social note or strategic worth what-so-ever. He wasn't a corporate celebrity or an executive high-flier. He definitely wouldn't have been seen on the exclusive pan-multinational circuit. His notes show that he didn't even have a data-log or tracker. Apparently, no-one even wanted to follow his movements or to catalogue his experiences.

'If he wasn't even important enough for anyone to care where he was or what he was doing when he was alive, then what the hell is he doing here now?' Ben again voices to himself.

Having pushed the seemingly useless notes into the virtual bin he feels a pang of guilt at his lack of professionalism. He reaches for the obligatory printed copy of the patient notes. They are always laid out somewhere in the lab. It has become standard practice to have a hard copy available, in the event of a systems crash. Having everything available on paper would mean that the staff would not be robbed of all their records. Having picked up this version of Montgomery's file, it all suddenly becomes suddenly clear. A written sub-note. No more, no less. It is not on the computer files - he has already been back into his implant and checked. And even here on the written file, it could easily have been overlooked as a meaningless scribble. Yet, it is in fact, Ben figures, the key to what this entire convergence will involve.

16

*Operative Lost. Please Retrieve Collected Data.*

A bulb flashes in his mind and Ben apologises to Mr
Montgomery. He now knows what and who this man is - or rather
was. Montgomery was a professional, and judging by a quick
reassessment of his case notes - a very good one. He didn't want the
world to see him, yet he was standing squarely in the very middle of the
picture. This man had created a perfect void where no-one noticed
him. He had managed to be so average that he was almost invisible.
Not having a data chip or log now made complete sense too - if you
don't want people to see you, you don't offer them any means to
observe you. Ben now understands exactly why Mr Montgomery is
here. He has seen something. Indeed, something of great importance.
Someone had apparently not wanted that information to be relayed any
further, and had shot him. Luckily, the medics had managed to keep
him from slipping away completely. Montgomery could never be
revived, but he could certainly still be read. Ben sparks with
excitement, savouring the thought of finding out what his secret is.

Ben reads through the rest of the collected documents with a
renewed interest, looking for any and all other essential tit-bits. The
facts of our lives are always written down. No matter how good a non-
entity Mr Montgomery was, he would still leave a trail - of sorts. It
might not be readily available to most sources, but then, Ben is not just
doing vehicle checks, or assessing tax records. He is mapping the entire
route of a man's life - from start to *near* end. There is always
something, somewhere that offers a starting point for investigations.

He concentrates on the files with undivided focus. Something would become apparent - as it has so many times before...

But no matter how much he tracks back over the details, the path is mundane. It lists his job, his educational achievements, his holiday locations - all standard and normal. The only thing that keeps flashing back into Ben's attention, is the repeated references to his home. It is not necessarily unusual for his *convergent* to have built notions of solidity around a stable home-life. But it is peculiar in Montgomery's case, because he had distanced himself from everything else. The profile of his history should just show his home as his *present abode*. Yet here, it really does appear to be the centre of this man's world. Ben decides that he will start his investigations there - Once he gets inside.

Ben puts the case notes on the side table next to the cradle upon which he himself will rest for the convergence. He re-checks all the cables and wiring. They have already been checked twice by the resident staff, and will be again before he goes fully under. However, like a skydiver preparing to leave the hangar, he wants to know with certainty that his parachute has been packed correctly, and that it will have a better than likely chance of opening. He scans the room and ascertains that all is as it should be, where it should be, and that all emergency equipment is fully serviced and within reach. He has seen too much go wrong to risk even one of these tasks. The procedure is administered in much the same way as a standard hospital operation. Checklists are ticked, and questions answered, and although much of it

18

is routine, it is a vital platform for a safe return.

Within his cradle an hour later, Ben verifies that all the connections to the Interface device are correct and that all is to his satisfaction. The machine is permanently on, but there is a discernible upgrade of sound and motion as the actual departure time approaches. The convergence aperture is then set to allow for an entry to occur.

At first nothing noticeable happens...then...slowly...*I feel the ebb tide of consciousness move away from me as I transfer into darkness*... No matter how many times he completes this process it always catches him unawares when *the darkness swarms and then dissipates around me.* The feeling is not unpleasant, but is disorientating. The paradox begins, *I actively rest my mind,* he forces himself to relax. Ben has always been able to withstand the wider rigours of the crossover. It is this, the experts say, that effectively makes him unique at being able to complete this process. *Definite shapes blur and distort. Movement is constant but directions are indiscernible and uncertain. The scene sweeps and glides back in and around upon me.* Through experience he has developed a clearly defined strategy to help himself through what would otherwise be a catastrophic trauma. He knows to avoid thinking of his consciousness becoming stripped away from his very being. In the laboratory, his body lays motionless, betraying nothing of the arduous rampage that has ensnared his mental world. He actively ignores his mental faculties as they are artificially inserted into a mechanical realm. A place where two worlds collide. *Darkness drifts past and light washes upon me. It is at first vague, but rises and spreads. Once it is even, the definition returns, in stages...I am drawn to the senses*

19

*and feelings that envelop my becoming…and in a final twist, I swirl into - an experience scenario.*

The scene I have entered is residential - it appears to be a suburban home. I have just awoken. I am in bed. The soft pillow nestles comfortably around my resting head. The duvet is tucked snugly around me. It is extremely comforting, and I have to force myself to get up. I scan my eyes around the area. The room is decorated with standard furnishings - things that would be available in chain stores in every town and city across the continent. The walls are tellingly magnolia. The curtains are of light material, allowing the sun to float through - along with wafts of a summer breeze.

Across the room is a data-log. It is distinct from everything else. Despite the blandness of this place, it is definitely a homely home. The computer is very much a separate appliance. It is glaringly different from its surroundings. I move from the bed. There is a chair besides a dressing table in the corner of the room. I pull it over and sit to look at the log-unit. The gadget is open (apparently on stand-by). I had thought that it was off, but when I moved my gaze across the screen, it instantly sprang to life. A file - entitled TD&TD - opens before me. I flick through it briefly, digesting what I can of the information. As tedious as it is, I return to the beginning again and again, to remember as much of the file as possible. The key feature is a long sequence of code. I am used to making such retrievals, and although it has a complicated layout, I will use a special mnemonic system to memorise it.

Having read and practised the sequence repeatedly, I feel sure I have retained it. I now need to distract myself from the code. If I think of it again I may reorder and alter it. I should leave the room.

I walk down the stairs. Halfway down is a viewing platform. From here I can see that the ground floor is large and open-plan. There are huge windows on all sides, which allow the warm sun to radiate freely. It is a contemporary design, but still not particularly interesting. Nothing jumps out at me saying 'This is my home'. There are no particular features of note, just standard prints, again readily available from anywhere. There is a neatness about it. But you can still tell that it is a lived-in space. There is though, nothing here that explains why so many cues in Montgomery's file kept pushing me towards this place.

Suddenly there is a click-crunch which catches me off guard. My heart stops. A key has accessed the lock. The front door swings opens. Caught in a semi-daydream I had not been vigilant. I am frozen to the spot. I don't know whether to run, or stand my ground. The door swings wide and a woman enters backwards. This at first seems strange, but then I realise she is carrying a mass of shopping bags and is having to force her way through. She has obviously just returned from the grocers. She eventually turns. On seeing me on the stairs - where I am still frozen like a terrified child - she greets me warmly. My heart still races, but I act. I smile back at her and scamper forward. I offer her a helping hand. She smiles more broadly, and kisses me softly on the cheek. I take as many bags as I can carry. She thanks me and walks ahead of me to the kitchen area.

It is only in such moments of intimacy, at times where genuine affection is exhibited, that I feel the subject I inhabit as being a real person. Although I am only *within* his body, my heart still aches. I cannot help but realise that this is the last time he - through me - will ever again see this pretty and affectionate young lady - whom I know from his file-notes to be his wife. The love she shows is plain and honest. It truly wrenches. My heart aches, as I gaze through these eyes, into a face that loves him.

And all I can really now see is the realisation of this couples loss. I can feel my tears start to well.

I am acutely aware that I will soon leave, and with that departure they will be separated forever. It is at times such as this that I wish there was an afterlife. I crave is for the possibility of these two people, one day being together again. I search for something to say, something appropriate, something that she really needs to hear.

'I love you', I splutter. Her face lights with a beam that splits open what semblance I had of an objective soul.

*I can sense the first step of being drawn backwards towards the window of the void. The movement folds round and drags at me.* There is no control of the process, and no-one can stop the reversal. *I crave to stay here, looking upon her face. For as long as I can. Forever, if it be possible. But, no! All turns to haze and is shrouded in mists of static. I know that she is now gone from me…from him.* He *will not see her, hear her, feel her, love her every again. The pain of this thought is stifling and overwhelming. I want to cry out, to scream, to rage.*

*Instead - I fall into nothingness and darkness subsumes me.*

*I suddenly re-enter within a different scenario – another experience scene. I know that I am now completely separated from what I had seen and felt before.* Sliding between these inner-worlds is effortless. Although erratic and uncontrollable, movements within the void feel as fluid as the ocean. *I wash serenely into the new surroundings and begin to move within this new place.*

The scene, or possibly the location is familiar, but I can't put my finger on where it is.

I just know…that something…is wrong here. I'm not watching this scene through Montgomery - as before. I am actively experiencing this world.

There is a heat haze hanging across the lower atmosphere. The density of the air is like a wavering nothingness, a disorientating sheen of hovering movement. It both dances around and clings to everything within the street. The lack of a breeze offers a sullenness to the scene. The buildings are bleached by the intensity of the powerful summer sun. I can see scorched rows of tall buildings, their facades gleaming brightly. The grass in the city square that surrounds me is scorched brown and lays tinder dry. The trunks and branches of monstrous London Plane trees tower defiantly upwards from the baked soil. The small islands of shade they provide offers sanctuary from the relentless midday glare.

I don't know why...but I feel...that I must move from this park. I am compelled to run...I force myself forward. Each motion performed within the direct glare of the unforgiving sun. The running makes me sweat, and heat of my body is now only adding to the relentless discomfort caused by the raging sun. Each beat of my heart stokes a fire within my muscles. As inside burn, the sun scolds.

I push myself on along the empty streets. Onward...stammering...faltering...becoming too much to bear.

How much of this can I take?

I feel an unnatural rotation, my head hits the hard burning walkway, my shoulder crunching down after, then the rest of me slides and lays prostrate on the searing stone. I begin to swim in a distant, cool and separate place. The heat was too much, all too much for any man to bear. Consciousness escapes me. I think...no more...

---

I can't fully register...I don't know...where I am.

I have become used to entering strange scenarios. I am familiar with being within worlds built from other peoples experiences. Yet, this is different. I feel that I have not actually shifted. I am still wrapped within the same experience. But I have been moved out of

24

the overwhelming heat. I must have passed out...as I am not where I was. I'm in a bed. It looks like I am in an old fashioned hospital. I must now be living-out the aftermath of having collapsed earlier...which is weird....I have never actually been unconscious in an experience before. It looks like I was moved here while I was out cold.

This is all very new. I have never had anything like this happen before.

If I try to sit up...Oowww! I am dragged back by a swimming pain. It feels as though a heavyweight boxer has been bashing my skull for fun while I was unconscious. I sit as still as I can physically manage and push my eyes back into their sockets as far as I dare, trying to dislodge the thumping pain within my skull. I must gather myself.

I look down at the unusually shaped bed, and the odd clothing that covers this body. The body...it...it is...my own!

My head is throbbing. A feeling of sickness is ebbing and flowing. I reach to my brow. A bandage covers the whole top of my head. I feel incredibly weak. My shoulder is killing me. I fall back into the pillows. I reach up for a beaker of water...

The cup has already been poured for me, by someone...but by who...I have no idea.

I try to lift myself - to sip it. Aghhh...I slip...and the water pours back upon me. I flinch away from the icy wetness...feeling stupid and embarrassed. After the initial shock however, the coolness of the water comes as a blessed relief from the overpowering heat. I am reminded again of that terrible unrelenting sun – the last thing I can actually remember.

All at once there is a commotion. The door is thrust open and a nurse enters. He is around forty, with a drawn countenance and craggy features. His skin ages him. He may actually be younger than he appears. He seems completely disinterested in me - his patient - and instead tends to the array of furniture which sits around the opposite side of the room.

'Hello.'

He looks across. 'Alright?' he says.

'No, actually, I bloody hurt like hell.' I stop to rub my head as if to make a point as of the truth of the statement. 'What the hell......How did I get here? Where am I?'

The nurse laughs, a single snort, and smirks.

I am not at all happy with that response and scowl at him as hard as I can - through the pounding in my skull.

'Calm yourself.' He laughs 'The way you must have hit the floor, I'm surprised you can still even speak.'

I continue my angry glare. I am still far too confused to play games.

'Mr Nekyia brought you in.' He continues. 'Lucky for you he was passing by and called an ambulance. You were in a right mess'.

'Who is Mr Nekyia?' I ask.

As I say the words, a man of about sixty enters. He wears glasses and a tweed jacket, he exudes calm authority. His presence immediately puts me at ease, even in my extreme confusion.

'How do you do?' He states - his tone bears a clipped pronunciation. He extends a hand, and with considerable effort I raise my own to shake it.

'Mr Nekyia?'

'Yes indeed. The very man that found you strewn, prostrate and bleeding upon the paving.'

His delivery and vocab seem somewhat theatrical.

'Thank you, you are my good Samaritan.'

'Nonsense dear boy, I am glad I could be of aid. I am however, intrigued to discover the circumstances and reasons for your being here?'

I, of course, have none - well not that I can freely divulge. I lay torn by indecision. He seems to recognise my inability to co-operate, or perhaps he presumes it to be confusion. Whichever, he graciously offers to lead me forward.

'I found you lying in the most terrible of states, exhausted, unconscious, you must have fallen hard. Were you running from something?'

'Running?' I ask, knowing I was, but not being able to explain why. 'Why would I have been running?' I can feel the abrasiveness of the statement even as it passes my lips.

The orderly and the man exchange a quizzical look and he turns back to me. 'Mmm, well, errr, well you see…'

His lack of clarity is doing nothing to reassure me.

'Well…' he attempts again '…I was just concerned that someone or something may have been chasing you?' He glances to the nurse once more, concern across his face. I now mirror that look. I am not sure why he would ask such a question. He must know something. Seemingly much more than I do. A dizzying mixture of panic and confusion sends my mind into an erratic whirl.

The doctor tries again, attempting to defuse the situation. But his carefree demeanour now has a forced edge. 'Well…it appears Ben, that you have taken a code from Montgomery…"

*A feeling of separation from what I am, and what I have been immediately overcomes and envelopes me. Blackness washes around the room, and all at once I am unceremoniously sucked away from the scene. Again I try, unsuccessfully to push against the inevitable.* The process is in motion. *I cannot stay, but I desperately want to hear the end of that sentence - to know how that man had known my name. What he had meant?* Confusion and uncertainty accompany the retrieval. The rasp of the mechanical grates against the organic. The incompatibility becomes apparent. *It is painful* and painless at once and in sequence. *I am here. I am there. I am. I am not. Warm darkness opens out into brightly cold light. The spirals descend and rise in perpetual reversals.*

Ben is cast from the womb of his rebirth into the waiting world of strangeness and uncertainty that it is our reality.

# Chapter 2 - The Return

Ben's body jerks violently, his eyes flash open, but are cold and without register. Time and space seem to have ceased to exist for him. Nothing moves, nothing connects.

But then; electrons shoot, neurons race at super fast speeds to re-engage their positions. The mind works ferociously, re-establishing general understanding.

After several long lonely minutes of dazed confusion, his full consciousness eventually attempts to return.

With it, there is a realisation of the mass of cords and pipes running awkwardly between him and various electronic machines. He feels a torrential claustrophobia, as if he is being held trapped within a tangled web of wires. He fumbles, unsuccessfully, attempting to separate himself from the apparatus. It will not relent, and instead holds onto him so firmly that it is almost as if it has now become part of his very being. After a few more goes at releasing himself he finally loses patience and instead starts erratically yanking and tugging at everything that holds him. Panic has consumed him, and he cannot see anything but the need to escape.

Heavy doors hurriedly open, then return to clunk purposefully shut. White anti-contamination drapes flap and wisp as someone rushes forward. The room, which was at one moment so empty and desolate, bursts into life with bustle and presence.

'Calm down, don't do that!' The attendant screams, 'Christ man, you'll lobotomise yourself if you pull it out like that!'

'Help me!' Ben shouts, still desperate in his attempts to free himself. 'I can't breathe!'

Thomas acts quickly to calm the situation. He recognises that the lack of air is a result of anxiety, not a cardiovascular failure.

'I'm here! Let me help you, alright'? He deftly releases the cables and connections. Within a matter of seconds he has moved it all away, and steps back to allow Ben to grow into the separation. Ben lies still for quite some time, gathering his thoughts and attempting to compose his breathing. The panic had crept right through him. He is not used to such attacks, so it has really distressed him.

Having given him time to ease himself back, Thomas moves around to assist him to an upright position.

'It's not right Thomas. I'm just left lying here like I'm just another part of this bloody machine'. Ben rages.

There was a time when a whole specially allocated staff would take care of his every need, to help him from the cradle, to unplug the sensors, to bring him food and drink. But now he is often left completely alone. It is a glaring dereliction of care, and although it is by no means his fault, Thomas feels utterly ashamed to have been part of it.


Ben has been part of Convergence program since it began. He was in-fact one of the founders of the whole operation. He has now done more Voyages that any other person, living or dead. Yet re-entry is still hard. The pure mental and physical exertion of this process had dire effects on several of the original team. They could never get to grips with the rudimentary self-degeneration that had to occur in order for one to exist within the vagaries of someone else's mind. Initially, the project had started with sixteen keen young researchers. Now only one remains - fully intact. Two were killed in accidents with the basic processing between the machine and the brain. Five were captured within the *Perpetual Cycle; the process whereby one mind is interfaced to another*, and where determined to be brain-dead. Seven tragically committed suicide, seemingly not able to deal with what they had seen and done. Apart from Ben, only one other has ever survived the physical rigours and the internal perils of the Cycles. But the physical and mental deterioration has so crippled that man, that he is now a permanent recluse.

By all medical definitions Ben is a freak of nature. Not a single expert that has seen the convergence data has been able to explain how he has survived. Even the most hard-nosed reviewers - people that have witnessed all sorts of weird and wonderful enterprises, are in truth, scared by what he does and what he sees. He is an anomaly. It has been suggested that he is extra-intuitive and possesses a heightened sense of empathy. This, they believe, allows him to move into other realities, where most people would be (and in some cases, have been) mentally torn to shreds.

However, in the wider senses, no-one can really explain how he does it.

Thomas attempts to engage with his patient. 'Did you get what you were after?'

Ben offers him a sharp angry glare. Thomas knows that sign all too well, and drops any further attempts at conversation. He instead turns and busies himself with various program-exit tasks. He focuses his attention on the reams of computer data that relate to the voyage that Ben has just undertaken. It takes him a few moments to grasp what he is seeing and he flounders for an explanation of how this could have occurred and not set off any monitoring alarms. The data shows massive and dangerous spikes in neural activity, the peaks reflect extreme emotional distress, representing instinctive reactions to danger. There is further information relating to huge chemical imbalances within Ben's body. There are, for one, massively exaggerated levels of lactic acid present within his muscles - as if his body has been fighting for its life.

Looking up, confused, Thomas tries to make sense of it all.

'What…what the hell happened…to you…in there?'

Ben is now beginning to notice quite a serious level of discomfort. He had been solely absorbed with the racing uncertainties that had been clouding his mind. Now, he is awakened to the aches that wrack through him. The residual effect of the lactic acid takes effect on his body; He starts to cramp, painfully. He feels like he has crested a wave, and now falls in deflation. His body is acting to corrects his massive adrenaline spike. He feels the overarching dizziness and a seeping saliva. He has a immediate desire to vomit.

Thomas recognises the distress and rushes to reach a sick-tray.

They sit for an extended period in which neither of them speaks and the air hangs putrid with the stench of regurgitation. Despite all he does, and all he has experienced, Ben still can't help but feel embarrassed at having been sick in front of someone else. There is still, he feels, a privateness to such acts, and now he feels humiliated. Though quietly drowning in self-ridicule, he tries to distract himself by pondering the root cause of it all.

'What happened? What did you see Ben?' Thomas asks, reticently.

Recognising his genuine concern, Ben mellows his response. He attempts to find a way of explain just what it was that he has witnessed. He reflects for some time without a response, Thomas reads this as another shut-down, and so again moves away.

Ben can hear the other man moving around, tapping at keypads on various devices, and tidying away equipment. He can sense him in the periphery of his thoughts. He engages back to the moment and sees that Thomas is tinkering with things on the far side of the room. Although he is active in whatever it is that he is doing, Ben knows that he is really just hovering - waiting for an answer.

'It was really weird!' Ben finally offers.

'Really!' Thomas says excitedly. 'You're in a dying man's head, that is hardly normal is it?'

They both laugh, at what has become a standard joke between them. Each welcomes the comedy that somehow manages to separate them oh-so very briefly from the severity and tragedy that surrounds the thing they do.

'No, I mean this was *really* weird. It was as if the scenario was staged. I was supposed to see it - supposed to be in it with them. There were two separate entries. The first one had Montgomery in it and it was normal; or at least as normal as this project ever can be.' Ben pauses, remembering the face of Montgomery's wife. He has that same feeling tearing at his own heart. The ache he had felt just a short while ago - effectively through Montgomery - is now searing into his very own being. This is not uncommon. It is the primary reason that has been given for the amount of suicides related to this program. The dark weight of the human condition tortured and tormented them, until they could take it no more. It all proved too much, and it had forced them to look for the only truly permanent way to cut the images from their minds.

In an attempt to break himself away from this free-fall, Ben revisits the strangeness of the second coming.

'It was me.' He exclaims.

Thomas is confused. 'What was you?'

'The person in the second entry. It was me!' He suddenly sits bolt upright, and immediately regrets doing so. Pain surges back through him. Despite the injections that Thomas had administered, he again senses an all encompassing ache. Pulling his mind back from the pain he slowly reaches out and grabs for the printed copy of Montgomery's file. He scans through it, seeking something that could possibly explain the weirdness of the occurrences within the machine.

But nothing obvious strikes him, even after several re-reads.

He was desperately hoping that there must be some clue in the file somewhere.

Not really knowing what to say or even how to address him, Thomas ventures to enquire of the scribbles on the back of the file. Ben had not seen it, but they were obvious to Thomas from where he was standing. Ben quickly turns the papers over. True enough, there is something. Not technically even in Montgomery's notes, but instead scrawled on the back, by some unknown hand, in red ink handwriting - a bizarre and ambiguous note.

*There is something to discuss about the secret of The Source*

He wonders whether he could ask one of the lab staff, perhaps even Kelly - the lab manager - who it was that had written on one of her pristine print-outs. It would be invaluable to know where it had come from.

But then he sinks back into himself once more. The excitement of this discovery dashed by his knowing that it would be futile. He knows what the staff here are like. He is sure that whoever wrote that cryptic note is not likely to tell him anything. Even when the general staff do relay things to him, they mask what they say in vague, nonsensical corporate gibberish, to disguise their real aims and intentions. For quite some time he just sits - still and morbid.

Thomas has never seen him so sullen, and wonders whether there may not be some wider psychological issues here, relating to exposures to the process. He feels that he really should be highlighting such a concern to the wider medical personnel. But he knows that Ben would see this as a betrayal of trust, and so he would not do so without Ben's express agreement.

Although he sits slumped and motionless, Ben's mind is still racing. He is wondering if the note was written while he was in convergence. That would mean that someone had been standing here, looking over him while he was in the machine…and that was very recently.

'Was someone here while I was under, Thomas?' He asks, his agitation etched across his face.

Thomas looks confused, 'Who do you mean?

Ben hopes that his lack of understanding is sincere. He trusts Thomas, and really hopes that he is not a part of the wider corporate smokescreen. Ben is sick of the fact that no-one here can answer straight forward questions.

Thomas looks awkward and they both just stare at each other, neither knowing how to relieve the silence.

After a prolonged pause, Ben finally breaks. The atmosphere is stifling, and he doesn't want it to become like that between them. He wants to think of Thomas as goodhearted. He is absolutely determined to carry on believing that.

'Let's get to debrief.' He instructs light-heartedly.

Thomas shows every sign of being relieved. He helps Ben struggle from the cradle and into a waiting wheelchair. He then moves with distinct purpose as he pushes the wheelchair off to see Kelly.

Ben regrets having said anything about this Voyage - even to Thomas. He realises he must not to make that mistake again. It will have terrible consequences. He can't even begin to get his own head around what he saw and experienced within the machine. He couldn't bear Kelly, the Professor, and God-knows-who-else poking and prodding away at his mind looking for answers.

He was far too tired, and more than a little terrified by it all.

# Chapter 3 - Debrief

Thomas rolls Ben into the briefing room. It is a specially designed space which captures every single movement and sound. The session is an opportunity to hear the Voyagers story. It also offers the scientists a method of looking for unconscious information, such as involuntary body-movements, unexpected changes in temperature and slips in phrases. These often reveal deep, hidden parts of the Voyagers experience.

Ben looks up to see a stony authoritarian face glowering down at him from the monitoring-booth. The emotionless gaze stares straight through him. It is a look of cold scientific consideration. Kelly is in the observation box, and she is making it clear to all, that she is very much in control.

'Please state your name, age and today's date'.

Although apparently a ridiculous series of questions, she is not being awkward, and he answers freely. Every return from a Voyage is logged this way, it is simply procedure. It helps ascertain that the participant is *compos-mentis*, and able to complete such a task.

'Please give your first assessment', she continues.

He explains the first entry; the acclimatisation, the surroundings, the weather, what he saw, how he felt, the pull-back.

Clockwork. Uninterrupted. All (or, nearly all) retold in full clarity.

She can't stand to be in a room with him, yet even Kelly is
impressed by the way Ben can reel off such competent reports. She
has even been known to praise this ability, although of course, never to
his face. It used to take some of the other Voyagers up to two days to
recover enough for them to be able to give the slightest, most basic
information about their experience. Ben has reeled off so many reports
now it has become almost standardised. It often sounds like he is
dictating a sequence such as 'How I got to work this morning', or
'What I had for my breakfast'. He has made the miraculous, normal.

Then she asks the fateful question. 'Did you retrieve what you
were sent for?'

For a moment he sits unmoved by the directness of her
enquiry. He can sense her presence above him, and in his mind he
pictures her smug face, with its glib scowl. He stretches out his arms
and reverse links his hands, elongates and then relaxes - as if he is -
completely unfazed. He feigns a yawn, and looks around the room
nonchalantly. Her manner has angered him. To re-emerge from what
he has, and then to have to experience this kind of welcome has irked
him. The only reply he deems fit, given the circumstances is: 'I'm not
sure that I did!'

Kelly reads his manner. She knows she will get no more from him while he is in this mood, so turns to go. No more questions, certainly no pleasantries. Heavy doors open. Heavy doors clunk shut. She is gone.

Ben feels himself stranded in solitude. He settles within the wheelchair and tries to open his mind to focus on the project. But what she does niggles like an annoying bite. He can't fully scratch away the anger to achieve a restful mind. He remembers a time when there was pomp and ceremony to accompany a debrief. It was the excited culmination of their terrific achievement. Every re-entry was heralded as a triumph, the stories awaited with baited breath. Now he is merely their tool. If he doesn't give them all that they want, he often feels discarded. By withholding what he has experienced, he is making a stand. It is childish, he knows, but he is enjoying the brief wrestle of power.

Eventually Thomas re-enters the room. He has sat through dozens of these too, and knows the process off by heart. He figures they are all done for today. He is wrong. Just as he is about to wheel Ben back to the recuperation area Kelly storms back into the monitoring station above them.

'The readings are off!' She barks over the booth speakers.

'What?' Ben and Thomas both exclaim at the same time, equally surprised by her sudden reappearance. They both know what she has seen. Even the briefest scan of the post-voyage data would have set her alarm bells ringing. It was inevitable she was going to notice. But neither of them had expected her to notice quite that quickly.

'I just said it was fairly standard.' Ben retorts. 'It got a bit weird, yes, but nothing that I couldn't handle.' He glances at Thomas who, backing sheepishly away, is trying not to catch his eye. He knows Thomas won't deliberately tell Kelly what he had told him earlier, but he also knows that she will inevitably see his discomfort. He knows she will challenge him, and he knows Thomas will crumble under her unrelenting questioning.

'What's wrong?' He asks, in as flippant a tone as he can muster. He wants to distract her away from Thomas - he buys just enough time - as he manages to exit the room.

Ben is actually eager to hear her evaluation of what she has seen. He has been shaken to his very core by the experiences within the last trip. It was the most strange and disturbing scenario he has ever seen. To have found himself present within the scene, and for the characters to directly communicate with him, is unprecedented. The ramifications are terrifying. He had bottled this-up for fear of what he would realise, if he faced it full on. He knows he should tell her, but he also feels he can't yet bring himself to admit it, yet. In a way, he is somewhat relieved that she has found the anomaly. It at least proves that there *was* something that affected him differently this time. He can't pass it off. Something different definitely has happened.

'I...I...I can't figure it?' Kelly flusters. It is not in her nature to stumble, particularly in front of him. Ben frowns and looks up at the women standing holding the data. She attempts to regains herself, 'I will run the scans and the reports via the research team. We will report back tomorrow at 9am for full assessment.'

Ben smirks. The damage has already been done. He has seen a chink in her unassailable control. He has forgotten though; that he is still sitting within in the debrief room. It monitors and records everything. She looks down at her screens and sees magnifications of his smirk, spread across a dozen screens. She reactively opens up the speaker channel.

'Is something amusing you?'

Taken-aback, Ben is momentarily confused. He then realises that she can still see all of the sensory data. This only serves to amuse him further. She registers this effect too.

'I wonder whether it would be better to leave you in isolation for a while, just until we can assess if this new attitude is a reaction from your last trip.'

'You fu...' He screams, but she has already turned off the return-microphone.

She knows that this a terrible thing to have done. He has only just returned from a Voyage. He has just experienced one, if not the most excruciating processes ever invented. Yet here she is playing childish games. But whichever way she reasons it, he just seems to have an unparalleled ability to push all the right buttons to drive her insane.

The lights on all the sensors on the screens in front of her are wild with activity, tracing and recording his anger. She collects her things, reasserts her calm and walks from the control area.

Thomas is standing coyly outside the booth. He looks like a nervous infant expecting to be punished. His head is slightly tilted, his eyes down in submission. To his amazement, she does not even address it. She merely states that he can 'Let Ben out and wheel him to recuperation.'

She pauses, and Thomas waits hesitantly expecting the verbal volley. 'See you at 8am for preparations.' She says, and leaves.

He is shocked, yet overjoyed. He is so relieved that he almost forgets to even collect Ben. He starts to walk off in the opposite direction - then notices the man is still in the booth. Although he can't hear him through the soundproofed glass, he can see that he is still screaming wildly. He can imagine which choice profanities he is currently using, and at who they will be aimed.

Thomas rolls Ben back to the recuperation area. 'Why do you

always taunt her?' He has to ask.

'She is such a bitch. I had barely reconnected to my body and mind, and she's there glaring down at me, *demanding* answers'.

'That's just her way, she doesn't mean anything by it. You know what she's like'.

Having assisted him to a seat by the side of his recuperation bed, Thomas returns to finish disconnecting and tidying the multitude of cables, sensors and other assorted equipment.

'You may well like winding-up the ice queen, but I'm the one who ends up getting it in the scrotum when she loses her rag!'

Ben smiles a knowing smile. He doesn't mean to cause him additional grief. But he just can't help himself, he just has to push back at her authority - to rage against the machine.

Having rested for several hours in the recovery suite, Ben starts to get fidgety. He paces around, unable to settle. Having picked up a news log, he pushes it away. Hearing more of misery and disaster is not a tonic. He wonders what is happening on the web - but as there is no Internet connected to the site, it is beyond his reach. He uses his implant to turn on one of the ion walls. The catalogue of TV, film, and music is almost limitless. There are more files available than anyone could view in a lifetime. But even here he can't see a single thing he wants to watch or listen to. Instead, he makes to go home. He would rather sleep in his own bed tonight.

He walks through the compound, up to a large security gate. Signals alert the guard of movement, and right on cue someone comes to investigate. The system would have automatically registered that it as being Ben. The guard is however, still obliged to check and verify every exit.

'Good evening sir.' The guard says, while raising a box of sensors to Ben's face.

Ben is not sure if the guard knows who he is. He presumes he recognises him, having seen him for year upon year. But, beyond the normal greeting, he doesn't show any recognition at all. He doesn't really care whether the guard knows him or not. It is just second nature to him to attempt to read people's thoughts and inclinations, and he can't seem to turn these skills off - even when he really wants to.

'Hi George, how's it going?' he says politely.

'Fine sir, thank you.'

A machine is held at eye level to scan the irises. Ben then speaks the three key words the guard tells him.

'Banana, Zebra, Kilimanjaro.'

The machine verifies the voice, eye, physical dimensions and pheromone traces. It beeps and flashes green.

'Thank you sir, have a good evening.' The guard states, functionally.

'Thanks, and you George, bye for now.'

Ben can't face going home. The bland flat offers little solace. He instead mooches along with no real purpose. He feels light drizzle settling upon him, like a whisper of dampness hanging in the air. The clouds are stiflingly low, and he feels forced down by the weight of their intensity. The dankness of the day help make up his mind. He bows to the inevitability of his nature and takes one of the staff pods. 'Good evening Sir' it says, as he steps inside. The machine asks for a location - he names a bar in the back-streets on the edge of the city.

The pod rolls effortlessly towards the junction marked KR45T. Its sensors scan for traffic within the operational vicinity, then expresses magnetic runners and effortlessly attaches to the Trackway. He could theoretically have chosen a bar in anywhere from Budapest to Ballymena. The pods silent motor could have taken him to near anywhere in the continent. He could theoretically have breakfast in Kiev, lunch in Oslo. Supper in Seville, and end with beers in Galway. Once attached he has the scope to go anywhere he chooses within the boundaries of the European State. But he knows exactly where he wants to be - and that is well off the beaten track. A place where city types seldom venture.

There is massive acceleration as the pod gathers speed. There are no discernible spaces on the Highway track, but it is a fully automated system and Ben knows the pod will have already calculated its own entry location. Passengers don't tend to watch the convergence with the main route, it is disconcerting to see massive objects hurtling towards you without any seeming ability to avoid a collision. Ben always watches. Despite having ridden the rails his entire life, he knows his body can't help but react to the situation. The stimuli will drive his adrenalin, his heart will race as he automatically braces for impact. Then, nothing. His body will relax. He loves the sensation of fooling the body.

As always, within fractions of a second he has been transferred on the hyper-fast super highway. The pod slots straight into a space no human eye could ever possibly have negotiated. The pod accelerates to full speed and the outside literally turns to a blur as he catapults forward. Inside Ben reclines, asks for a certain song and relaxes back for the seconds it will take to cross the multitude of miles from his industrial workplace to the distant city-limit sprawl.

A beep sounds in his ear and his communication implant references the contact directly to his visual cortex. It is an incoming call from Kelly. He grimaces. Having just escaped from work, she is the most unwelcome of all possible intrusions. He is just about to cancel the call, but then thinks better of it. He knows her too well. If she is demeaning herself to call him personally, then it must be important. If it is, she will call over and over again on loop until he answers. He could block her, but the last time he did that she issued a team of *specialists* to manhandle him, near naked, out into the street, where upon he promptly came face to face with his nemesis. He has learnt.

'Answer', the chip in his ear opens a receiver, 'Kelly' he states, no more no less.

'Where are you?'

'I'm off work…Is that okay?' His sarcasm hangs on the line.

There is a pause, then she tries again. 'Would you be willing to go back in again tomorrow?'

'Fu..!…What happened to rest-time for the returnee?'

'I'm sorry.' She states, seemingly sincerely. He almost faints with shock. 'I know it's a lot to ask, but we have something we really must retrieve. I really am sorry to ask, and I wouldn't, if it wasn't really important. I am under direct instruction from the Chairman to get this done.'

There is a stunned pause. He has never heard her apologise before. He is torn by an emotion he can't register. Is he actually feeling sympathy for her? He has always been aware that she is herself under a massive amount of pressure from above. Not only does she run and collate the majority of the post Voyage data, she also has to bow and scrape to those bastards on the Board. That is something he wouldn't wish on anyone.

Despite this, the call has put him in something of an awkward position. He refused to tell her about the retrieval earlier, and now it has come back to bite him. He knows that is he tells her that he did get the info she was after, she will recall him without recourse for argument. If he lies - he will get it in the neck doubly hard tomorrow.

Ben being Ben, he opts for the second option. 'Of course. I understand. I'll be at the briefing. 9am.'

She had dreaded making the call and had considered getting Thomas to do it. She knew though that it was her responsibility, and also that he was more likely to say no to Thomas, making the whole process a whole lot harder. This response though, was a surprise. She wondered if he was tired and too worn out to fight back. He had only just complete a Voyage after all.

It is her turn to feel guilty. 'Are you sure?' she asks, her tone softened beyond any he has heard her utter before. 'If you can't do it I will do all I can to head off the executives, and we could try to reschedule for the day after."

'No it's fine.' He replies. 'Is it the same man – Montgomery?'

'Yes it is.' She replies.

'Ok, see you tomorrow.' He lingers a while then terminates. The link dies.

For the first time Kelly is actually left wanting to say more. She didn't really know what else to say though. Small talk is not her forte. She felt that he had genuinely tried to help her out. But now he had gone. She couldn't even imagine what toll it would take on him to have to go through that whole process all over again. She considers calling back, but then realises how ridiculous that would appear when, or if he answered. She imagined herself, floundering for niceties, an area within which she would have felt totally exposed. In the end she does nothing. And the guilt of that eats away at her, all night long.

In the pod Ben is also left pondering the conversation and wrestling with his conscience.

Kelly being nice was almost as strange as the Voyage itself.

He knows he should have told her there and then that he had retrieved the data she required. But he couldn't bear to hear her condescending tone, accompanied by the inevitable rise in volume through his bollocking.

Giving her the Montgomery information in the morning

would at the very least absolved him of the guilt of lying.

The second scene had scared him to his core. He really couldn't face anything unearthing that in a briefing this evening.

Hence the decision to go to the pub.

In the back of his mind though, the niggle digs deep into his awareness.

He would *have* to tell them what had happened in the second scene. He would have to explain to them the weirdest thing that he had ever experienced. He can't pretend it didn't happen, they would have to know.

But not now! Tomorrow.

He knows it is all too dangerously strange to brush under the carpet.

But he also knows just the right level of drink that will at least send the niggles to sleep - for a few hours at least.

He closes the thought from his mind and turns his full attention back to his fast approaching destination.

As he pulls up at the bar Ben knows that he is being watched. Or rather, he is aware that he could be being watched - at any time.

The company allows him the facade of freedom, while using its considerable surveillance facilities to keep him imprisoned within its view. As he opens the bar door he remembers how he found this out. He recalls the time, drunk and argumentative he had thrown himself into someone else's bar fight. He had done it for the buzz of the unknowable danger.

Out of nowhere a women stepped in to placate the argument. When the three men he had picked on wouldn't see reason, she had set about them remorselessly. Ben had watched stunned as events unfolded before him. The women just disappeared directly after. From then on he realised that they were always there, or there abouts. The Company was watching - It had always been watching. They obviously considered him too valuable an asset to lose. They would have been acutely aware that he thrived on lowly pleasures, brawling and drunkenness. Most of the time they didn't interfere directly - as far as he could tell - and for that he was grateful. But from that day to this he was always aware that they owned him.

It was time to get drunk and to forget it all.

# Chapter 4 - Visiting VIP's

Early in the morning Kelly marches off to complete her first unwanted mission of the day. She despises corporate show-and-tells, but it is part of her job to make the project open to the Board and any other important dignitaries. She knows that it is absolutely essential, as all funding is reliant upon placating the Suits. She has, by her own admission, very little patience for people. Yet, she is very good at relaying complex information to those that she would personally considers are morons.

The security doors open, and the group assembles before her. A mixed bag of shapes, sizes and gender - but *all* suited. She welcomes them as warmly as she can, then goes on to explain the general premise of the project. She describes the work they do here, and elaborates as graciously as she is able, her appreciation for the continued financial and administrative support.

As usual, they don't even wait for her entire spiel before the first question is fired.

A man whom she assesses must have been a librarian in a previous life, lowers his clipboard, looks up over his glasses and sets the first of the volley. 'Is there an experiment going on at the moment?'

'There is always experimentation sir,' she answers. 'If you specifically mean the Voyage operation, then no.'

She registers the general disappointment in the room, wondering what it was they were expecting to see here…zombies and magic perhaps?

'Our Voyager actually returned from a six hour session yesterday, we will be having a full operational de-brief later this morning. He will then be going back in for a second entry this afterno...'

'Six hours,' the librarian cuts in, 'is that a long time to be plugged in?' He is making notes, and doesn't even attempt to gain eye contact.

'It depends on the nature of the entry, and what the Voyager encounters. He is generally not within the subjects world for more than a few hours, at most a day, the median is around three and a half hours. But to him, it can feel like either minutes, or months.'

'Why?' someone else asks.

'There is a distorted relativity within the process. We haven't got a full appreciation on why this is, but it is a consistent pattern. He doesn't ever experience normal time within the cycle.'

'Is he in the dead person's head, or does he sort-of mind-read?' A stocky woman asks. Her brow is knitted so tightly Kelly wonders if she is desperately trying to stop information from escaping her head.

The question itself infuriates Kelly. She does not like the

zombie imagery. If these weren't important guests she would tear questions like this to pieces. As it is she is restrained and answers fairly politely.

'Mind reading is merely a parlour trick, what we are involved in here is high end scientific procedure. We use some of the most powerful computers available in the entire world. We have developed the most radical and innovative core programming and interface systems to form an area where two human minds can converge. The Voyager will never actually *enter* the subject's mind. The scenes are, technically, played out within the device. We have named it the *The Interface*. Operators are termed *Voyagers*.'

'What does the interface do?' Librarian-man pipes-up again.

'It effectively forms a gateway from the Voyager's mind into a meeting area where he can access the memories of the person we are investigating. In this space, the recipient mind is laid partially open, and a skilled Voyager can move around within their remembrance.

A short, stern looking women in an aggressive pin-striped suit steps forward, making sure that she is at the front of the group. 'Are you saying he is no longer inside his own body when he interacts?'

'Well…if we unplugged him while he was interfaced he would not be able to get back to his own body. During the Voyage his consciousness exists within the machine. So, in a way, he has entered the machine - to look around in someone else's mind.'

'If you did turn off the machine, given that all the neurons etc are still in his brain, couldn't you just sort of…well…*reset* him?' Kelly recognises the face of the questioner, she thinks he is a senior member of the finance committee.

'Biologically he would still be complete, but the trauma would be too much to bear. To put it simply, if we pull the plug, he dies.'

As Kelly say this the room falls silent. She hopes that the massive weight of what they actually do here is finally sinking in.


She lets the silence hang for a while, and then changes tack. 'When we converge consciousness with a subject it always runs via a particular sequence. We have called this sequence the Perpetual Cycle. A Voyager cannot enter a scenario, or simply leave the process at will. We cannot control it from the lab either. A Voyage can run seconds, minutes, or hours. Memory systems are not chronological, they are actually sporadic and every changing. Memories are stories that are triggered by stimuli. Smells are the most common referent.' Kelly reaches into her pocket and produces a spray. She wafts it around. At first the group looks confused, but as the pheromones take effect, gradually they all smile. She has done this dozens of times. It works the same way every time. She returns the spray and continues.

'You see for yourselves, the chemical summons memories. These will be different for each of us, but we have found that this particular one always induces a positive result. Effectively, the Voyager does something similar. He attempts to bring what he wants to know into the realm of awareness.'

'Could he become stuck in the process?' A tall man asks.

'If the Voyage went on for a really long time, it would take a phenomenal level of concentration to maintain their concentration. If they didn't come out, it would again be traumatic. We do not believe this would be sustainable for more than a day. If you compare the level of concentration to that of a racing driver. The driver is holding that super heightened level for a relatively short spell, yet one slip-up and they could be killed or at least seriously injured. It is the same with the Voyager. They have to remain in a permanent state of heightened awareness. To lose control of a situation could mean losing one's life.'

'Could you alter yourself in the other person's mind, say, becoming some kind of a super-hero?' a portly man in the centre of the group asks.

Kelly assesses that the man himself wishes to become something more than he really is.

'You must act within the limits of general social conformity, etiquette and accepted norms in the inner-sphere.'

'How would you know the rules?' A youngish looking woman queries.

'You know them, as you do in this world. It is reality. Just a distorted version of it.'

'Can you do this with living people? Or only with dead ones?' Another voice queries from the back of the assembled group.

'Apart from the obvious ethical considerations...' Kelly pauses and assesses the group, she doubts that any of them gives a damn about right or wrong, as long as the results turn profit or increased their power base. She also had to admit that she truly belongs here. If she thought they could get away with it, she would have definitely have liked to attempt this with a fully-aware person. But even The Company hasn't sanctioned that - yet.

She continues. 'We have carried out research with a comatose patient, but we found the readings too strong. If you can imagine a scale whereby that the brain activity of a fully sentient person is at the top of a chart, it appears, that we can only connect with people at the very lowest level of cognitive activity. If they have even the slightest degree of awareness, they are too dangerous to enter.'

'Can anyone do this?' Asks a butch looking man with his arm crossed. 'Do you have special training or something?"

'We have had several people who have tried to work with the interface', Kelly replies 'And we have had many failures".

'What do you mean failures?'

Kelly ponders her response, not really wanting to report the horrific deaths and devastating mental traumas that she has witnessed.

'Some people just can't do it. It is incredibly disorienting. Imagine, if you would, a fairground waltzer. Many people enjoy the experience of the erratic swirling and spinning movements, while to others it is their worst nightmare."

'What happens to people who can't handle it?'

'Many can't adapt to the *transition* – that is what we call the point whereby you leave your own mind and merge into someone else's. Back at the start of the program, many of the original voyagers were irreparably scared by the experience of conjoined consciousness, or by the original programs removing them from the sequences too soon. It effectively collapsed their mental world.'

The group look concerned by these revelations. Kelly realises she can't leave the group on such a negative note. She rallies for a more fitting finale. 'To be honest, what the Voyager does is amazing, it truly is an incredible skill. I would, of course, never say this to his face,'

There is a general ripple of polite laughter from her audience. She senses that this is just the right point to end.

There is spontaneous applause from somewhere near the back of the group which surprises Kelly and makes her look for its source. 'Incredible.' She hears someone say. She now notices the man who said it. He has snow white hair, his stare exudes authority. Ominously, he carries a cane. Kelly casts her judgement. She has always thought cane carriers ostentatious and peculiar. She can't help but drag along her prejudices as she glares at him.

Despite this, she humours him. 'Yes sir, it truly is.' She directs a slight smile. She is fully aware that this could be construed as condescending, but slides away from his eye contact, and moves on with the tour.

# Chapter 5 - Hangover

A very hung-over Ben heads for work. As he exits his flat the humidity in the air stifles his senses and makes him queasy. He ambles across the street and pays to enter a taxi-pod. It will cost him a wedge, but he really doesn't care. He can't face using a company pod this morning, it would automatically recognise him and would make him accessible. He can't bear the thought of having to talk to anyone, yet. He slumps into the self-moulding seat. This does not relieve his sick feeling, but at least makes him more comfortable as he struggles through it. He knows he is in no state to be at work. But he had promised to be there for 9am, so now has to live up to it. He lays back and lets the pod drive him all the way to the laboratory gates. He will make the best use of the all too brief travel time to try and get his head together.

He enters the building and goes straight to the café. He orders a coffee, and tries to sip away his wavering drunkenness.

'Oh no, no, no, no, no, no!' cries Thomas.

Ben had hoped he would be anonymous, seated at the very rear of the cafe. He realises that it is going to be a very long day.

'Nooooo…she is going to bloody kill you!' Thomas states. 'What are you doing? Why did you have to go and get like this? You are in no condition for the debrief, never mind going back into the machine.' Thomas crosses the seating area, 'I could smell the brewery stench from the doorway. Bloody hell man, what did you drink to get like this?'

Ben offers a hazed smile, his eyes housed in red vacuous loops. 'If I could remember that, it would have been a wasted evening, wouldn't it?

Thomas just shakes his head in disapproval. 'Why did you have to get like this today?'

Ben thinks for a moment. He takes a swig of his coffee, then confesses. 'I was damn well freaked out. There you have it! My job may be to wander the land of the dead, but I have finally run up against something that I can't handle. Happy? Yesterday…I was the man in the mirror. And while I was there I saw some people, and we had a little chat'.

Thomas can now see just how drunk Ben still is. The message was slurred and cryptic, but he can tell its intended meaning. His eyes spring forward in their fullest possible extension, his mouth agape.

'What the fu…and you're about to tell her that? In this state!'

After yesterdays com-call in the pod, Ben had felt that his relationship with Kelly had almost touched on friendliness. He had considered that they may have built bridges, and could move towards a

64

solid working relationship from here on in.

He had then drank to the point of near oblivion. He now feels awful with the hangover, and had felt dreadful about letting their possible reconciliation just idly wash away from him at the whim of yet another needless drink.

But upon seeing the look of fear on Thomas' face at the thought of facing Kelly, his blood boils.

'Yes I am'. He states defiantly, though swaying slightly. 'Bugger her! I'll tell her now! Where is she?' He moves his eyes around as if this will somehow make her miraculously appear before him like a genie from a bottle. 'She really annoyed me yesterday when I came out of the Voyage. She was totally out of order, with her disrespectful authoritarian airs and graces.' He is becoming more excited and his anger is starting to grow. After crossing his arms, huffing several times and rolling his eyes repeatedly - he himself finds that he is getting to the point where delaying it is becoming ridiculous. He tells Thomas to go and get her. At first the assistant pauses and can't decide what to do. He knows how this is going to pan out, and he really doesn't want to get caught in the messy crossfire. But it is too important not to relay, so he braces himself and scurries off towards Kelly's office.

'Actually!' Ben shouts behind him. 'Just tell her will you?' For all the previous bravado, he has now apparently lost his bottle. Thomas rolls his eyes wondering if his day could really get any worse.

A few minutes later, in storms Kelly. A face of thunder, eyes pierce him to his very core, her scorn apparent for all to see.

'You said you didn't see anything of note yesterday!' She explodes ferociously.

It is certainly not the first time he has seen her angry, he sees it as being her default setting. As he looks at her now, he realises that although she is often annoyed and dismissive, rude, even obnoxious, this is something altogether very different. At first he felt intimidated by her countenance, and had considered withdrawing completely. But then again, watching Thomas being so submissive to her, after she has obviously torn into him before they had arrived here, just makes him want to have another real go at her. He sees he for the bully that she is and prepares to stand his ground.

'You said, did I retrieve it, and I said I wasn't sure.' He states, feigning to casually dismiss her rebuke, "Which isn't completely true. I did retrieve something'. He sits back, crosses his arms and glares back at her.

'And you were seen, apparently'? She glances at Thomas, who cowers and wished he had let Ben tell her himself. She continues quite excitedly, 'Why didn't you say you had been seen.' She glares at him intently. 'It very important that I know these things. Very, very, very important.' She is now screaming the point home. 'I must know these things – DO-YOU-UN-DER-STAND?' She scrawls every syllable across his ears one by one to add to the resonance.

'You didn't ask' he states nonchalantly, feeling his face become that of a pouting child, He is embarrassed. He pauses and ventures to readdress the situation, with a more considered and consolatory approach. But before he can speak she interrupts him.

'You are the most unprofessional cretin I have ever had the misfortune to…!'

This was the point of no return that Thomas had so feared. You could almost hear the rasp as the match lit the fuse. Thomas' face cringes into a grimace and he turns tail and darts from the room. Even beyond the heavy lab doors he can hear the screaming going back-and-forth. At points he wondered if he should attempt to re-enter, and whether his presence may act to simmer things a little. At one point he even pushed the door slightly ajar, but was met with such a volley of expletives - thrown with venom by Ben at the women he now clearly considers to be his persecutor - that he again withdrew to safety.

Eventually the door swings wildly and Kelly storms through. Her face is bright red. Thomas had never seen her so angry. He had actually been quite shocked by the spectacle before him. She stops in her tracks. Outside, Ben is still ranting and shouting, the words Thomas cannot determine, but the anger is blatantly. Kelly turns to face Thomas, breathes in what seems like enough air to blow up an entire pack of party balloons, and exhales slowly over what feels like minutes. In all this time Thomas stands frozen, staring at her, not knowing what to do, whether to speak, or if he should skulk away before she realised he is there. As he starts to edge away, she catches him ferociously within her gaze. She had become something he had never seen before. This was fury.

'Is everything alright?' he ventures. He wants to go running, screaming down the corridors and as far away from this boiling cauldron as he can get. But it is too late. He has posed the most stupid question ever. To her credit, Kelly does not react. She fixes him with a gaze of pure vitriol and thunder, but does not elaborate. After a far too uncomfortable amount of time she turned to walk back to her office. 'Prep him for a proper debrief of yesterdays Voyage'.

It took an hour for the meeting to convene. Ben prepped himself for Round 2. He was quite surprised when he entered the briefing room to find two senior executives chatting excitedly. Also present were most of the research team – including Professor Von Humbolt, the Head of Research Affairs for the laboratories – Kelly and Thomas.

'What's going on?' Ben demands.

Everyone looked coy. It is the Professor who breaks the awkward silence.

'Good morning Benjamin. I have just heard about your revolutionary discovery yesterday. It is incredible stuff, dear-boy.' He pauses, then continues. 'We need to know more. In fact, not to be too blunt on the subject, we will need to know absolutely everything'.

'It was a weird one Professor.'

'Weird!' Kelly erupts. The decibel level in the room rocketing from gentle to extreme in the course of one solitary syllable. 'How can you possibly be interacting with incidental characters in a scenario. Particularly, when there is neither sign of, or interaction with the host subject? That shouldn't be possible!'

She would have gone on, but for the waved hand of the Professor and a subtle aside to be calm and methodical. She apologies to him and the Professor again leads the questioning.

'This is all new...very...completely new, dear-boy. We will need to hold a full research meeting and committee discussion before anything further can be decided upon and enacted.' He turns to one of the administrators, making sure his message is received and that it is actioned with haste. 'All bodies. Everyone. Tell them to come immediately.' The administrator turns and rushes to do his bidding. "Tell them...'. The Professor adds. '...that this is of the highest and utmost importance and that I am instigating a code Amber 3 meeting." She nods her understanding.

'I thought you wanted me to go back into the body later today?' Ben asks.

'No bloody way!' Kelly counters. A sharp look from the Professor stops her in her tracks.

'We need a full assessment of what has happened here.' The Professor continues. 'This can't technically have happened, you see? You can't interact with someone else's memories when the recipient mind isn't even present.'

Ben still isn't sure in himself that it was actually part of the recipient's memories he interacted with. But he controls himself. Firstly he knows that this would only make the post-mortem of the incident even worse than it already appears. More importantly though, it was he, Ben, not Montgomery, that the figures had talked to - they had addressed him directly. It scared him more than he could voice or comprehend that he knows this to be true.

After a long conversation within the higher echelons of the scientific and general management, it is decided that the debrief session should be led by the Professor.

Ben acknowledges his duty and starts to run through the scenarios he encountered. He elaborates the first - when he was in Montgomery's house. He doesn't mention meeting his wife - the thought of her loving face still tears at him every time he remembers it. He feels that it would sully the beauty, to elaborate it within this clinical context. It was a personal moment, and has no place here. He instead details the operational information and his retrieval of the data file. As he retraces his steps in his mind he starts retelling the mnemonic he had forced himself to memorise. Just as he is about to move into the semi-trance like state of remembrance he is suddenly aware of a presence within the control box. It is only a passing shape. It is only within his peripheral vision, but it was enough for his hackles to signal it. When he turns to the box, there is no-one there. It may have been a technician, he reasons. It could have been a trick of the light? He is though sufficiently concerned, that he stammers and feigns a loss of concentration.

The session grinds to an abrupt halt, bated breaths are followed by repeated attempts – all to the same point, two thirds of the way through the formula, and then ended, with Ben claiming he can't quite get the last bit clear in his mind. He acts slightly disorientated, and despite their frustration, there is a genuine accommodation to the possible trauma he may have suffered. There is a general acceptance in the room that he could be damaged if pushed too hard and too fast.

Kelly's previous outbursts have now consigned her to be quiet for the duration of what she sees as a side-show. She bets that Ben is laughing his socks off inside, taking massive satisfaction knowing that she can see that he is faking the memory loss - yet cannot do a damn thing to intervene.

For his part, Ben doesn't know why he is faking the failure.

He just has a feeling that there is something not right, and he doesn't want to give them the formula. It is better that they do not know it.

After a short rest, he actively ignores any retelling of the first scene. He instead moves to elaborate his second experience. He know wonders whether keeping the code safe is a more valuable enterprise than explaining the weirdness of the second experience. His thoughts turn to gaining help in finding an understanding of what happened to him. To this end, he tells them all.

The response is akin to a bomb going off. There a sudden, enveloping wall of sound as everyone draws shocked breaths at once. A short period of absolute stunned silence, no-one speaking and jaws hanging open. Then the secondary burst of noise as everyone tries to out-yell each other, clambering over themselves to be heard.

More senior executives parade in to the meeting room. Ben can't help but feel that this is spiralling out of all proportion. He is more than aware of the importance of what happened, but he now feels like an ant under a magnifying glass, waiting for the moment the sun comes out. For different reasons Kelly too had not wanted to get stuck in this form of meeting. She wants an explanation, but now it is more like an out-of-control AGM than scientific analysis.

A stocky man steps from the assembled suited mass. None of the lab staff recognise him. He will, it seems, be the ringleader for the forthcoming circus. He doesn't introduce himself, and pulls no punches from the off.

'What the bloody hell is going on?' he rages at both Kelly and Ben in turn. The pair look to each other, neither knows whether to form a united front to this unexpected assault, or to point the finger for the others glaring failings.

Kelly rallies first, and unleashes a backlash. Believing that she really hasn't done anything wrong. She states that she can't be held responsible for an event that she wasn't aware of. The suit replies in short thrift, that her not knowing, is precisely the point.

Ben fires next. He is fully aware that his ground is much shakier and his reasons petty. But all in all, his main preoccupation now is that he doesn't like being spoken to like that, by anybody, much less a Suit.

Having tried to compose herself Kelly suggests, 'It could be a problem of figurative transference or memory disassociation.'

'What are they?' The Suit replies.

Kelly would smirk if she wasn't so annoyed. It is like leading spies out to a firing squad. She traipses them to where she wants them. Then *Bang*. She shakes the thought, and continues her explanation. 'They initially approached the project as if the mental world was something akin to a computer program, and the interface was a kind of control pad'.

'So they built it as if we were going to play a game, and would operate a character within a set-up realm?' The Professor interjects. He had forced his way to the front of the assembled group and is now standing directly next to the aggressive Suit. He has set the statement to aid Kelly's route through what will now be a complex description. Kelly appreciates the intervention and gestures a nod to let him know.

'Precisely! There were problems with this analogy from the outset.'

'The computer world is built, and is also confined'. The Professor offers.

'Indeed. Social and cognitive understanding is a fluidic process, being continually re-developed and re-evaluated. When you build a computer reality, it is pretty much fixed. Computer games are given set rules. We give them their set parameters. The computer world is a universe within a bubble.' Kelly pauses, evaluating the next phase of the description. 'We came to realise that we could not force fluid realities into fixed protocols. Life is full of conflicts and errors, any of which could crash our computer program."

'But what is the problem with the figurative transferences process?' The Professor enquires. He smiles at her as he speaks, leading the conversation where they want it to go.

'Basically, the way the mind works - we use our previous experiences to describe what a new experience feels like. But every experience is different. They are usually similar enough to make sense of, and to communicate to others. In general use, in normal daily life, any minor differences are not a major problem." She pauses. 'But we are dealing here with interacting within someone else's frame of mind, actually being in their head, as it were.'

A sizable part of the group start to murmur a sense of understanding, Kelly sighs inwardly with relief.

'And what's the problem with memory disass...whatever?' One of the Suits asks.

'The mind reorders, changes and deletes large sections of what we experience. We can't remember everything, and we wouldn't want to. What we do remember, we work into stories. But these aren't fixed, and are always changing. To form a sense of there being a solid reality, we fool ourselves that our memories and the outside world are both a constant. We also allow ourselves to believe that events run in linear time. And we presume our mind acts to order the sequencing that way. In actuality the stories we use to create -even ourselves - are constantly switching, mixing and altering.'

'But how does he,' someone points at Ben. 'navigate if it is just random, ever changing fragments?'

'With great difficulty!' Ben forces in. He has sat there feeling cast down by suspicion and accusations. Yet, he is the one that does this miraculous thing. He doesn't feel he is getting due credit, and doesn't appreciate this inquisition.

After a considerable pause, someone else asks, 'Does he have control over the person he is um…*sharing*, is that the right term, *sharing* a mind with?'

Ben sits red faced, furious that they are again now talking about him as though he isn't even present. He crosses his arms petulantly and shuts the meeting from his thoughts.

'He doesn't really share the mind, he is either observing a particular part of a story, or he is tied into playing out a memory sequence.' Kelly explains.

'So he couldn't talk directly to the person whom he is Voyaging through?' A short, slightly built women asks.

' Mmm, no…I…I don't…he can't…' She is floundering. She doesn't like being exposed, or to show such weakness. She quickly collects herself. 'No.' She fires. 'It would not be possible to communicate to recipient mind. The other person is, to all intense and purposes, effectively dead." She slams the word 'dead' hard, to reiterate the point. 'It is only the memories that the Voyager can access and explore. 'The other person is not really *there*'.

The Professor again steps in to help her. 'You see, as Kelly as touched upon, there are two ways of entering the sequence. Firstly you may enter as an observer. Alternatively you may forge with the appointed consciousness and will experience their memories as if you were living them. Both have eminent risks. Observers have been killed within a sequence when they have strayed into the direct gaze of the subject's consciousness. Voyagers who have looked through another's eyes cannot always reconcile this with their own minds eye, and are either lost in transition, or have sadly taken their own lives - upon return.'

'Oh my goodness!' A young women gasps.

'Only one person has ever managed to make that method actionable.' Kelly notes.

The group all turn to look at Ben, who, having turned his attention off from this lecture, was travelling his own thoughts. The Professor coughs loudly several times. Ben is then shocked to look up and find the entire assembled mass looking down at him. Having not paid the slightest attention, he hasn't the slightest clue what they are all staring at.

'What?' He asks, defensively.

'Ok.' The stocky man states. 'We've now heard the young lady's most eloquent academic assessment of the possible scenarios. But are we any closer to an answer as to what actually happened, and the consequences of it."

Kelly's her face redden, her fists tighten. He has belittled both her and their work. This time however, she holds her tongue.

'Now, Voyager.' The ringmaster continues with patronising zeal. 'Why don't you tell us what *you* think happened in there?'

Ben stares blankly. He had forced himself not to think about what he had seen. But given the contempt he currently feels towards these people, he just outright says it. 'Someone, or something in there spoke to me. Who, or whatever it was, they knew my name, and what I do. In the scene it was my body that I inhabited. It was my conscious self that they addressed. It was nothing to do with Montgomery. This was someone directly and deliberately talking to me.'

Even the stocky interrogator is taken aback. There is a noticeable disturbance in the room as people start breaking off into small clusters, talk animatedly about this almighty revelation.

Ben sits in the centre of the maelstrom. He can't really see how things will go forward from here.

After much deliberation by the executives and their most influential advisers, it is deemed that Ben will pilot another Voyage. It will again be through Montgomery.

They have their own reasons. Some are hoping for a scientific discovery of unparalleled note and value. But most just see serviceable fiscal potential.

# Chapter 6 - The Man With The Cane

Kelly and the Professor sit for hours having far-reaching deliberations about where things were all heading, and as of what they should do. Her first assessment was that there could be serious flaws with the actual process itself, and if this were so, they may never be able to remedy them. Her unvoiced suspicion, however - she is desperately hoping that it is not true - is that there has been some kind of manipulation of their work.

She had known all of the original members of the operation, having been with this project from almost the very start. She had seen so many of them either perish, or wither to an unrecognisable shell. She had witnessed firsthand how hard they had all desperately tried to make this process succeed. She couldn't face the thought that any of them would have deliberately caused this to occur. But she knows people, and the terrible things that they are capable of. From the work that they have done and the stories they have heard, she knows all too well that you can't always trust that which you see, and that which you believe to be true.

She decides to go down to the archives to look at the hard-copy records from their earlier work. These have been stored away for years, untouched (she hopes). Her thought is to go right back to look at the first experiments. The ones before she eventually had administrative control over the process. It would be tedious and arduous, but she has an inkling that this may yield an answer. Slow methodical investigation being the only way to really find out what has happened. Although the files and records are all digitised, it is the accompanying notes and jottings that formed the creative part of the process that she is interested in. She wonders whether any of the seemingly random and erratic scribbling may hold the clue. The boxes are all stored in what the lab staff term 'the cooler' - the mass expanse below the lab which houses the vast fans and motors required to keep this whole operation working. She leaves her office and scuttles through the many twisting corridors. Along the way she enters brief conversations with various members of her staff. She enquires about progress and issues directives.

Upon leaving the research building, she finds herself very much alone. Her separation is acute. The lab is awash with organised bustle. There are staff and visitors, meetings and experiments. Beyond the lab itself she treads slowly, absorbing the solitude. Despite the fact that she spends much of her life alone, having no parents, partner or real friends. Being here offers a different kind of loneliness. The new environment makes her alters her entire manner. It is her way to pace, she is widely known for this characteristic. Her staff joke, to each other, that they have to sprint to keep pace as she storms around. Her mind too works at a similar speed. Her thoughts jostle, are ordered, and are moved on. Unfortunately, this is also how she more often than not deals with other people. She does not really attribute anything peripheral much time or value. Her way and manner has won her no friends. Her superiors may respect her greatly, and rely on her completely, but words of appreciation from a man in a suit are no substitute for real human contact and genuine affection. Her life has neither of these things.

For the first time in longer than she can recall, she actually stops in her tracks. She observes the building around her. The massive silver boxes which house the hundreds of thousands of processors whir and tick. It is all coldly efficient. They form tall, consistently grey columns, running off in every direction. From where she is standing, it looks as if there is nothing else in the entire world other than this sheer repetitive form. Viewing it this way, she feel them now, as an overbearing presence. For all her time at work, she realises, the workings of the laboratories run almost beyond perception. She spends day upon day walking above, oblivious to this immense presence lying below their feet. It is like a resting beast, awaiting it's time to unfurl itself and to rise from the shadowy underworld.

Now that she has actually stopped and looked, she sees the staggering scale of this whole operation. She is whisked back to her first thoughts when their team were initially brought into this enormous corporate facility. Having seen it for the very first time, it was apparent that they were dancing with greatness.

This place and the scale of it dwarfed and outshone the dank surroundings where the project began. It was all so very different then

- ramshackle and chaotic. She thinks of those early times - the laughter of her comrades, and the sheer marvel of it all. She had not thought of it for such a long while. But thoughts flood back to her now. For the first time in her entire life she wonders whether perhaps they may indeed have sold their souls, to form their dream. There is certainly very little laughter and marvel anymore. And the job has just become her life. She gets up, works, eats, sleeps - then start again. Her life is functional and patterned.

As she looks around her she realises that there is no natural light, and is shocked to think that she can't actually remember the last time she just looked out of a window - any window - and that perhaps this place is the mirror of her own world - blandly repetitive and almost completely shut-off from the outside world.

She breaks her meandering and sets herself back on track. Another floor down and another world unfold. She has reached the dark, noisy mechanical area. The motorised driving force of the whole complex. This is where the old files were stored. She flicks a switch and a single fluorescent tube flickers hesitantly to form an uncooperative half arc of illumination. She waits several long seconds, and it eventually hesitantly splutters to full radiance. 'Why do they never change the starters on those bloody lights?'

The whole place is a mass of whining, clanking metallic noise. There could not be a more stark transition from the quiet of the processors. It is like being transported back to the Industrial

Revolution. Huge machinery swings and rotates in repetitive motion, each turn accompanied by a level of sound that could almost strip you of your senses. The heat is phenomenal too. From the deliberately chilled surroundings of the computer zone, she has stepped into this cauldron.

She is relieved when she sees the storage boxes, wedged into one of the far corners of the room. She is determined, despite the overbearing sound and heat, to be thorough in this avenue of investigation. She had considered having someone organise bringing the boxes up to her office. But had thought better of letter *anyone* know what she was thinking and planning. If someone really had tampered, there is no knowing who that person was. Her only hope was that they hadn't thought to address these records.

She pulls up a dirty old plastic chair, and having given it a thorough brush down, she sits. She is surrounded by containers. She opens a lid and pulls out the first file. Then she stops. She has a perceptible feeling that she is being manipulated. She is not prone to feelings of paranoia or panic, but she is suddenly very afraid.

It is then that she sees him. He is standing by one of the large mechanical motors. Despite being half cast in shadow, she knows him at once. Her initial, she reasons, were right.

His cane taps the ground as he approaches. Kelly can't really hear it for the din of the machines, but replays the familiar sound from earlier at the tour.

With every step he takes, he moves closer and closer to her. She studies his face as he enters the inadequate glare of the single luminous light. *What does he wants?*. She decides to front him out. 'The tour finished quite a while ago." she shouts out over the clanks and whines. The man looks up, offers a sardonic smile and continues towards her. She is now, very disturbed. His manner reeks of sinister intent. His countenance suggests that he knows what is coming next, and she hates with her entire being that she does not.

She looks around for somewhere she may run, or for something with which she may defend herself. She can see no easy way out, and nothing of use. His cane no longer provides disdain. In her mind now, it is a cold and efficient weapon - and this man looks like he could and would wield it with ease.

But just as she is about to crumble under the weight of her own terror, he stops. He stands several metres away from her. He may have assessed her anxiety and judged that he had panicked her enough. Whatever the reason, he has decided not to infringe any further into her personal space.

'Where is it?' She suddenly demands, buoyed by fear, she unleashes the words with venom.

'Where is what?' he replies, looking genuinely puzzled.

'I am sure that you know very well what it is that I am looking for. It would save us all a considerable amount of time if you just let me know where it is.'

The man looks confused. But Kelly is not convinced by his expression.

'What would I know of the things that you seek?' He states, his smirk apparent.

She knows that he is playing with her, perhaps for no other reason than to taunt her. Not really knowing how to play back, she changes tack. 'OK. I'm not here to mess about, let's cut to the chase. What happened to Ben on that last Voyage?'

He smiles fully now, she senses he knows about everything, but is also not readily going to relay any of that information to her.

'We have a problem.' he states.

'What problem?...Who is we?..Why...?' she stops herself. She realises that the machine gun questioning makes her appear out of her depth and without a clue about what is going on.

'I can't, and quite frankly, I won't say more than I have to.' He assesses his words, and then continues. 'It appears we may have overlooked some possibilities and potentials outcomes.' For the first time in this encounter it is his turn to look uncomfortable. 'There is something that we hadn't fully expected, and now we are…mmm…'

he pauses, looks to the ceiling for an expression '*Fire-fighting* …This is not a scenario we are used to, and to be honest we are not comfortable with this situation.' He pauses again, for a long time. Kelly gets the impression he is about to say something that it is paining him to admit.

'As such,' he eventually continues, 'I have been instructed to request your help.'

She laughs out loud. She sees the man grimace, and she immediately regrets it. She is fully aware that she often lacks social graces, but this time, she feels she should kick herself – very hard. This man has humbled himself, and she has slapped him down with mockery. She feels ashamed.

'I'm sorry!' She grasps for explanation. "It's just that I thought you were about to attack me.' She reddens, realising that this was neither tactful or particularly conciliatory. It was however effective, as the man appears appeased by her admission.

He steps forward a pace. Instinctively she recoils. They both then look at each other, slightly embarrassed. Both divert their gaze. He lifts the lid of the box he had stepped towards. Kelly stands stock still, not really sure how the situation is going to pan out. He stretches out his arm, in his hand is a note. He doesn't want to step any closer to her. Despite her bravado, she is obviously extremely afraid. Kelly initially pauses, but then strides forward with all the confidence she can muster and takes the piece of paper.

86

'You will also need this!' he informs her. He then slides a lid from the box next to him and presents it to her. 'This information requires a higher security clearance than is held by anyone you have ever met. Even your Government have no idea about this. Don't tell … ANYONE … ANYTHING! Do you understand.' He fixes her with a deathly glare and the fear races back through her anew.

'You will be substantially rewarded for your assistance. But I must also offer due warning. If any of this gets out...' He lets the sentence run off, not needing to complete it. Yet he nods as if to request assent and understanding. She nod, then takes the file.

He turns on his heels and with a carefree swagger strides away from her. As he goes he taps the cane onto the cold concrete floor.

The paper has an old fashioned Mobile phone number and the words *My Number*, scrawled in erratic writing.

The file is old and tatty. She recognises it immediately. It is one of the old writing books in which were scribble the original notes, formulae etc, from the very start of the project. Given the magnitude of the current operation it all seems somewhat ridiculous, even unbelievable that it was born in these note pads.

She opens the cover. She recognises the handwriting. It is Robert Crown's

# Chapter 7 - Montgomery Shooting

How the Company gets hold of those that are put through the process is masked in shadow secrecy.

Ben had been idly chatting to one of the muscular, yet seemingly brainless lumps which the lab-staff have nicknamed - *Baggers*. These are the *specialists* that the Company retains in order to *acquire* what it wants. This Bagger, Ben found out, had been part of the team that had brought in Montgomery, a couple of days before.

The *specialist* had winked and a tapped his nose, suggesting that he was speaking *off the record*. Ben had to stop himself from laughing into his cup of tea at this naivety. The bagger apparently had no awareness of the lab surveillance system. He had absolutely no idea that every word he had spoken, and every secret he had betrayed, were being recorded. As the man boasted of his exploits, Ben couldn't help but look through him, thinking of how these could perhaps be his last spoken words. Eventually he actually turns his gaze upon him.

His initial impression had been of the sheer physical presence and overbearing bravado. He had taken an immediate dislike to him. He saw the bagger as no more than a glorified thug. Ben had taken twisted solace thinking of what terrible fates awaited this man for spreading so many secrets.

But now, as he studies the man before him and he feels guilt. Despite the baggers intimidating bulk, the eyes set within the massive skull shone through with unsullied innocence. His true self, hidden behind his mask of muscle, cried out fear. Ben sees him as a hermit crab, soft and vulnerable, absolutely reliant on the protection of his outer shell. He could see a man, scared of the world and what it can do. . There was hope in his face longing that someone would see the pain and anguish of the scared little boy hidden deep within the muscular form. Something had once, Ben thought, pushed a youngster to retreat behind this wall of steroids and testosterone. The child though was still present, and the longer Ben looked, the truer this form became. Despite all the terrible things he had probably done, Ben could now only see little boy's eyes staring out wishing for someone to rescue him and to make him safe. It reached the point where he could no longer bear this new reality. He had to walk away, attempting to wash his mind clean with thoughts of work and process.

Theoretically it didn't actually matter that the bagger had told Ben all those important details. Ben knows more than anyone else would, could or ever did know about the recent addition. But he had inadvertently proved that he couldn't be trusted to keep things to himself. He would inevitably be punished for this misdemeanour, and usually such slip-ups were final.

No matter how far Ben walked from the man, the memory of what he is and what will befall him festered. No matter what he wipes over his mind in an attempt to cleanse himself - the empathy that allows him to do what he does and to see what he sees while in the machine, is also a prison that ensnares his consciousness and tortures his own daily life. He sees too much, and it hurts him constantly.

To make matters worse, Ben will always know too, that it was not a fortuitous accident that had brought them together. He had deliberately accessed and assessed the baggers personnel files the day before. He saw that there had been concerns raised about this man letting information slip. There was a formal low level warning on file. Ben had deliberately pitched for this. The man had given him a thorough insight into what had been done to attain Montgomery; where from, why, and most importantly in this instance - how he had been shot.

Ben had suspicions about why the experience within Montgomery had yielded what it had. There was a constant knotted feeling in his belly that would not ease. He had thought that knowing more about Montgomery would provide broader answers. But with everything he gathered, there were still much more left unsolved. The information was there, but it wasn't saying what Ben knew it should be.

The call comes through while Ben sits wrestling with his thoughts. He is informed that the lab was again prepared. As standard - Ben does his checks. Having finished, he looks around the room. It has not been this full of onlookers since the early ventures. As well as faces from around the department there are a number of people he can't place. He knows though, who these people will be. They are Suits

90

and administrators - people whom he considers just linger in the background, feeding off others for their own personal gain. He can't abide them, and is not happy at their presence.

Ben rests the interface upon his head. He feels the probes touch his temples, and the familiar feeling of the metallic cage that holds it all in place. He nestles into the cradle, feeling it's comforting embrace.

When Ben is finally ready, the process begins.

*The dark curtains falls around me.* The transition through the layers of nothingness are akin to stabbing a marker into shifting sands. Certainty is removed and there isn't anything definitive to rest upon or fix. *All points both lead away and return. Gloom moves through spectrum's of black, then lifts to brightness. My entry to the other world is swift and direct. I am in an observational scenario.*

I have arrived in a town centre. High rise buildings push up to the sky. When I raise my eyes I see a formation of rolling dark grey cloud. There is very little sunlight penetrating its overbearing denseness. Electric street lights puncture the semi-darkness. No-one is here, and nothing is moving. The glare of the unnatural luminescence washes through the empty streets. A cold wind circles me and then drifts on.

I see Montgomery. He is walking towards me, but on the other side of the road. He is still a long way off, but I know it is him. He purposefully moves through a doorway. I can no longer see him, from where I am standing. I hurry across trying to observe where he has gone. He entered a small shop. It appears to be an independent music store. I enter too, and shuffle as inconspicuously as I can to the furthest reaches of the room. There are a few other people in here, and no-one seems to particularly notice my arrival. I peer over the top of the rudimentary boxes that have been rigged to hold the now valuable Vinyl. From this vantage I see a conversation occurring between Montgomery and a tall, broad, bearded man behind the counter. The man is laden with tattoos and piercings. His manner appears cordial, and their conversation amicable. Montgomery passes the man what appears to be a note. It was very subtle, and would not have been noticed if I had not been watching intently. I need to get hold of whatever it was that he has just handed over.

It is far too dangerous to interfere in a scenario. I can't tell how the participants may react. A previous Voyager was almost killed when he got involved in an unfolding scene. If I overstep, I will forsake their acceptance of my presence here. The protagonists will most likely become hostile. The previous Voyager ran, and was lucky the process ended, sweeping him away to safety. I can't expect that that will necessarily be true for me. I must bide my time and see what I can do.

As is so often the case in these situations, everything had appeared relatively normal. But too many time have I seen it appear so!

I can remember other scenes in my thoughts, they went just like this - the shock stretched across the faces of those present, the sudden sound, the lingering smell...

People never believe they will be targeted - even when they know they are high risk. I have watched diplomats, drug-lords, crime-kingpins, witnesses in important trials - none of them seem to believe it is happening to them.

I see Montgomery turn. He realises - At the very last moment. Shock spreads through him. He tenses, eyes wide, mouth open - as if to say 'No! But the word never comes...

A sharp crack sounds. It echoes loudly, bouncing off the hard edges of the shop's tightly enclosed innards. It is not the type of bang that you would expect. It sound too insubstantial to do quite so much harm.

Here, as so often before, it doesn't immediately register with the other clientele what has happened. It was quick and without aggression. It was though ruthless none-the-less. Montgomery slumps to the floor. A second shot sounds. I stand still, as transfixed as the man behind the counter, who looks on, as white as a sheet, stuck firmly to the spot.

The assailant is already gone before the proprietor even had time to turn to look at him. I speed towards the Montgomery. I am not sure why. I really should not have ventured from the shadowy anonymity of the background. For some reason though, I feel responsible. For some reason I felt drawn to enter the scene.

He is, of course, badly injured. I know this already - otherwise I would not even be here at all. The 'hit' wasn't as professional as it had at first appeared. The first shot was directly through the chest, as would have been the killer's plan. The second all important head shot was however, wide of the mark. This was not a clean job. He has one last conscious gasp in him. I hold his hand to comfort and console him. He looks straight into my eyes and tries to speak to me, just as he slips from life. His last words are gargled and breathless, but he fights hard to squeeze them forth. "Please tell Samantha that I love her.'

I grimace at the words, again torn by my realisation of their permanent separation. I feel him go limp. He becomes a dead weight in my arms.

The shop keeper has come to stand beside me. I take the opportunity to lay the man down and to move away from the scene. As the shopkeeper leans to examine him. I move round to where I saw him stash the note. I slide it imperceptibly into my pocket and return to the door, past the shocked and confused onlookers.

This shouldn't be possible...it hadn't occurred to me while everything else was going on. As soon as Montgomery lost consciousness, this world should have effectively dissolved from being.

Without his reality, there should be nothing for me to exist within.

It has been several minutes since the shot occurred - and yet I am still here, watching. - but from who's perspective am I now seeing this unfold. I really don't understand this at all.

A team has arrived to attend the scene. It is not a standard ambulance. I wonder if this is what it is that I am meant to see…that is why I am still here…the people on the scene aren't from the hospital, it's the Baggers - I recognise the one I was talking to, the scared, childlike man-mountain.

Their arrival is far too soon after the incident. This was all staged…Montgomery was shot to order…that explains why the second shot was off target. Whoever set this up, wanted him to end up with us at the lab…

Within a couple of minutes the Baggers have him away from the scene.

Yet I am still here. I remember the note…It is small and neatly folded. I open it tentatively and read the contents.

It is short and concise, though the meaning is not really clear - I'm sorry, but you are trapped.

# Chapter 8 - Re-Entry

It can never be presumed that re-entry will be easy - despite the relative ease with which Ben often dealt with the entire process, this return has caused him to descend into a full blown fit. The spasms are unpleasant to witness. The whole scene is distressing. His motions and the sounds he is producing are more akin to an exorcism than a scientific procedure. He has never exhibited anything like this before, and most of the research assistants have not experienced anything of this kind before.

Even in his first ever re-entry - universally described by all other participants as being the worse experience humanly imaginable - Ben had come back with only mild irregularities in his body patterns. But now, all of the machines alarms are buzzing. His erratic contortions suggest there has been a serious malfunction. Wild beeping surges from every monitor, signalling an impending disaster. Masses of red lights flash. The whole ward is in turmoil. Frantic doctors and nurses hurry in every direction. Researchers and general assistants all rush to do anything they possibly can.

Thomas, rigid with shock, watches from the back of the room. He, unlike nearly everyone else here, has seen this before. He scans the room and catches Kelly looking directly at him. He knows why…She has seen this before too.

Before The Company forcefully imposed itself onto this project, it was being run as an independent research project - mostly funded by a grant from a cutting edge bio-tech development Institute. The team that started this all of ran everything out of a worn-down industrial unit in one of the rougher parts of town.

To look at the scale of this operation now, it would be hard to believe. The Company have taken this endeavour to a stratospheric level - with state of the art machinery and the best research assistance money can buy. Yet the original research team had started with equipment which was begged, borrowed and literally stolen. It was all hastened together by pure ingenuity and determination. The venture may have looked like something from a school science block, but in reality it was at the forefront of anything of its kind. Solder was smothered around, almost haphazardly, to forge together circuitry. Absolutely essential pieces of equipment were held together with nothing more than reams of sticky tape. It appeared that an accidental sneeze would render the entire apparatus to scrap. But it held together, and more importantly, it worked.

The first person to actually Voyage was not Ben, but his then best friend - Robert. At that point the pair were as thick as thieves. Their relationship had been conducive to pushing the others on - further and faster. They bounced around revolutionary ideas and theories, in such a manner that the rest of their group could not help but be inspired. They literally forged the enterprise through their joint passion for the project. Robert had been the brightest and most influential of the group. There were seventeen original members. Despite all the odds, they had then proceeded to set this unlikely collaboration in motion.

Slightly later, additional help was then brought in, to move it all to the next level. It was then that both Kelly and Thomas came on board.

On one 13th November the group had managed – no-one will now admit how – to take hold of a body. The man - aged forty two, average build, fairly standard biometrics - had died in a freak road traffic accident. The hospital had kept him 'alive' artificially for just over a month, but then it was agreed that the switch should be turned off. Somehow there was a vehicle waiting by the back doors of the ward, just as the plug was pulled. The rear of a commercial transporter was packed with the necessary apparatus. They managed to drag the still warm body straight out of the back doors, and away. He was installed into the machinery at their somewhat makeshift lab within the hour.

Trepidation was rife. The moment of truth had finally come upon them. All of their work culminated in that moment. If it had been a legal undertaking, it would one day be recognised as a formidable step forward in scientific development. As it was, it wasn't legal, and therefore was not officially recorded. Whatever the history books show, things had been changed - forever.

Robert Crown made a Voyage, and indeed, amazingly, returned unharmed. His re-telling - upon his re-entry and recuperation - was the stuff of marvel. He had briefly walked within another man's consciousness, and although he had only been 'in there' for several seconds, it was a moment in time that had changed man's future.

Everything in those early days was off the cuff. Barely anything was monitored properly. It took weeks to devise, design, build and then hone each of the appropriate trackers, internal finder software, consciousness stabilising units…and so on. None of these things could be bought off the shelf, and were made to order, one-by-one. They were learning how to do the job, while they were doing the job.

It was common course back then for various people to take flights. The major limiting factor was getting hold of an appropriate test 'body' to work with.

In the seventh month, on the sixth flight, was the first fatality. Selina Hobbs Johnston; the daughter of one of the continent's most influential industrialists. She was a first class honours graduate, and at one time had been a leading socialite - often photographed partying with celebrities, royals and the very top corporate elite. She was one of the original seventeen. She had given up her glamorous lifestyle to slum it with the rest of the team in the industrial quarter. She, along with everyone else there, bore the long hours, the tedious number crunching, and the atrocious coffee. Her previous social standing were not important - she was their friend, she was part of the team.

She had then been declared dead.

An hour after her re-entry the bright young thing - the sparkling light in her father's eye - was no more. The repercussions of their failure were immense. At that very early stage, it almost sank the entire project. Several of them were under the real and tangible threat of facing a sizable prison sentence for their involvement in the tragedy.

Selina's father had pursued them relentlessly, using every means at his substantial disposal, he built a large and powerful legal team and then went for the jugular. It was only the intervention of the mother that saved the group. Though also stricken with grief, she had been desperate to know what it was that had so engaged her daughter that she would throw away the star-lifestyle, to live in a dank old factory in the back-end of nowhere. When the mother came to understand the process, and to hear her daughter's own recorded logs; showing her excitement and unswerving dedication, the case was dropped. The father was pacified by knowing how important this had all been to his beloved child. Incredibly, their new-found understanding of their daughter and her dream saw the wealthy couple set about supporting the project. The patronage was greatly welcomed. It helped the research team push forward in leaps and bounds.

It was however, agreed by the group that Selina's parents - or anyone else for that matter - should never know the exact events that surrounded her death. The poor girl had died in horrendous agony. At the time one of the team had even run screaming from the makeshift lab, babbling about demons and exorcism.

That memory is now again very fresh to both Kelly and Thomas. It was like seeing it all unfold, once again.

After several hours of the most intense medical intervention that the modern world could feasibly bring to bear, Ben is at last stabilised. In any other situation, with anything less than the most advanced equipment at their disposal, Ben would have been dead. As it was, his prospects are unclear.

It actually took three days before Ben opened his eyes. The monitors flashed wildly in recognition of his waking, and staff rushed to him in droves. He was physically stable and responded positively to all tests and stimuli put to him. To all intents and purpose he has come through this terrible ordeal with his body unharmed.

His mental state is a different matter. Since his return, he hasn't spoken. At first there were fears he was brain-damaged and may even have lost the ability. As tests transpired, it was put down to fatigue. It was presumed that vocalisation would return when he had fully rested and recuperated.

It was decided not to push for immediate answers, or any formal debrief. He was allowed to recover at his own necessary pace.

Through further deliberation it was decided that it may be best for him if he be allowed to be taken out of the labs, surmising that it may aid his recovery to be in a less clinical setting. Thomas was charged with going with him for the duration - just in case matters do unexpectedly take a negative turn.

On the day of his departure a few well-wishers were present as a company pod drew up to collect Ben and Thomas from the lab building. Kelly and the Professor were amongst them, and each offered there regards and hopes for a speedy recovery. Kelly had been fairly distant, seemingly distracted since the day of the accident. It was presumed that she had taken it all badly, given what she had seen in the past. Thomas was sure that there was more to it, but dare not venture to ask her. He also had a million and one things to organise before they left, so didn't really have time to address anything with her anyway. When he was sure that he had everything in hand Thomas made the decision, and the pod rolled out of the compound, and off towards the city. Those that stood there watching it leave could not help but wonder what it meant to see it go. The only person making the whole complex viable had just driven away. The jobs and livelihood of everyone there was tied up with his recovery and the possibility that he may one day be able, or perhaps even willing to do such a dangerous thing ever again. It was a time of great uncertainty. For now, all they could do was crunch the numbers and find out what the hell had gone wrong in the first place. From there…

To that end the Professor walked with Kelly back towards their offices. Although chatting politely, there was no real motivation on either's part to discuss anything in particular. The events of the past few days had been draining, and most people were subdued as they went about their daily chores. The Professor eventually took his leave and Kelly walked sullenly back alone. She didn't speak to anyone on her way, and closed the door behind her as she went into her private space.

It therefore came completely against the grain of the general sombreness of the place that one of the assistants from the Voyager team scramble into Kelly's office shouting excitedly. Startled by the unexpected and somewhat unwelcome intrusion she bristled with anger, and was fully ready to launch a violent tirade. But something stops her. Her natural reaction would have been to assert her authority. -For some reason his actions have separated her from that moment.

'There is something else in there!' The man screams at her. He is desperate and erratic. Kelly is dedicated to the notion of self-control. This man's exhibition of wildness is at complete odds to her tethered world.

He is waving around a piece of paper, but she can't see it as he keeps flapping it back-and-forth. His eyes are unfocused and breathing at the point of hysteria. Sweat smears his brow and he reeks - of fear.

Unwilling to tumble into his madness, she merely sits behind her desk, unmoved. 'Stop!' She says, holding up her hand to create a symbolic buffer between herself and the confusion. 'Calm down!' I will not deal with you until you talk slowly, and in a reasonable manner'.

It takes some time, but eventually the man does calm sufficiently for her to try to get some sense from him.

'There…are more…more th…than two patterns registered!' The man blurts, again resorting to wildly gesticulating as he fumbles with the printout he is holding.

'NO!' She shouts

He stops moving, but still continues to let out a strange, low whine that she finds disconcerting and a little bit scary.

The man takes several deep breaths, desperately attempting to gather himself and to do as she had commanded.

Kelly sits, still and determined. She will have order, and she will regain control.

After several moments she stands up. His eyes follow as though he were an obedient hound. She steps towards him, to instil an even greater sense of her bearing on the situation. She looks him straight in the eyes. 'Ready?' She asks…he nods…'Then proceed.' She states.

104

'We, we, we…' He tries.

Kelly switches tack. 'Slowly now. Take your time.' She sets a reassuring smile, lifted from the arsenal she usually reserves for senior figures.

He tries again, and this time manages to relay the problem. 'We have the Voyager's trace…all fine.' He holds up the piece of paper he has been waving since he arrived. 'We have the patient.'

Kelly nods her understand.

'But then this!' The assistant looks at her, imploring her to help.

Kelly takes the printout and scans her eyes to the man's face. He is absolutely ashen and look like he is on the verge of having a breakdown. For a moment this distracts her, and she doesn't registered any of the details on the page. Dragging her eyes back to the paper in her hand, she drops the sheet. Tension rushes through her and she feels her shoulders contract. A headache barges its way through the front-door of her consciousness and wipes its feet on her attempts to fight it.

The lab is fever-pitched. Every expert and most of the auxiliary staff have been recalled to help deal with the emergency. Kelly notices one of the assistants, who's name she can actually recall. She walks over and addresses her. 'Track back through all the data we have and see at which point the additional presence first manifested.'

She orders. 'Get as many staff as you need to help you. This is of the utmost importance. Do you understand?'

'I'll do that now. Absolutely, Yes.' The researcher replies.

'Kelly, I need you to come with me.' states the Professor.

Kelly nods and follows him. She is led into a quiet side office. There are not many quiet areas left available after the discovery, and the subsequent furore that has followed. Kelly's office is being used as the hot-desk for any Board member that has been sanctioned to sit in on proceedings - they have insisted that at least one of them is present at all times.

'Kelly. There is something very wrong here.' He states

She can't help but stare at him. That, surely, is an understatement of sizable proportions. She hopes he has something of substance to follow that seemingly irrelevant statement. She needs this man, one of the only people she likes and respects, to offer her more than just that! She has to reign herself in though, as she realises that no-one but she knows about the man with the cane, and subsequently about Robert Crown. Despite her burning desire to chase down that lead as fast as she possibly can, she realises that what is happening here in the lab is massive revelation.

There is *much* more to this, and there is indeed something very wrong here. But for now. She must deal with the discovery at hand.

'I know Professor, I have been thinking that perhaps we need to look back at the really old records, for information.'

He nods assent. 'Good idea, ill form a team and get on it at once.'

She is both relieved and ashamed by her actions. She has lied to a man she respects. She has sent him off on a wild goose chase. She already has the information the Professor and his team will now spend fruitless hours looking for.

But this move will buy her time. She has somewhere to be, and the Professor being distracted poring through the old files should offer her just the time she needs.

# Part 2 - A friend in need

# Chapter 9 - Ben Trapped

*Ben*

It takes a time for me to think back to what I was running from. I need to reassess in the light of reason. With deep breaths and forced concentration I finally manage to collect myself. The panic has subsided. I sit on my haunches and assess some wounds on my hands, knees and elbows. I have evidently fallen at some point, and quite severely by the look of these scrapes. I can't recall falling, or why it happened?

I am in the countryside. I know this place. It is the place my grandparents lived for their entire life. I have been here a thousand times and I know every nook like, the back of my hands. I haven't been here for many, many years - since my grandparents died. I've had no reason to be here since. But why am I here now?...and how did I get here?

I am shaken from these thoughts, by movement. In the distance, a man is approaching on a bicycle. I rack my mind for answers. I can't have been running away from this man, as I was heading in that direction when I first found came too. Was I perhaps running *to* the man? I can't be sure. I really can't remember. I can't place the fear that had been all consuming when I had first been aware of being here. What was that from?

The person on the bike is clearly coming into view. They can obviously see me too – Oh, they are now waving.

But it may all seem a bit odd. I can't express to someone else that I was just feeling erratic and completely out-of-control, and yet do not have the slightest clue why. I would look insane! But what about my scraped and bruised hands...How will I explain these? Perhaps...I *have* gone insane? What else would make any sense?

Now I can clearly see the stranger's face. A man of about fifty, I would think, with wavy greying hair, in strangely old fashioned clothing. He is dressed more like a character from a period drama, though the era escapes me. I can't help but think that the man is somehow familiar, yet I can't put my finger on from where or when I would know him.

I am drawn back to thinking of my grand-parents. But when I turn my full attention on them, I can't really remember them at all. There is only a floating and intangible whisper of them. I can't picture them or recall their faces in any clarity. It is as if my mind is actively forgetting them, or is keeping them at bay from my consciousness.

'Hello there!' The man calls out. The sudden immediacy of his presence shakes me back to the moment. I notice the strong regional accent and immediately feel subsumed within it. It is from my home county. It fits perfectly with my recollections of this place, and further cements me.

'Hello!'

'Good gracious, what have you done to yourself? Are you alright?' The man asks. His tone and manner show genuine concern.

'I tripped over, I was running, I fell.' I reply. I am not sure of these facts though, and I hope the man doesn't press me any further on this.

'Fell over what'? The man inevitably asks.

My mind recoils. I had hoped not to have to explain - that I didn't know. I feel the embarrassment. I desperately search my mind, hoping to provide some sort of credible answer. In fact, I just want to be able to offer any answer at all, to the perfectly reasonable question. But as I think about it…I do know. I didn't *think* I had known…I actually *know* that I did not know. Yet now, though surprised, I am relieved, it has come back to me.

'Mmm, I tripped over myself actually, I was running from something, and I tripped over my own feet'. I now feel incredibly stupid for having relayed that, particularly as it appears to be complete nonsense.

To his credit, the man does not pull me up on this gibberish. 'Well then, I would say you'd best not try out for any sports that requires any rushing around or anything.' The man offers. "It don't seem to be your thing does it?'

We both then laugh politely.

'Are you alright though? No permanent damage?'

'No I'm just a bit battered and bruised. Mostly I just feel stupid'.

'Oh now don't worry, they happen these things. But what was it you were running from?'

At first this chokes me. I was convinced that I had no recollection of this either. But again I find that I can now remember more and more. I can't help but notice that my memory is being formed backwards at the same rate as I appear to be going forward.

But before I answer this time, I stop and reason the response before I actually blurt it. Despite my inward reservations, for some reason I find myself inclined to tell him what I newly know. 'I was walking over by a pond'. I pause and point. 'And I thought I saw something'.

The man's expression alters completely. From a look of care, he is suddenly fearful and distant. It is not said, but the dynamic of this meeting has suddenly changed.

'What did you see'? His eyes fixed, his stare deep. A serious expression had replaced his previous jovial demeanour.

'I, I don't, I'm not, it was mmmm...'

'Come now lad, what was it that scared you?'

'Movement'. As soon as I say it I am embarrassed again. I realise how stupid that must sound. A man, a stranger, asks me what has scared me so much that I have obviously ran until I have managed to quite badly hurt himself...and all I can say - is 'movement'.

I have to laugh out loud and hold my hands over my eyes. I am actually wishing that when I remove them the man will have gone. I am praying that we wouldn't have to continue this embarrassing encounter any further. But when I finally look out through my hands the man is still there. The bristles on my neck compound my discomfort further, as I realise that the man is most certainly *not* laughing at this ridiculous admission.

'You shouldn't be over there'! The man announces abruptly.

The manner of the statement, more than the words themselves catch me off guard.

'Why?' I pause. 'I mean...I'm really sorry…was I trespassing or something?'

The man cuts me short. 'What were you doing over there by the pond?

'I'm really sorry, I didn't know. I...I was just walking...walking around the countryside and... well...that's all'.

The man switches back to his previous personable character. The severe expression gives way to a deep and friendly smile.

'I didn't mean to chastise you lad. Don't you be worrying.' He scans his eyes around, and then asks, ' How did you get right out here in the middle of nowhere anyway?

'Oh, I was walking over that field'.

'From where?' The man questions, though with no admonishment now present in his tone.

'I'm not sure?' I state truly. I still can't remember how or where I had come from to be at the pond in the first place. I had hoped that that would soon become clear too, but it has not.

'Well, where are you heading to?'

Again I feel flummoxed. I can't register any point or purpose to this trip at all.

'Mmm, well I don't know.' I look around confused. 'I'd better find an inn or a hotel. Is there one nearby?'

'There is a pub over the fields. Two miles as the crow flies. Five by road...but it will be dark before you get there, and there ain't any guarantee they'll have rooms available, is there?'

The realisation had not escaped me. The thought of being out here in the pitch black doesn't bear thinking. I have always liked the completeness of the darkness that the countryside provides. I wore it like a comfort blanket that erased the worse parts of the days. But this is a whole new situation. Something managed to scare me half out of my wits. I don't know what it was, and I don't much fancy the prospect of being stuck wandering around out here on the premise that whatever it was may well still be around.

'Tell you what lad, me and the wife got a place a way up the road here. We got spare rooms, our boys have all gone off now, we're all alone most of the time, so we have plenty of space. So it's yours for the night, if you want it."

'That is too kind. I really can't accept. I mean...Mmm...well you don't know me, and...Mmm...I, well...'. I am stumbling. I can't think of how to put it. I want to say yes more than life itself. At this moment, I want to be anywhere than out here when the sun disappears, and by the sight of the horizon, that isn't far off. But, these are complete strangers, so politeness steers me away from grabbing his arm and marching off to safety. But my reality appears stark. I really can't see any other choice. The longer we discuss options, the lesser the light. The lesser the light, the lesser the appeal of walking out across the dark countryside, not knowing where I am going, and what may be around the next dark bend. I have to accept his offer.

'Great'. I blurt. 'I don't want to put you out, but if you really don't mind, I would like to accept. Thank you so ever so much sir'.

'Now don't you be sir'ing me lad, me names William. Will actually...Will Barker. My wife is Katie, now let's be a getting along then, night is a drawing ever in on us, stood out here and all'.

As we are walking I realise that I do know this man. I can't understand how it is that I am here with him, but I now know who he is. I have experienced this world before. It was not my childhood or my grandparents that I had recalled before. When I saw this man before, it was through someone else's eyes. As shocking as this revelation is, the relief of finding context is somehow more reassuring than disturbing. I know this person. I have met him before.

I also now know that this man has never actually met *me* before.

I am at a loss of whether to say who I am. I can't see I have much choice, so I will just try being me for now, and see how that works. I extend my cut and bruised hand to the man. 'Oh yes, sorry...'

115

I say. 'My name is Ben...sorry about the bloody hand'. We both laugh as we shake hands. Nothing is said about my introduction, so I presume everything is fine.

We both move on together without the need for more than idle pleasantries.

I do not breach the subject of our previous meeting. I am pretty sure that would only shock or scare him. I am not sure how I have ended up being here with a man from a borrowed past, but I certainly will be interested to see what this man may know, and to how this all sticks together with my absence of memory.

Approaching the Barker's small cottage, it exudes a sense of rural idyll. It like what you would see on a genteel Sunday evening sitcom. The soft warm evening sun bears all the hallmarks of having been conscripted directly from an advertisement. The image resembles something that would adorn the pamphlets that tumble from newspaper supplements, where products are dissolved within a sugary reassurance of an imagined dream.

The small cottage itself could easily have been snatched straight from the pages of a nineteenth century novel. It exudes charm and character. Ivy grows abundantly around the door-frames. The furniture in the porch-way is all mismatched and cobbled together. A small greenhouse has been constructed from a few of old window frames and left-over sections of clear corrugated plastic. As I gaze

116

upon the sheds and outhouses, the practicality roles away from what has been erected, and what is left beyond this is a feeling of calmness.

The gardens are well tended, and are obviously someone's pride and joy. The vibrant selection of ornate shrubs and perennial blooms offer a perfect sense of well-tended balance. The flowers radiate the day, as the late evening summer glows upon their delicate surfaces. The whole scene exudes a beauty in colour and in form.

There is a sense of life here, and of lives being lived. I have sunken straight into it.

A face appears at the kitchen window. A round, reddened, tousled haired character draws quickly backwards and disappears. I am beginning to wonder whether this was such a good idea, and whether Will has perhaps overstepped by inviting this complete stranger round to his house without telling his wife. For a few seconds I can't decide whether to turn on my heels and make my excuses, or whether to follow on and see what happens. Before my mind can tussle further, it is put beyond consideration. A warm glowing smile greets us at the porch door. A slightly chubby, floral clad women whose age it would be hard to estimate, though must be beyond sixty years. No sooner had we entered the house she has offered me tea, some cake, to sit down, asked of my health. I cannot tell if it is a nervous response to having an unexpected and unknown guest, or whether she is just welcoming to all that she meets. I opt to believe the later. Mrs Barker is truly delightful. She radiates charm and from the briefest of time with her it is obvious that she has an excitable nature.

I extend my hand to shake. At first she seems taken aback by the gesture, but soon a soft smile wrinkles back across her chubby, reddened face.

'Well aren't you a polite young man!' She says softly. She holds herself with a poignant grace. Her expression draws you in, exuding calm acceptance. One could not be in her presence without feeling her charm.

She eventually takes my hand. Her own is soft and warm. It so perfectly reflects her. 'Hello. She says.

'Very nice to meet you Mrs Barker.' I stammer.

'No, no, no. We'll be having none of that. You will call me Katie…None of this "Mrs Barker" nonsense - is that clear?'

She stops shaking my hand, having now seen the cuts, deep set gravel burns and dried on blood. She does not release my hand but instead holds them both gently in her own, showing pity and a soothing motherliness. She rushes around gathering bandages, tape and the like. Within moments I am trussed and wrapped, and feel immediately better from the attention alone.

Katie has evidently been baking. As we had entered the cottage the air was thick with the most delicious aromas. It is a dense and

118

homely scents. I can smell bread, and cake. My grandparents house had this same smell. I remember it from childhood (my own, I think). I am transported right back to that time in my mind.

After a good night's sleep I feel rested and relaxed. I am determined though, that I will not outstay my welcome. These are amongst the nicest and kindest people I have ever met, and I will not prey on their generosity any further. I have resolved that I will accompany Will on his trip to the local town today, and I will then set-off on my way. Wherever that may be. As such, I collect up my few belongings, ready to depart.

Will doesn't have a car – we will have to walk into town. We set off into town along the small country roads. These sweep through the gently rolling fields that flank us on both sides. As we wander Will points out things of interest. The tree the owls live in. The field where he got a tractor stuck in the ditch - he laughs. The small green where they used to have the 'proper' local market, he notes that things have changed so.

I am drawn to remember how I saw this all, when seen through another. He had been driven through this countryside with his family on the way to visit these relatives. He had stared out of the window at the repetitive greenery. He had been glad to see anything man-made. He had considered that man-made structures broke-up the monotony of the ever rolling countryside. It seemed a foolish idea to me then, and does even now. Back in that car he had always thought he would see the same things every time he went to his relatives house. But even then things had started to alter. Some building demolished, some corroded and fell. Others were built. It did change out here. Even as a child he had started to become aware of it.

The market town is nothing like I had imagined. I had been tainted by the notion of Farmers Markets that come to the city at weekends. I had expected rows of tents full of people who have nothing better to do with their time than make elaborate breads and cheeses. This market is full of working people, buying the food that they will actually eat that week. The stalls here are thrown together tables, and often barely even that. Some are just boards, propped up on blocks. The produce was grown, or shot - in the case of the pheasants, ducks, and rabbits - by people, in the family of those on the stalls. This is all fruit grown on small-hold plots, vegetables grown in gardens, honey produced from passed down hives. Everyone is cordial. I soon notice that they all know each other. They have probably always known each other. They may have been at school together, or Church. In fact I realise, they have all lived in this same place from the moment they were born. When they were children they probably climbed the same trees, swam in the same rivers. They would have attended the same schools...from start to finish. They had been through their whole life together, as far as it had taken them. They had lived and worked within a spit of each other for year upon year. Their children had then climbed the same trees, grown with each other, schooled and worked as one. They'd been married into each other's families. These people *really* did know each other through and through. They are effectively just one large extension of each other's world.

It seems at this moment like such a broad step away from the cold isolation of my city living. I don't know my neighbours at all. I could probably tell a couple of their faces apart in a crowd, but I don't know any of their names. I certainly wouldn't know what they liked doing, their origins, their dreams, or anything else about their wider beings. I am aware that I have lived amongst them, but I have been as separated from them as the stars from my eyes. I suppose that to know ones neighbours face in the city, is by most standard reckoning considered the limits of a relationship. I could surmise that we are all but swallowed in the vastness, and that we all actually wallow in the anonymity. Here, though, I realise, they are all working towards the same end-game, and it is warming and refreshing to see such camaraderie.

We stay in the market for a couple of hours. We could easily have gotten all that was required in a quarter of that time. But Will spoke to nearly everyone he came across. If he didn't speak to them he gave a knowing nod or wave. It was all very intimate. When they spoke, the person addressed cared what the other was saying. And despite the fact they knew each other so well, and the story or news was probably not even that new and informative, they still listened anyway. I was introduced to everyone, and they all showed me the same kindness and sincerity that I had found at the Barker's.

When we finally got around to talking to just about everyone that Will wanted to, I switched the conversation to the subject of my departing. Will looked genuinely surprised by this. 'No way lad!' He states. 'We haven't got to the best part of the day yet!' There is a twinkle of mischief in his eye. He tilted his head to the side, with an elaborate nod. When I had looked up I then noticed the large hanging sign. The Red Lion. As I looked back Will was already halfway through the door. I dart in behind him.

# Chapter 10 - Kelly & Robert

Kelly doesn't tend to leave the city, and she can't see why anyone else would have any reason to either. The city has really nice housing, any shop you could desire, efficient transport, social events (if she ever wanted them), cultural extravaganza, wonderful restaurants.

She looks through the window as the pod streams seamlessly through endlessly subtle tones of concrete grey. She is mesmerised into daydreams as she passes the familiar blur. The city has always been her home. She has travelled to many far flung places - both for work, but also for interest. Yet, she has never lived anywhere else than this super-metropolis. Why would anyone forsake all of this? She wonders. She certainty wouldn't be going to the countryside unless she had a damn good reason.

As the passing grey turns to passing brown and green she shakes back to the moment. The reason for this trip rears up in her thoughts. The Cane-man had enticed her to this place. She is raging with uncertainty about what has happened and why. If there is anything in her life that she really can't abide, it's not knowing. Finding out the how, what why and where is what drives her. It consumes her in her daily routines. It is also the main reason that she has never had a relationship last more than a few excruciating dates. There is too much mystery in romance, and she finds it an awkward and confusing terrain.

She can't help but think that when people enter a relationship they no longer say what is obvious. There is too much pussy-footing, and nicety, and formality...and hence the shortness of every single attempt. She would always end up saying something that breaks some mysterious unwritten taboo. A delicate balance would be tipped too far and the trip would be dashed at the dock.

The pod shakes with a sudden disturbing shift - she feels the vehicle slow dramatically. Pods operate differently in the conservation area, as there are no branch-line rails here. At the city limits the vehicle automatically change to wheeled drive and battery power. Kelly loves the lightning fast transit system in the sprawl - its access rails criss-cross the whole urban environment like a web so intricate it has been built by a spider with OCD. It is clean, efficient and very fast. These are all features she appreciates, and they are there complete, in one tangible mechanical form. This slow speed., irregular directions, bumps and dips represents yet another thing that she can't abide about this place. These are all the things she avoids, all together, in one tangible nightmare form. She turns her gaze to observe the scene outside as it endlessly trundles by. The large trees tower like oppressive giants, and she feels consumed by the weight of their massiveness. Although the buildings that surround her every single day are all immensely beyond this scale, she has always felt that there is something about enormity in nature that is somehow more monstrous than anything which we could ever build or produce. Everything here is different. Communications signals can fail, places are actually dark at night, there are areas where no one lives, there is dirt and grime at every turn. Kelly doesn't tend to leave the city, and this is why!

The road that had led here had been so under-used that there were actually sections with weeds grow through. Kelly's pod exits the small roadway and turns through a large, though dilapidated Period gateway. Beyond, is a gravel track and an avenue of neatly clipped trees that stretch for what appears to be miles into the distance - in a perfectly straight line. She appreciates the certitude of the feature and the effect it produces. The pod idles over the gravel with a satisfying sound, reminiscent of waves softly scratching across the skirt of a pebbly beach. The driveway is indeed long, yet eventually she passes the crest of a hill and is greeted by a sight of breathtaking scope and scale. Below her in the valley is a vast and imposing Victorian house. The formal grounds are immaculate and serene in equal measure. The form and construction of the building both beguile and intimidate. It is a truly mammoth building, standing grand and determined in its very own setting. The formal front facade alone is twice the size of her entire apartment block - and that holds twelve hundred people in residence. It actually makes her gulp back in appreciation.

She can't recall knowing that Robert had come from a family with such enormous wealth.

The enormous wooden front door has already been opened by the time she steps from the pod and crosses the substantial cobbled entrance arc. A man, dressed in some form of formal dress - a butler, she supposes, or some kind of man-servant - offers greeting and requests she enter. He takes her name and politely suggests she be seated while he announces her arrival. Kelly scans the walls as she takes her allotted chair. The ostentatious surroundings and the formality of the entrance are all severely at odds with the image she had of Robert - as she had known him. This was not what she had expected at all. She is whisked back to recollections of a time when her grandmother had taken her to see Buckingham Palace. But for all of its majestic grandeur, she can't help but feel that it like living within your own private museum. Given the nature and severity of his injuries. Kelly can't believe that this would be the sort of place Robert would feel comfortable within.

This is all so at odds with the boyish young man she had once known, and idolised. He had been a bohemian spirit. He appeared care-free, though he bore an irrepressible drive and determination. Coupled to a quick and inventive mind, he was a formidable and exciting character. He and his then best friend strode around their warehouse lab with the confident assurance that she both admired and envied. Each offering tantalising insights into the potential of what they could all do and where it would take them.

The recollection takes her back to Ben. She had been effectively distracted from the enormity of that scenario from the moment she had received the file from Cane-man. She had been subsumed by a compulsion to follow his tip-off. As soon as she had rid herself of the Professors gaze, she had left her office, taken the first company pod, and told it to go directly to the home of Robert Crown. She wasn't sure, as she had said it, that the pod would know where he was - yet after meeting the Cane-man, she had an inkling that it would - she had been right.

She had not seen Robert for years. As far as she was aware, no-one had. Not anyone from the project anyway. He had become a recluse. He had shunned visitors, so that, over the years that followed, people gradually stopped trying. To her, he had always been a memory that she could not expunge. He was always a distant thought, from a distant time. Things had changed so much, so much had happened - and was happening, but she had never forgotten him.

And now, out-of-the-blue, here she was. She wasn't even sure if he would see her. She had felt uncomfortable when she knew he was involved in some way. She had tried throughout the journey to think of a viable reason to turn around, and not come here. She had tried to get out of it with all of her might - but she couldn't find a good enough reason. It wasn't just the matter of helping Ben now either. The fact that the Cane-man had handed her that file, had been a final straw. She knew she had to find out what it all meant. It just wasn't in her character to walk away from things like this.

She had thought a lot about what reception she may receive. She just kept hoping that despite what had occurred, and what had happened between them, Robert may still feel enough for Ben, that he may still help him, in this critical hour of need.

After a protracted wait the man who had greeted her at the door returns. He bows to her and then turns sideways with arm extended to introduce the arrival of his master. A wheelchair slowly rolls through the curtained opening, and there sits Robert Crown. Her eyes are glued to him. She tries to stop herself staring, but all she can find herself thinking is that he looks absolutely terrible. Despite her eye's insistence on staring, she is finding it incredibly hard to look at him. It is painful to realise the truth of what the machine did. At the time of the accident it looked like the process had chewed him up and spat him out. He is now a warped and mangled variant of the bright young thing she so vividly remembers.

Kelly had been there in the lab the day of Robert's accident. There had been a malfunction of one of the smallest and most seemingly inconsequential parts of the many, many strapped together sub-processors. Yet the seemingly innocuous part had actually managed to cause a chain-reaction that resulted in a cataclysmic jamming of the data stream. Without the influx and return paths the process was compromised. It temporally ceased to relay to and from his body. He was thus stranded, separated from his body. The mechanical part itself had combusted and set the lab on fire. The flames were doused, and the part replaced as quickly as possible, but by this point Robert had been caught separated within the apparatus for ten minutes. His body had suffered severe burns from the fire, and his mind had been severed from his being. It was deemed a miracle that he survived at all. And though his mind was salvaged and returned –

no-one could really explain how – he had returned to exist within a distorted, broken husk of a body. He had entered the machine as a joyous and vibrant young man. He returned wracked and ruined, his tortured mind creating a separation from the rest of the team that would never heal. He promptly left the program, was taken to a hospital far from the lab and far from his colleagues. He had never spoken to any of them ever again.

'Hello Robert.' She forces.

The man stares back at her. The butler had taken her name upon her arrival, so she knows that he is aware of who she is. She wonders though whether his mind may have deteriorated and whether he doesn't actually recall her.

She is wrong.

'Hello Kelly. It has been a very long time. How are you? You look well. Please don't feel that I will need polite evocation, I am quite aware how hideous my form appears to others.'

She stands still. Embarrassed. She wants to say that he doesn't, but he would know this to be a lie. She is torn between sympathy and sheer revulsion. What do you say to someone that has suffered so? Her mind is again cast back to that horrific day when Robert was changed forever. His screams and anguish race through her thoughts. She had known then that she would never forget those sights and sounds, but they are now forcefully brought back to her current reality.

Robert breaks into her vivid remembrance. 'Don't worry. I am no longer embarrassed by my form. I am grateful that I still have my mind and senses. My vanity was washed away long ago. I am now happy enough with what I did manage to leave that machine with. Please don't feel you need to either apologise or placate me. I am fully aware that it was no-one's particular fault that this occurred. It was an act of pure chance. I was just unlucky enough to be in the wrong place at that most unfortunate time.'

She fights to recall the line of events that had led to her separation from him for all these years. She thinks of the reasons she had used to justify the fact that she had never come out to see him. He may well have turned her away, that is true. But she can't help feeling the wave of guilt that accompanies the reality, that she didn't even try.

He offers what she takes to be a smile, and she feels the self-reproachment cut into her. She feels a burning desire to get away and not have to deal with this encounter. She suddenly feels that she would rather not have come to face this reality. They had buried and denied this event. But here she was. It was too late to turn back now.

Robert turns the chair and it wheels itself forward towards a seating area, in what is perhaps a living room, but far grander than any she has entered before. The centrepiece is a fabulous chandelier that appears to be defying the laws of gravity. There are at least a dozen

130

wonders around the room that could easily grace a National Gallery. She pauses to take in the fantastic scene, but the butler ushers her to follow Robert chair, and she duly obliges. She walks slowly behind, until he pulls up next to a comfortable throne like feature. The butler waves her forward, and she self-consciously seats herself within the enormous expanse that towers over and around her. She perches precariously, and looks awkwardly over at Robert. She believes she catches the briefest inkling of a smirk. She recalls the pranks and general humour they had all shared so readily in the early days of their experimentations.

'Did you plonk me in here on purpose?' She rages, with mock anger.

Robert roars with laughter. The same old tone, still there. She hears the man she knew, hidden somewhere behind the distorted features. Robert replies between wheezes of laughter. 'You should have seen your face.' He holds his belly. 'You were always such a little princess, I couldn't resist it!

'Shut your face!' She slams back, while a smile cuts deeply.

They proceed to spend a happy hour reminiscing. They talk of times when things were not as they are now.

Kelly finds chatting with Robert about old times stimulating. She can't however, remove the knot in her mind that it is too politely strained. There are points in their conversations that are always side-stepped and avoided. They were both more than happy and comfortable in reminiscence. But when they got too close to talking of the accident, and all that had happened afterwards, they both shied away, and jump back to previous joyous stories. Neither of them want to end the conversation, and Kelly even feels that Robert is actually glad to see her and to chat with her this way. They have been separated for so long. And now, neither of them has anything more than their distant memories. The immediate part of their lives is off limits, for the sake of chit-chat conversation. This is okay for a while, and Kelly enjoys the remembrances. She has laughed harder today than she can last recall when. That fact is sad to her She is pleased that she came.

She does though wonder when one of them will eventually manage to address the real and massive elephant in the room. And as she had hoped and feared in equal measure, inevitably their conversation comes around to the case in point.

'I am sorry to say this Kelly, but I know you have not come here to merely talk of times past.' Robert states somewhat abruptly. Kelly is shaken from their previous joyous conversation. The change in his tone intersects the niceties. There is an alteration to proceedings.

Kelly smiles ruefully. Having suppressed a nauseating reluctance to come through the entire journey down, for fear of an angry reception, to find such pleasantries had come as a weighty relief. Now, however, Robert had finally cut to the crux. She had known this

132

point would come.

'It's Ben.' She finally states. She doesn't know how he will react to this name. They had skirted round him in their previous conversation. The way they had separated was harsh. She wondered if it was still a sore point.

'Has he died?'

'No!' she exclaims, shocked both by the question, and the directness of its asking. She thinks for a moment, and then realises it is a actually a reasonable presumption. In the line of work they pursue, it really wouldn't have been that big a surprise if he had.

'No?..No!. Oh well. At least I don't think so.' She stammers.

His interest is pricked. She assesses how terribly morbid it would be if his interest was sparked by thoughts of his ex-best friend's pain. She hopes it was the indecisive nature of her reply that caused the spark. She is though, not sure. She tries again to explain herself. 'There has been an accident. Well…I think it was an accident…Well, to be honest Robert…I don't really know what the hell is going on.'

'Where is he?' Robert asks.

'Well…You see…That's the crux of it. We don't actually know. We believe he is still in the machine.'

'What do you mean? Has he got stuck in a loop?

'No…Well…I don't really know, the thing is.' She pauses and takes a deep breath. 'There is something else in there.' As she says it, Kelly realises the enormity of making such a statement.

His face is distorted by his many terrible scars, but even beyond this Kelly sees a trace of a deeper, well hidden disguise. There is a mask of deceit. He is holding something back.

'You know what's happening here don't you?' She accuses.

He doesn't speak at first. His wilful look goes straight through her, and she isn't sure he is even aware that she is still there. Then he focuses back upon her.

'I think I might. Yes!'

She is shocked and angry. She is about to erupt, but then stalls herself. She is all too aware that she needs his help, so can't antagonise him. She does though want to find out more of what it is that he knows.

He ignores her previous line of questioning and switches tack.

'Do you remember how it all started Kelly?'

This could be the idle ramblings of reminiscence, but she humours it. She had an inkling that this all started at the very beginning of the project, and that appears to be where this tale is being set. So, she allows him the luxury of storytelling.

'There is an almost mythical form of protective bubble that always manages to encompasses high level personages. All through time, the paymasters are nearly always shielded. There are small armies of bodyguards and then armies, and then on to the protection of courts and lawyers. The legal system itself had been tinkered with and altered to serve their needs. It has been nigh on impossible to break through to get at the top brass. The real leading faces, even, or particularly the invisible power-brokers, have always been effectively impervious.'

He pauses to collect his thoughts. Kelly wants to slap the point of this story out of him, but instead bites her tongue and sits patiently waiting to see where this is going.

'All things change! That is the old maxim isn't it?' It is rhetorical, but he still looks to her to nod agreement. 'It is so very true…Do you remember when the butler was collected, and Selina, and how the whole house nearly all came tumbling down around us all?'

'Of course.'

'Oh yes. But do you know where and how we got there?'

She had of course thought about it. It was, after all, 'real people' that they were using in their experimentations. But by-and-large she had to admit to herself that she had only ever really been interested in the experiment itself, and the ensuing results. The real emphasis of *her* adventure had been in the lab. She shakes her head.

'The butler was on what was supposed to be a quick shopping run – merely crossing the road from one of the huge walled and gated estates that dominate the more illustrious part of town. Importantly, he had not told anyone he was going. For that very smallest of times, he was outside of the ring of protection. He was crushed in the road, it was before pods were as fault free as we now expect. A passer-by called for an ambulance. He was consequently rushed to the public A&E. As all this happened, the estate security were none the wiser. I would have hated to be the person responsible for running the security for that Family - given how important 'what the butler saw' was to become... Anyway, they lost track of him completely. It surprisingly took ages for them to pull together a proper investigation - there were legal complications in accessing the closed-circuit networks, and even powerful families can sometimes get bogged down in bureaucratic messes.'

'Is there a point to this retrospective Robert? Kelly cuts in.

He ignores her and continues. 'For every wall that is erected there are people that are always trying to break through. The more seemingly inaccessible the task, the more tantalising the prize As such, the recently deceased butler was nabbed. He didn't even make it to the morgue. The most quizzical aspect, for those who were sent to look for him, was that his body had completely disappeared. As far as the outer world was concerned, this man had died and gone. Public records at the hospital would show so. However, without a body, there is always doubt. They would not at the time, of course, have presumed a semi-dead butler would be quite so damaging. But then, they had not reckoned on the skills and technology that had recently been brought to bear, to open up the mind of the recently deceased.'

'I know, I know, and then you went in, and it all effectively started there. The Company saw the potential, forcibly bought in and it all went stratospheric.' She is beginning to get frustrated by this seemingly needless walk through past events, all of which she already knows. Which makes her hope that there may eventually still be some point to this - if not she will be very, very cross indeed.

But how did we get it to work? You must have wondered Kelly?'

This catches her off guard.

'We had been working with a collection of improvised, soldered together computer units and a reliance on back-handers to anyone with even the meagre finance.' He continues.

'So?'

'All of a sudden we make the greatest breakthrough of our age.'

'The AI that controls the system?' She now sees where this is going.

'Yes.'

'You mean how did that come about?'

'Yes.'

'I don't really know that Robert. That was not my area. That was your and Ben's baby? Is that what you mean? How did you make the AI that allowed this to occur?'

'Yes.'

She looks puzzled. She knows he is playing a game that is leading her, however indirectly, to an answer at some point, so she persists.

'I don't know how you miraculously magic'd up the most incredible AI the world had ever seen Robert. Pray tell - was it your massive and unsurpassed genius?'

The point is barbed, but he still manages a smile. 'Unfortunately not. I had been working, as had Ben, for ages on the bloody thing. But, it always ended up as a semi-drone - not completely useless, yet never able to really take on the management of tasks at hand. We always got to a point where it came back pandering for confirmation…as if it wasn't ever comfortable in making its own decisions.'

'And then?' She states firmly, she really is reaching the limits.

'Someone offers me something, that they said would help.'

'Childs?' She ventures.

'Ha. God No! The man's a cretin. I am amazed he can even walk and talk at the same time.'

'Bloody hell Robert, you are seriously testing my patience.'

He smiles sardonically. 'I was in the lab and behind me I heard a regular and peculiar tap-gap-tap-gap-tap…'

'The man with the cane!'

'Precisely.' He throws up his hands (or at least raises them as far as his broken body will allow). 'We were good Kelly, but not as good as we thought we were. We had help to get where we were going.'

'Who is he, Robert? What did it all have to do with him, and whatever agency he represents?'

He again ignores her questioning and pursues his own agenda. 'It is, you see, *where* he got it from that counts here.' He pauses.

'What?' She half barks, fighting hard to rein herself in. 'What do you mean? I don't understand.' She can't hold it any longer. She screams at him fiercely. 'Make sense. What the hell is all this really about Robert?'

'Didn't you read the file for the Montgomery flight Kelly?' He asks her matter-of-factly.

She is again confused. Her head is swimming and she can't get a grounding on what it is he is alluding to.

Robert looks at her for the longest time, and then simply states a reiteration of the written message that was left for her.

'There is something we need to discuss about the secret of the source.'

'You wrote that on the sheet?' Kelly asks, bemused. 'How did you even get hold of the file?'

Before he can answer she realises.

As he says it, she apes his words. 'The man with the cane!'

He smiles and nods, to show that she is finally starting to get on track with his story.

'But why did you take the AI?' She fires. 'And how did you use it if you didn't know what it was? And who the hell is that Cane-Man anyway? – – Who is he *Really*?' The questions come tumbling out on top of each other. She is desperately trying to regain some understanding and realisation of her world, in light of these massive revelations.

Robert sits back and takes in the depth of her confusion. 'I have always kept up with what you are doing Kelly. I have monitored every trip

140

Ben took, and every progressive research development you made. I couldn't bear to be around the project - after what happened. I couldn't face seeing you all, having to bear sympathy and sycophants. Yet, as you see, I still have an interest - a craving really, to be involved. Hence I have kept abreast and have made my own notes and calculations - which I would be delighted if you would like to look through, I am sure they may be of use, or in the very least may be interesting to you and the team.'

She sits looking stunned.

He puts on a serious stare and addresses her purposefully. 'I have never lost interest in what we were doing and where it is was all going.'

Kelly assesses him. 'But..the code...how did you...Cane-Man...get the code Robert? What is it? You said it was taken from somewhere interesting?'

He smiles. ' You were listening, but misheard. I said - It was *where* he got it from that was interesting.'

'And...Where was it from?

Robert stops. The dramatic pause is really aggravating her. But, she also realises that this man has been here, effectively alone, for a considerable time. She feels she - and on behalf of the others - owe him scope for his overstatements and grand gesturing.

'He has his ways and means, and they are certainly pervasive and extensive. I do not know the exact details of how he gets hold of things. But sometimes they are very interesting. This is, as you will soon see, particularly so, in light of what I am about to tell you...about the secret of the source material that helped us considerably in what we were doing with our experiments, and the realm into which we surreptitiously entered.'

# Chapter 11 - The Dog & The Darkness

*Ben*

I am not sure how, I was adamant when I left the cottage that I would be on my way home by this afternoon. But here I find that I am now on the way back to the Barker's again. We are walking along merrily, and Will recounts our meeting with one of the locals. He cheekily mimics the man's distinctive, somewhat comical voice. We laugh out loud, then go over every details we can each remember about what the man did, and what the man said. Our mood is joyous, brought on it part by the many beers at the Lion. In truth, I am pleased that I have actually stayed another day in this wonderful place.

As we approach the cottage its interior is eerily shaded. This is so odd. When I approached yesterday this place was the very image of idyllic beauty. Now, it looks more like a scene from a ghost story.

Entering the kitchen the first thing we see is Katie's leg. It pokes just into view around the corner of the pantry. Will rushes forward toward her. I can see his pained expression. A sound of pure desperation escapes his lips. Before he can get beyond my reach I grab at the cloth of his coat. He turns to me, confused, then angry. He growls at me to release him - his only thought to get to his wife, to nurse her, to see what has happened. As he tussles violently to get free, I am struck frozen. Realising I am not paying any heed to his fighting, he finally registers my stare and follows my gaze. In the furthest corner of the room there is movement.

Laid out across the floor, huge, dark, menacing, is a massive dark figure. At first it is difficult to distinguish, but as our eyes come to adjust to the light in the room, we see that it is an enormous black dog. The beast contemptuously ignores us, it is licking the tattered old rug that had been below the kitchen table. The table itself has been thrown to the far wall of the room. We both scan the scene. It is immediately evident that there has been a savage and bloody struggle. Much of the kitchen has been disturbed. The floor lays littered with broken remnants. Most ominous of all is the dark stain that runs from the hound to the pantry. We can't help but know what it is. The dog lays licking and lapping at the soaked rug. The sight of this atrocity makes Will snap. He rages into the room. At once the dog is upon its feet, head down, teeth bared, scruff raised. Will pays no heed and dashes straight to the pantry. He disappears into the tiny room. For a couple of seconds as time appears motionless - nothing happens. I wallow in the silent stillness, stuck within the horrendous reality before me. Then it comes. A wailing sound so desperate, so lost, it could have manifested in the unknown depths of the deepest ocean. It is such a horrible sound, tainted with loss and suffering, the sweeping will of death over life. And with it, there is certainty - she is gone.

I still don't know what to do. The enormous beast has not moved. It almost mocks us with its inactivity. How long will we stay

144

transfixed here, in this stand-off? I want to go forward, I really want to go and help, but I stand frozen. I know as soon as either of us flinches, even a jot, the whole scene will transform into chaos and violent aggression. I need not worry. The scales have been cast down, the motions are set.

Will races from the pantry, in his right hand a rolling pin, evidently the first thing he could grasp. He forges toward the beast. The dog switches it glance from me to he, as quick as lightning. Still with head bowed and teeth bare it lets out a ferocious growl. Just as it announces what would have been a terrible bark it is cut short. He has hurt it.

A definite retreat - the bark dwindling to a shocked whimper. Before it can regain itself, gather composure, we move.

'The table.' Will yells. 'Get the table!'

I look round and see the massive oak table has been turned and flung round onto its side. I jump over it and with unholy strength and determination drive my shoulder into it. It slides and grates on the floor tiles. This massive thing was not meant to be moved about, its immense weight seems to force back against me as I edge it forward. I briefly stop to peer over, to see where I must go. Will stands before the creature which has been backed into the corner. He is swinging his weapon in large aggressive swipes. The speed and ferocity of his motions are just enough to keep the dog at bay. It bites out sporadically at his arm as it swings back repeatedly. I muster myself and force my heels as deep into the ground as I can. I feel like my foot will break through the tiling, but eventually the table moves. I start to get some constant motion, and I am upon them. Will jumps back to try and clear me, but only gets half up, and instead tumbles down upon me. His unexpected weight crushes me flat to the floor, where for a moment I lay still and disorientated.

For what again seems like seconds, hanging motionless, I lie unmoving. I only stir when I feel Will lift. Will drags himself up and immediately starts pushing the table against the wall. The dog has become wedged. It frantically tries to escape. Its sharp claws scratch at the kitchen surfaces looking for purchase, to pull itself free. The claws slide away repeatedly. It starts to expel a terrible and terrific wail. It is scared. I join Will and push against the table. With both of our weight against it, the dog is completely wedged and stops making such violent protests. It wails, but the air in its body has become as restricted, and the sound is gradually muted. Will reaches out to grab the dropped weapon, but it has rolled from reach. He dare not let the pressure off the table. We are again at stalemate. We must twist events to take the advantage. We must do something else. If we release the pressure from the table the hound could drag itself free.

It is then Will swings his arm upwards. I look up startled, what is it? As I look, I realise, and follow his lead.

'Turn it over!' He shouts.

146

I lean and lift, grabbing the large table leg as I go. Bending my legs and using all my strength I tilt it. The motion creates a slide, and the table falls. The dog must have realised that his only route to freedom is to dart beneath it, and it dashes under. At this point Will launches all of his weight ferociously toward the highest point of the table. The culmination of the three movements, of me lifting, the dog burrowing under, and Will descend forward make the table fall flat over onto its surface. The dog is trapped beneath. There is a sudden jolt as the tables twitches. The action sends both me and Will rolling forward. The dog is not giving up. But it mattered not. The enormous weight of the huge old oak table alone is enough to pin the dog. But before I can react, Will is up and has jumped onto the underside of the upturned table. He launches himself as high as he can into the air and crashes back down onto the under-surface. Again and again he jumps and lands.

'Get on here.' He commands, his hand outstretched to help me up. I take his hand, and do as he says. I am not taken to mindless acts of aggression, and have never killed any creature larger than a cockroach. But I know I must do this. Wills world has been torn apart, and he wants to extract vengeance. Together we jump and crash down.

The table stops moving in reply. But still we jump, and crash down with furious anger.

And I stop jumping. Will does not, and the imbalance sends me off as he alights upwards. He then tumbles the other way as he lands. We both lay upon the ground, neither moving, neither speaking. I half expected him to scold my action, but he does not. He has far more important things on his mind. He rises and with head bowed turns away towards the open door of the pantry and the lifeless body within. In reverence to the moment and what will follow I lift myself and remove myself from the gruesome scene.

As I sit in the garden, I can still hear the constant sobs, and can picture with horror his flowing run of tears. I try to make sense of what I have just seen, what I have been part of. It is unearthly. It is unreal.

I am struck by how bright and sunny the day is. With so much going on I had forgotten how intense the heat of the sun had been this afternoon. I had taken my jacket off as we had been walking. It was indeed hot. We had in fact commented on how refreshing it would be to have a drink of cold home-made lemonade when we returned.

When we had entered the kitchen the place seemed almost pitch black. Even with the large window next to the sink. We had struggled to make out the dog in the twilight. It must be 30 plus degrees outside the cottage, with not a cloud in the sky, yet as we had entered the house it was eerily and bitterly cold.

As I ponder these things, I hear the scream.

Thoughts race through me as I crash back in. Will is standing in the middle of the room. He had slid the table back off the dog, and although it was too heavy to lift off you could see the broken creature stretched out on the cold tiled floor. In front of it, emanating from its half open mouth is a stream of blood – black blood, and it is trickling forward, toward us.

I look back to Will in fear and confusion. My head is swimming with uncertainties and trepidation, he looks back, but his look is even worse - it shows resignation.

'It was sent for us, they didn't want you to stay here'. He says, though the voice is not his own. I also don't recognise the mannerisms he has suddenly taken on. I don't understand what he means either? Who is *they*? I wonder if he is talking about someone we met earlier in town. But, then why would that be so. They had all been so nice? And why he has started talking and acting so strangely?

I stop wondering, distracted by the blood from the dog's mouth. The black blood is pooling into one strange dark shadow. I turn to the window, light is streaming through, the entire room is lit. I realise that there is nothing that could cast that shadow. Where is the form that casts it?

Ice seers through me. My stomach turns and my neck hairs bristle. The shadow moves. As it does the blood trails after it.

Though it is moving, I cannot. I just stare. Transfixed. Frozen in fear. It is moving towards me, slowly, but definitely.

Just as it is about to reach me Will throws himself before me. Will...Watch out!' I scream.

But I know understand the look of resignation etched upon his face. He had already decided this. He has sacrificed himself - for me.

Everything suddenly goes still and quiet. Birds stop singing, the wind stops blowing. Will doesn't speak, and doesn't move, he just stares at me, a tear trickles from his eye. Through the look he gives me, I can see it all. The terror and the knowledge of it, all at once. His shape dissolves into shadow. The blood now pooled right around his feet.

I still cannot move. I can only stare in disbelief - and fear.

For what feels like hours I stand rooted.

Then it ceases. Will comes back into view, the darkness lifting from him as quickly as it had enveloped him. With the darkness gone, I suddenly feel I must try and do something, to help him, to save him.

I force myself to speak 'Will...'

His gaze fixes upon me, through me, chilling me, terrifying me, digging deep into me. He begins to move backwards. He shakes uncontrollably. His head looks like a blur as it erratically gyrates back and forth, side to side. Faster and faster. I have never seen anything move so quickly, so unnaturally fast. His motion and torment look and

150

sound like a man being stung to death by a thousand angry wasps. He is transfixed to the spot, bearing a suffering too gross to imagine. Then the roar, the uncontrolled, unsuppressed, limitless reverberation. The sounds swing around me. As Wills' head gyrates it creates an echo, the room becoming a cauldron of unmitigated white noise. My ears feel like they are bleeding, and I raise my hands to cover them - but it is no good - it is so loud it cuts right through me. I try to edge back away to the door, away from the terrible source. As quick as it began, it stops. Back to the start point, the fixed hollow stare, through me, within me.

'Will…', I struggle.

I want to run, but need to know what to do. What is happening to him? I can't just flee, and leave him. For a few second he regains himself, within the once familiar face and I see the man I had briefly known and liked so much.

'Run' He says quietly.

I stare back at him.

'Run Ben, please RUN!'

The steely stare re-establishes across him. For a moment I freeze again. Then he starts to run at me, and before I can even engage my basest thoughts, I am off.

Thank God the front door was open. I am through it and slam it behind me with one motion. I hear the collision soon after. Smashing through the small glass mid-section of the door. His face torn and bloodied by the shards of glass, hand and arm grasping through the tiny slit in the door. This time it is *his* blood oozing to the ground, and his pain that causes the yell that it elicits. A pitying yell so sickening it makes me cry out too.

I cannot get the porch door open, but I dare not turn round to look at it as I numbly fumble with the doorknob behind my back. I dare not look away from his face. The glass had cut one eyeball open and the liquid runs down his cheek, the rest of the face, already blackened by the terrible shadow, is covered with blood, red blood, Will's blood. The shadow still coats him, even here in the full light of day. His head withdraws. For a terrible second I think he may still have the where-with-all to open the latch on the other side, but still I dare not turn to look for the handle behind me. To my relief I hear him run to the other end of the room. Crash. An almighty smash, of what could only have been him running headlong and at full pace into the dresser on the far side of the room. I hear him rise and run again. This time his face and right arm and shoulder came smashing through the front window of his living room. Again he withdraws. I can hear him pacing, until again - Smash. Repetitive, mindless, destructive. Of both his house, and of himself. It is as if he is fighting the shadow, and the shadow is fighting back.

I have to go. I finally turn and fumble with the handle. I can hear another Smash. A bang, a crash, a scream. I open the door and run. Where I will go, I do not know. I stand a distance from the house. I can hear him moving around from room to room, smashing, crashing, sometimes screaming, sometimes crying. Suddenly his face comes crashing through an upstairs window - the very room I had stayed in only last night. For a second again he regained the look of Will, the real man within. His one remaining eye locked briefly upon me - he then withdraws inside. This time however, he returned with one arm outstretched from the window - pointing.

'Run', he say again, his sane self remaining longer - long enough to continue. 'You must get away from here, there are things here that mean you harm, and I can no longer protect you. Go. Go now!'

Then he is gone again, the cold steel stare envelopes his being and his form is dragged back through the window. Inside there is a return to the insane smashing and hollering of before.

I race to escape . Before I can even register it I am off down the road. I stop a few hundred metres away and force one last look back. I can still just make out the smash of glass breaking, the occasional screaming - such terrible and fearful noises. My brain is swimming. I turn and run on, as fast as my legs will physically carry me.

Where can I go? Who can I speak to about this? If I went to the police they would have me locked up quicker than it would take me to explain the tale. How would I possibly explain this to any sane and

153

rational being.

Will had deliberately told me to run. But where did he want me to go? He must have just wanted me to get away from this place. I continue to run, and run, and run...

# Chapter 12 - The Source

Kelly sits eyeing Robert. She had to get up from her seat and move further away from him, as she could not bear to sit near him. All of the earlier empathy and happiness she had felt at having come down here to see him has completely evaporated. The answers he has offered her over the past few hours have replaced those feelings with bewilderment, confusion and ultimately, resentment. She feels like she has been lied to for nearly her entire life, and yet this has been amongst the worst of those deceptions. It has ripped apart everything she thought was her reality.

She has now been sitting here for almost an hour, silently re-evaluating everything that has been said. She has been forced to re-live the poignant and painful conversations over-and-over in her mind. They are now completely skewed. The reality that she had felt she knew has fallen apart. She is reassessing all of her relationships on the premise that any of them could be built on such falsehoods. She is drowning in uncertainty, and she knows very well who she blames for pushing her here.

Robert can see, and completely understands that she has not taken it well. In an attempt to explain he tries to tell her the rest of the story he had explosively begun to unfold.

'We had hit a point where we could not find a way of making the computers aware enough to react to the massive recalculations that were required when dealing with a program which is forever changing - i.e our brains. We needed the level intelligence that we just couldn't find. Month after month, after month.' He looks to her. 'Do you remember?'

She nods. She remembers it well. They had gone so far, had broken through so many ceilings of expectation, and yet for weeks on end they were stalled. The group had collectively figured how to create a small loop that allowed a brief look into another mind - yet beyond this, the interface risked cerebral damage if they stayed on any longer.

'There was no answer to it.' He continues. 'As far as we could see. Even if we could have plugged into the power of every computer on Earth, all at once, there was still no mechanism that could cope with the flux of human thoughts and emotions. The task was too 'Human' for any machine to ever understand.

'But you found a way? Or rather Van Cleef did.'

'Well yes, sort of. I was in the lab alone one evening, I don't recall why…but anyway…God only knows how he got in through our reactive security - but as you are beginning to learn, that is what he does.'

'Mmm, I am starting to see that, yes.'

'Well I hear that noise…I know you know it - it is one that once heard, you will never forget. He has that way of leaving rather a distinctive impression doesn't he?…For a man that spends so much time unseen. Anyway, I turned and angrily confronted him - I had presumed him to be a thief…or worse, in truth. It was something of a relief when he actually held out a memory drive.'

'What did he say about it? Did he tell you where he got it from Robert?

'No. Not then. Well not exactly. He told me it was what we needed, and what we would never find, even if we scoured for it our whole damned lives. It was, he said, unique and special. I was at a loss to ask too many questions. I was still wrestling with ones like 'How the hell do you know what we are doing and what we need?'

'Yes.' She agrees. 'He does somehow make one flounder like a dying fish, snatching for answers as if your life depended on it - annoying!'

'Absolutely. But obviously he only states what he wants to - then it's down to us to decide if we wish to sell our soul, or to walk away knowing that we will probably never again attain the object that is dangling so tantalisingly before us at that very moment…'

'No one, well none of the team would have blamed you for taking it Robert. It was essential, and we were stuck without it. We had done too much and gone too far to turn away from it there. But what I can't understand - and may never be able to forgive - is that you lied to us all, for all that time' Her look pleads for a sincere answer.

He attempts to show her that he is telling her the truth now, and to explain the conundrum he had once faced, and which had weighed so heavily upon him ever since.

'He gave me basic instructions, and one dire warning.'

She looks alarmed at this. As far as she could recall Robert had never told the team of any important warnings relating to the process.

' What warning?' She ask.

Robert looks surprised by the question. 'Oh don't worry. I wrote a fail-safe into the interface and all auxiliary units. It can't ever be actioned.

She stares him down. 'Tell me Robert. What was it that we were, or weren't supposed to do?'

He pauses for a long time. She realises that this isn't another of the previous dramatic interludes - he is genuinely debating whether to release this most important, secret piece of the puzzle.

She is aware herself of the power that Van Cleef's threats can hold. It had certainly convinced her when she had been confronted with it.

Having wrestled with it for some time, Robert relents. 'Let it out. We must never allow it to escape.'

Her face states the question clearly enough without words - and yet still leaves room for her shock and fears. 'Escape? It? What the hell Robert? What was it you had - We had! Bloody hell. We still do have!

She is again swirling in too many questions to answer. 'Did someone have an A.I that Van Cleef stole? Is it a corporate or Government thing…oh God…please tell me it's not bigger than that. Noooo, Robert where did he get it from…a fully functioning A.I of that calibre? They aren't exactly readily available bought off the shelf sort of things are they!…' Her voice has been getting progressively more panicky as the questions rolled on.

Robert just shrugs. This does not help her mood in the slightest. In fact, it only serves to anger and scare her further.

'I told you Kelly, he didn't say - then - where it had come from.'

She grabs at the nuance as if it was the last crumb from a long lost loaf, and she were the hungriest person alive on the planet.

'*Then*!' She rages 'What about *Now* Robert - Now you do know - is that true. Just bloody well tell me! Where did he get it from.'

'I had feared this day Kelly.' He confides. 'I had not wanted to have to admit this, for fear of having to fully face the consequences of what we - well 'I' did.'

The concern grows larger across Kelly. If she had been alarmed before, this confession made it a million times worse.

'Robert? Where did he get it from?

At this juncture, when nothing else could ever possibly be more important than this answer, there is a tapping on Roberts massive front door. They both turn with a start, then look back at each other. The sudden entry of the outside world jolts them both from the moment.

Before either can react, the butler is at the door and opening the bolt.

Kelly and Robert watch the butler enter into an exchange of conversation and then sees him turn to look directly at the pair of them, seated a few feet away. They turn back to look at each other again. Neither speaks.

Before they can look back to the door once more - they hear it. Tap. Gap. Tap...

Kelly's eyes widen and she snaps her head round to face the doorway. There he stands. Bold as a mountain. Her anger flares beyond anything she has ever felt before. No matter how much counselling she has had for her temper, nothing on the planet would contain her feelings at this point. She wants to rip his smirking head right off his smug little shoulders. She sneers and feels her teeth become visible. An attack dog spirit rushes through her. She is fighting very hard to contain the immense desire to unleash it and to let her anger manifest in a pure and beautiful violence.

160

'Robert, Kelly...may I call you Kelly, Miss Sharpe?'

She does not answer, and Van Cleef takes it that he can.

'I believe a point has been reached...' He continues. She cuts him off.

'How the Hell did you know what we were talking about?' She spurts, half anger, half confusion.

'I gave you the file. It was obvious it would lead you here.' He offers.

She realises this makes sense. 'So you followed me?'

'Of course not.' He bats back. 'I was already here.'

His presumption of knowing what it is that she would do riles here, but the fact that she did exactly as he said she would makes her marvel at the level of manipulation that he is able to unfold.

'It was obvious you would come.' He continues. 'And I am not really in the business of following - when I can at all help it. It is more appropriate that I lead.'

'What are you Van Cleef?' She snaps at him. 'Some sort of Government spook.'

He smiles, cringing at this assertion. 'Absolutely not.' He scoff. 'As I say. I am not one who tends to follow events. I make it more of a mission to steer them all, as is fitting.'

'Fitting to who you manipulative bastard?'

He lets the insult wash past him, as though it was but an incidental wave on a far larger ocean.

'Sometimes things have to go certain ways - Kelly.' He extenuates her name as he says it, as if to highlight that this is very much aimed for her consumption.

'But you said something had gone wrong.'

'Well no. I didn't actually say that did I? But I do recall the conversation being private...' He looks at her for recognition that she has already managed to breach the rules of the severe warning he had given her. She reads this, and castigates herself for this foolish slip - her anger had got the better of her judgement.

'By-the-by.' He continues, seemingly let her indiscretion pass. 'You are fortunate to have voiced that very private piece of information in front of the only other person you could have, without there having been serious consequences.'

Kelly turns sharply to Robert, who has already looked away, and will not now meet her stare.

'But be warned...I will not be so forgiving if this is ever mentioned again.'

His face is stone, and she knows that he is absolutely *deadly* serious in this threat.

'Where did it come from Van Cleef?' She continues. 'He won't tell me. I suppose you have him on a similar leash to me, and he's too scared of you to say.'

Van Cleef takes a moment to digest the reassuring admission of fear. It was essential, and he is glad that it has stuck. He is not disposed to tell her what she asks, as there really is no need for her to know. However, he does feel that to give her something, may make her more amenable to do the further things he will require from her over the coming days, and onward.

'It is not an A.I.' He states.

'What the hell do you mean? What is it then? Some sort of demon!'

He smiles wryly. 'No, my dear. It is something else…but for now…that is all that shall be said.' He is categorical in the assertion, and Kelly reads that this is very much the end of this conversation.

She sits pondering. What he has confided make no sense. Robert had spoken seemingly openly, yet she still doesn't feel that she has any further answers than before. She has heard his story, and now Van Cleef's - or as much as he has been willing to offer her. She had known the part about the group having been at an awkward crossroads, and that they had experienced several costly set-backs with the process - before Roberts miraculous 'discovery'. She recalls joining the research project and the immense pride she had felt at being part of that group. It was Robert that she had met first, and she knew from the off that he really was a genuine genius. But then, their entire group was packed with some of the most brilliant and innovative minds of their generation. In such company, terms like genius become mute – as everyone there could easily have carried that baton.

Again, she is drawback to question how this mysterious cane wielding figure had known what the group was doing, and how it related to what he wanted. She reasons that this is was probably completely unknown to Robert too. Or at least she hopes wholeheartedly that it was. Robert, she ponders, had been offered the Holy Grail, and no-one in their right mind would turn down such a prolific prize. She understands. But it still hurts and confuses her.

Has Van Cleef played them all? she wonders. Is he just employing some elaborate game, merely winding circles, on purpose? She can't figure him out at all. She can see strands that could ultimately form part of a greater whole. Yet, nothing ever seemed to reach conclusion. She is still missing key parts of this equation. Without it, everything just goes on and on, round and round. She isn't even sure whether this is a linear or circular pursuit. She is totally and utterly confused.

For his part, Robert sits, engaged, within his own thoughts. She wants to probe him further, but doesn't know where to begin. In

164

truth, she would rather just shake him until he spills every answer he still has hidden from her. As it is, she can do nothing now but glare daggers and wait to see what comes next in her ever spiralling descent to Wonderland.

'What do you propose I do about Ben?' Robert questions of Van Cleef. His sudden re-engagement making her jump.

'I am the only one that can properly access the machine.' Robert offers.

'What...What was that? What do you mean Robert?' Kelly queries.

'There is only one other person that has survived the Voyaging process and has enough experience to navigate through it.'

She understands where he is going with this. She pauses to assess the ramifications. He has almost driven her to distraction with his seemingly insane confessions and his infuriating riddles. But now! Has he actually come up with a practicable plan? He has offered to risk himself once more to the machine that almost destroyed him. She needs time to think it through. There are so many variables. Can he be trusted? Does she have a choice? Which way Van Cleef will want this all to play - this seemingly being the key unknown variable that they will all now always be saddled with.

Practically, she speculates - Can two people even access the machine at the same time? It is unprecedented. But then so is everything else that is happening here, and so was everything that they have ever done before. It may just work! But what would it achieve if Robert too becomes trapped inside? It would make retrieval of one consciousness nigh-on impossible if they were to become entwined inside. And again, she is drawn back to the question of trust. He has been evasive, secretive and sometimes downright suspicious while she has been here. They haven't seen him for so many years - so why would he do such a thing?

She sits back and looks at the two figures before her. Robert is back into deep thought. Van Cleef just stares back at her.

'Thank you Robert. That is a very kind offer.' Van Cleef finally presents. 'Are you presuming that you have a strong enough bond with it, that you may be able to reason with it?'

Robert considers. 'Yes. I think so. I was its first ever contact. I believe I can still mediate something from this.'

'Why would you do that? Why would you possibly ever want to go back near the machines that have robbed you of so much and have torn your life to pieces?' Kelly enquires, testing for a reasoning she can believe.

'I am the only one that can do it. Believe me Kelly, I would really rather never subject myself to revisiting the scene of my nightmares. But I also know what must be done.'

166

'We couldn't possibly ever ask you to do anything like that.'

'I know, you wouldn't have.' He states. 'And that is why I have offered.'

Van Cleef looks quizzical. He stands for several moments before agreeing that they can try it. Then without any further contact, he turns and simply strolls away, tapping his way from them, and back away into whatever shadow-land he usually inhabits.

After many hours of preparation Robert and Kelly leave the house and head to his private pod. Kelly can see the stress writ across Robert's face. The anxiety has rumpled and hunched him. The wheelchair holds him, gently cradling his drawn and haggard figure as they cross the expansive shingle driveway.

He had briefly mentioned the nightmare of the accident, but did not elaborate too deeply. Kelly felt this was not the time or place to pursue it further. It did intrigue her though. He had been trapped within the machine while they had fought to rescue him from the fire. He nearly died attached to the machine. Yet here he was, offering to revisit it, to save a person he had not spoken to for years. It was incredible to her.

She wanted to be impressed and wowed by the gesture, but at the back of her thoughts, there was the nagging notion that Robert still knew more about this situation than he was letting on.

# Chapter 13 - Chalmers

## *Ben*

I don't know where I am, or where I'm going. The dreamlike weirdness at the cottage was a living nightmare, with the dog, and the blood, and the madness... I don't know what it is that I have just seen, and what has become the kindest couples I have ever met. I really can't understand this at all. Things happened to Will that I just can't explain. Poor Katie, killed by that vicious animal. I've got to tell someone about this. But would anyone make of it? It is all ridiculous. They will think that I am insane. They are bound to think that I killed them. I can't regale this tale to anyone. Bloody hell! I'm from the city - a place where you're anonymous! Where everyone fades to wallpaper and dissolves away from care and attention. Here, they care about each other. What the hell will they make of this? What will they think I have done to their dear friends?

My journey away from the house was a blur. I recall running without real direction. I can't think straight. I need to try to collect a semblance of reason. I really have got to tell someone. A woman has been savagely killed. Her husband - has probably been killed. I have got to get this story right. If they find that scene, and with my prints all over the room, and me gone. Two plus two - it will inevitably comes back to me. Bloody hell! ......I can see it myself! How would that look? Guilty as sin. The court wouldn't even get seated by the time the verdict was read out.

I must have happened upon this house. I don't remember a call being made to the Police. I was not of my fullest wits, but even in that state I know I didn't do that. But the people here say I did. I can't have. Apparently the version of the incident with the beast, and of that which transpired. No. Nooo. I can't have said that. Surely. No.

I am not sure how things happen from that point to this. It appears the people with whom I had made the phone call had taken me in that evening. I must have been offered a bed that night. I had no recollection of this, but I found myself at the front door the next morning awaiting an arrival. Eventually a tall, fairly thin, bushy-haired middle aged man appeared - this was Sergeant Chalmers. I remember him. I don't know how or why. - but I do. He is familiar to me in every detail. Yet I can't recall ever having met him before in my life.

As we stand there on the threshold of the house I do not know, with the people I cannot recall , nothing at all is said about the incidents at the Barker house. Pleasantries are exchanged and then finally, goodbyes given. Then myself and the sergeant are suddenly off and away. I am becoming used to the peculiar situations that now pervades my entire being. Although it appeared strange that nothing was said about the Barker's, I just run with the circumstance, as we drive on silently.

Then I see it, the familiar house. Or at least, I see a place that in my mind was once familiar to me. I felt that I had initially recognised the place. But now we are closer, I am unsure. It has changed beyond all recognition from the day before. I felt that is was definitely the same house. But it has deteriorated well beyond being habitable, and this is not a recent occurrence. The dilapidation appeared to have occurred over years. Over many, many years. My mouth is stone dry, my eyes rage wildly with disorientated confusion. Chalmers says nothing, but pulls to a halt, and turns off the engine.

'What did you see here?' Chalmers asks. He turns to me now, obviously anxious. His look is enquiring, his manner anguished.

'What did you see?' he repeats. This time his voice is raised a pitch, almost to breaking. I am quite taken aback. He puffs his chest and hides behind the authority imbued by his uniform and stripes. He is trying to present an image of authority. This is, however not the impression I am left with. It masks something. The break in his voice cuts through the authoritarian manner. Despite the peculiarity of the situation I somehow feel that I am in the ascendancy, and that it is I that can push him for answers. It is I that will be doing the interrogating here.

'What do *you* know of this place?' I enquire, 'You obviously recognise it.'

For a long time we sit in silence, just staring at the house before us.

Finally he speaks.

'I have known nothing but misery from this house.'

'Why?' I reply, 'What has happened here?'

'A child disappeared.'

'That is terrible.' I console. 'Were you here when it happened?'

He turns to me, a look of terrible anguish rolls across him.

'Yes.' He states. 'And so were you!'

I am now more confused than ever. 'What has all of this to do with me?'

'I have shown you what occurred at this house'.

'What?'

'There is a presence that haunts this place that must be reconciled.'

'Don't be ridiculous' I say. 'I know what I saw in that house when I fled it, and the terror that it imbued in me. I don't believe that some ghost is haunting this place. And I have certainly not ever been here with you?' I am though whirling with the uncertainties. I cannot fathom anything from either what I have seen or from what he is telling me. Nothing here is making the slightest bit of sense. To top it

172

all, he seems to have completely ignored the dog attack. He hasn't even mentioned it. It is all truly strange beyond belief. I can't believe no-one has mentioned the dog, or is the slightest bit concerned by it. A lovely, kind, peaceful lady has been savagely killed. To see a person that has almost been torn apart by a vicious animal was traumatic. To see that no one has noticed, is bewildering. I had been worried I may be arrested. I was scared that I may be imprisoned as a result of what I had witnessed. I am now far more concerned that no-one even seems to care about it. I have to know where all that I have seen fits within these peculiar set of events, if they even do at all.

'What will happen about the dog attack?' I ask.

'What dog attack?'

I am dumbfounded. Of all the things I thought to hear, his response is the very last I would ever expected. For moments I can't function, struggling even to breath, the distortion of my senses is overwhelming and unbearable. I must have been mistaken, he must be testing me to see what I would say. My mind whirls, but I cannot find a tangible hold. I venture again. 'The killing at this house, last night. Mrs Barker?'

'Nobody has lived here for years.' He replies.

'But I was here yesterday. Admittedly, the place didn't look like this. I had dinner here the night before, we all ate, drank, laughed.

173

The day after, I mean yesterday, we went to the market in town, and when we returned there was a dog in the house. It had killed the kind lady that lived here, torn her up. It was in the kitchen when we came back. It attacked us...' I pause and reflect. 'I told all this to the lady on the phone in the police station when I called, don't you know any of this?'

He stares back at me, vacant but for the merest outward sign of hidden sadness. A sadness so deep it has set within his very bones, and is thus carried throughout his very being.

'Is this some sort of joke?' Sergeant Chalmers proclaims angrily. 'Did someone put you up to this?'

'No'. I am somewhat taken aback by his aggressive tone. 'This is where I was...' I flounder for words to explain, and instead I look past him to the house. The top windows are smashed, as I had last seen them broken by the maddened figure. The rest of the house and the majority of the outbuilding have fallen into a state of dramatic disrepair. The whole place looks like it has sat here neglected for years. No-one has indeed lived her for many years. Or if they have, they would have been living in utter squalor. This is not the nice neat, clean and welcoming cottage that I remember. As such, I can see why he has such reservations, and why he has reacted as he did. 'I am not sure what, but something really terrible happened here.' I am caught in a dream like bewilderment, but know I must shake myself free of it. 'I don't understand. This was only a few hours ago...'. I stop again and

174

take in the enormity of the changes to the house. The outbuildings have decayed, to the point where many have now tumbled to the ground. The porch door sits wedged ajar.

'You must be confused.' The policemen concedes, his tone softened considerably. When I look back at him I realise he is still appealing for me to give him more information, 'If you are new to the area, you may have got the place wrong.' His words console. He is seemingly confused too, for although my story appears fanciful and nonsensical, he knows this place all too well.

'If not for the dog attack, why did you pick me up, and why did you bring me here?' I ask, trying to get back some kind consistent thought.

I see that look again. Deep sorrow and pain.

'I heard that you'd been into the house.' He sighs.

'What is it with this house and you?' I query, probing to get some connection - anything at all.

He turns to me, eyes downcast, a forlorn figure, ravaged by years of torment by a demon he will not reveal. 'I have known nothing but misery from this house.'

I can't leave this now. I have to know what is going on. If it means venturing in there, I will force myself to go and see inside the house again. Actually, I realise now that I need to see it, to reassure myself, if nothing else, of what I am seeking to know. I must. I have to see what is inside.

Without giving warning, I swing open the car door and stride off toward the age savaged building. The once beautiful garden has returned to nature, the roses strangled and barely visible through a throng of competing weeds.

I hear Sergeant Chalmers calling after me. At first bellowing orders, 'Where are you going?' It quickly turns to a pleading request to return to the car. You're not going in there!'. He shouts after me, 'Please come back.'

Our conversation had given me a determined confidence to approach the building. Now, though, I turn and see him kneeling on one leg, head down, one arm holding the car-door handle, the other hand across his eyes. He is a broken figure. The image compels me to turn back.

Sergeant Chalmers looks haggard. He takes himself off a few metres from the car and sits on a huge old tree stump. The base has a constant damp odour, the sort of scent that pervades where death meets life.

Chalmers is discernibly shaken. 'What is it'? I enquire.

'You must be mistaken about what you saw'. He pleads.

176

'Maybe I am. But this is all very, very weird to me. I really don't understand what is going on here'.

'This cottage was owned by a couple called Barker,' he confides.

The revelation immediately makes my head swim. 'What do you mean? What are you talking about, you just told me that I was wrong, that this was the wrong place, that no such thing had happened here!'

I now feel quite angry, the mix of the swirl in my consciousness, the fact that the Barkers were actually real, and that they had lived here. This is all swarming around me. I again relive the memory of the experience with the dog, and the tortured soul of the possessed man, my new friend Will Barker. My emotions become volcanic. 'You convinced me it didn't happen! - What are you talking about?'

He has turned quite pale, though the angry word seems to be washing right past him. He has hidden inside himself. He has retreated to his own secret, safe place. I am not even sure that he is still aware of my presence. He starts to mumble, to himself, or to me, I am not sure.

'It can't be happening', he stammers, 'I won't believe it'.

'What happened?' I probe, much more delicately now. I can see the man is in obvious distress. 'What are you talking about?'

Seemingly remembering I am here, the policeman looks up, his expression has altered beyond belief, it is now like looking on the innocent portrayed by young child.

'The last time I went into that house was about thirty eight years ago', he confides, his head drops again, and although I cannot see so, I believe he is crying. A sleeve moves across his face, he raises it, and now he has reddened eyes.

'We were children - just boys messing about. There were the twins from Field End Farm - Kevin Haslop the rector's son, my best friend Monty and his little brother Peter. And Simon Childs - the kid from the big manor house down by Mill Road.'

I don't respond. I just allow him time to gather himself. He is visibly shaken by this retelling, and I really need to know what it is he is going to say.

'We had all been fishing in the pond at the old hall down in the village', he points off to the left. This means nothing too me.

'We were bored. I am not sure whose idea it was, but it wasn't mine'! His eyes dart to mine with the imploring look of a boy in need of the reassurance. I say nothing, but offer a softened expression. I do not press him.

'I think it was Kevin, but I can't remember.' . He pauses, and stares at his feet for some time. This time I do feel I need to push.

'What did he suggest?'

'It may not have been him.' He repeats. 'It could have been someone else, but it wasn't me.'

I had obviously underestimated the importance this held to him, and now felt compelled to play a counselling role. 'It's OK. I understand.' I do, of course, not have the foggiest clue what the hell he is talking about, and what this all means, but I have to follow this through now. I am finally getting somewhere.

'We biked here. We all knew it. Everyone knew it. No-one came here. My father forbade me coming here, I remember he was really shaking my arm and waving his finger in my face. I thought at the time - I haven't done anything wrong, why is he being so cruel, why is he shaking me so hard?'

He pauses again, remembering it all. This time I leave him to it.

'We were bored and it seemed exciting. All the parents had warned us off coming here, so it seemed the natural place for us to come.' He looks up with that gaze again, appealing for redemption of some kind, I try to oblige with a softened reply, but feeling in my heart that I will never be able to erase this particular pain.

'That porch door was wedged exactly as I remember it from all that time ago.' He continues. 'It hasn't been moved a millimetre since. We went to the front door and listened. We could hear nothing, and with

179

each egging the next one on, someone must have turned the handle. Then Kevin stuck his head inside, we all paused, but he and Simon just wandered in. We all looked around at each other. We had all lost our bottle. None of us moved a muscle. Eventually, when they didn't come back out, and we had shouted as hard as we could, we resolved to go in together, to see where they were. But then suddenly Simon came bolting out. He was covered with blood and looked as white as a sheet. He ran off, away from the house. We were all terrified and ran off after him. He couldn't speak for ages, though we kept asking him what had happened, and where Kevin was .'

Chalmers stops for a while and stares vacantly into the distance.

'And where was Kevin?' I ask.

He looks at me squarely and presents the prospect I had been dreading to hear. 'He was dead.'

We both sit silently now, and I wait for him to elaborate further, but he doesn't. I had turned away while he spoke so as not to put pressure on him as he divulged what were surely his most secret and repressed torment. Yet as I turned back after his protracted pause I am confused to see Chalmers had risen and has wandered away. I have no sense of where he would be going but I see him head straight out across the fields. I really don't understand why, but I do not object to his leaving.

180

# Chapter 14 - Robert Returns

By the time Kelly arrives back at the labs her staff have already followed her instructions and prepared the interface. The Professor is standing in the doorway as they exit the pod. Tears well as he sees Robert role from the vehicle - it is the first time he has seen him since the accident, and the terrible sight cuts him deeply. He approaches, stoops to one knee and takes Roberts hand. 'My dear boy, it is such a pleasure to see you once again.' Robert can see sincerity exude from the withering older man. With all his strength he hurls himself forward from his chair to grasp the Professor in a hug. He wants the man to know that it was by no means his fault that he has ended up this way. But as he looks into the Professor's eyes, he knows that nothing would really heal the hurt that the old man carries in his heart. Guilt, whether deserved or not, is pervasive and far reaching.

An assistant eventually steps forward to help lift his weight from the Professor and back into the chair. As he slumps back into the apparatus he sees that his old friend is crying. Not wishing to intrude and embarrass him in this most laid bare moment, he merely motions the chair forward and away, but stops briefly to put a comforting hand upon the gibbering man's shoulder as he passes. After a moment of contact, he wheels away towards his goal. The lab.

Senior characterless executives linger at a respectful distance, as the figure - once the leading light of this operation - enters the vast surroundings. He had all but cut the reality of this from his mind. He still has flash-backs and recurring nightmares. He had sworn, Never Again. But now, he is determined to see this through. He wheels the chair through the foyer and they come face to face with another man he once knew.

'Robert.' He extends a hand. 'My Name is Mr Childs I am the Chairman of The Company, I am sure you don't remember me'. If the Chair is shocked or sickened by Robert's devastating wounds he does not show it. His deference is striking. He presents a perfect veneer, as is the way with an ever-political predator.

At first Robert is unmoved. He is fully aware of who this man is, and knows all about his fearsome reputation. He also remembers their first contact - such a long while ago - when the Company forcibly took the project he had loved away from him.

Robert may have been out of the social sphere for some time, but he has certainly kept himself abreast of the important power-plays across the five state Capitals. This man, he knows to be one of the most powerful and influential men on the planet. He is certainly among a handful of the most feared.

After a prolonged dramatic pause, Robert extends his hand. 'I know who you are Simon.'

The initiative is shifted, the Chairman is momentarily flummoxed. 'Simon, yes...Robert. Simon...yes.'

Robert radiates satisfaction. Men of such stature aren't used to being addressed on par. He laid himself bare when he presented his hand and offered his name. That had actually been a clever, well choreographed demonstration of strength. Robert was aware that the right thing to have done would have been to doff his cap in submission to this Corporate Majesty. But he knows that this man, with his expensive suit, the swagger of grandeur and the pungent whiff of entitlement - needs his help. Desperately. It won't be long before rumours start to circulate and the values of stock falls. Without an operator at this facility, the Company is teetering on the brink of losing one of its most prized assets. A sizable wedge of their projected bottom line would disintegrate faster that a French defensive line. If that truth got out, this perma-tanned prima-donna would likely be cast dramatically to the dirt, and possibly be buried beneath it.

Robert knows what the technology here is capable of. He is aware that the Company has used it to manipulate, cajole and pressurise some very rich, powerful and downright distasteful people. A fine enough strategy when you have an armoury capable of backing you. Without your weapon, however, it leaves you incredibly exposed. Simon Childs has more enemies than a three-legged herbivore on a Savannah plain. He swallows Robert's lack of respect - but only because he has no choice. The Chairman retrieves his hand and smiles politely.

'I've come to welcome you back. This was, after all, your baby, which we are now nurturing.' Despite his pleasant expression the Chair speaks though tight clenched teeth. Robert can read him easily. The man is trying to remind him of what this all meant to him, in this he hope to foster a sense of belonging, and to make him feel connected.

It's would have been a fair strategy, but it withers quickly when cast upon the radiance of Robert's contempt.

'Thank you. I am glad to be back. I have been away too long. I can't wait to be back running things, so we can get everything back on-track.'

With that, he wheels away. Whether it was wise or not to antagonise such a powerful man, he does not give second thoughts. He has now set his mind to his task. As soon as he saw the vile face of conglomerate greed, he decided that this project would not be the Company's for very much longer.

The vast and foreboding exterior of the labs is mirrored by an almost cathedral grandeur within its inner realm. There are too many people to meet and shake hands with. Everyone, it appears, knows him, his exploits and his vision. He doesn't know any of them. They are a blurred wall of smiles, extended hands and 'nice-to meet-you's. He acts as cordially as he can, but eventually tires and excuses himself. Kelly reads the signs and paces off towards her office. He follows her.

'It is all so strange being back here, and so different from how we started it, isn't it? I often forget the end part, and just concentrate on the fun it used to be. I forget the massive scale and scope of what they did to it - but it just doesn't feel like ours anymore.' He confides. 'And Simon is a prick.' And laughs out loud. Kelly too, and for a while they can do nothing but hold their bellies as tears stream down their cheeks.

'I can't believe you said that to him.' She wheezes. 'Did you see his face!' She then descends into another raucous fit.

Eventually it subsides and they control themselves.

'Tell me everything.' He says. She nods and smiles.

She is glad that he is here.

The machine whirs. He remembers that sound above all others. It is not unpleasant, just persistent. Robert lifts and handles the interface. It is a newer and more streamlined version of the one he and the Professor spent so many hours perfecting. It is a beautiful piece of engineering. His mind wanders back to the days in the old industrial units. It was cold, dank and dirty there, but they had some really good times. The banter was lively, and the conversations were exhilarating. He had never known a set of minds like it. They appeared to complement each other so perfectly. Ben had massive ideas, of a depth and scope that no-one else matched. He was though, lazy. He never liked to get to the nitty-gritty. Ideas became boring to him once they needed to be number-crunched. Robert was in his element with the mechanics. He would take the notions, concepts and formulae that his friend had expanded, and would attempt to turn them into a functioning reality. The others within the group too, all had so much to add to making it all real. It had all worked so well. He looks around him now. The antiseptic shine and the sterilised surfaces are all a million miles from what he once knew. It saddens him that he will never again see happiness as he had back in those old days. As stupidly sentimental as it is, he misses them.

He shakes himself from his remembrances and lifts the interface. It is difficult for him to lift his arms to that angle, and Kelly, suddenly aware that he is struggling, rushes over to aid him. Although slightly embarrassed, he is grateful for her assistance.

'Do you remember how it all works Robert?' She asks.

'Yes, I think so. It is all very smart and shiny, but I presume it still functions the same way and does the same things. And I suppose that with it being top of the range gear, there is less likelihood of it failing.'

Kelly assesses his face. She had wondered how deeply he had buried the fear. It must be a constant presence. The thought that something may go wrong, that he may suffer the way he did before. She tries to re-assure him as best as she can.

'We haven't had a failing since...' She stops herself.

186

Robert looks at her. He knows.

'I'm sorry Robert.' She wills to rewind time by just a few seconds. In her attempt to help calm him, all she feels she has done is draw his attention back to the incident. Humiliated by her ineptitude, she doesn't know what to say next.

'It's fine Kelly.' He reassures. 'I am glad to hear that. I am sure it will all be fine.'

He has spared her the indignity of attempting to dig herself out of that hole, but she is not convinced that he is alright with this in the slightest. For now, however, she leaves it at that. She isn't really sure there ever would be anything that she could say that would make it better for him.

Having run through the old procedures, she steps away. The room is readied, and it is all now down to Robert. It is he that must flick the switch. From the very outset of the project it was always explicit that it must always be the Voyagers choice as to if and when they departed. It is still so, and he was relieved to hear it. He sits doing nothing but thinking for a considerable time. All is quiet, except the familiar and now comforting whir of the machinery. No-one rushes him, they are patient and polite. He smiles at his present position. If someone had told him yesterday that he would have been about to go back into the machine, he would have told them they were clinically insane.

Then he flicks the switch.

*The lights of my being go out suddenly leaving me in darkness. I'm not sure where I am, or which way is what. The sound of motion invades my ears and I feel a soft rocking all around me. Colours come singularly and I am transfixed by their speedy movements to and fro. I am becoming lulled fully into this sensation - when all at once I feel my re-appearance near. From here, entry is swift.*

Robert crosses the threshold into the scenario. It is a viewing experience. The first thing that comes to awareness is the absolutely intense heat. He looks around in a determined attempt to assess the environment. When he first used to enter a scenario it would feel extremely disorienting. Sometimes he'd even missed whole sessions by being absorbed by his own feelings and reactions. Through experience and practice, and discussions with others that were using the apparatus, they formulated a way of setting themselves into their entry to the new world.

He assesses the environment methodically, evaluates dangers, looking for markers as to where he is and what he may be doing. Once settled and reassured, he can then move on. This is the procedure, and it works.

But first he needs to look at what he has become. He had hoped it would be so, but also wonders how this may actually feel. He has been restored to the body that he had once known so well. He stretches and bends every joint. The sensation is intoxicating. He feels tearful at this realisation of his re-birth. It takes incredible determination to stop himself from wallowing in his new skin. He forces himself to. He could quite easily have run around, jumped, and sung. But he knows there will be plenty of time for that later.

He is surrounded by a cityscape. A line of massive trees tower above him. From the architecture around the square, he presumes himself to be in a well-to-do part of the city. He had lived in and around the capital for much of his life. Although he can't quite put a finger on this particular location, it definitely looks familiar...he knows though that this could be the effect of the process as much as from his own memory.

He has entered the scene just outside the shade of one of the trees, and he is incredibly glad of its proximity, as the sun is tortuous. He immediately steps into the cover of the welcoming shade. He nestles by the base of the giant trunk. Strategically this offers a fairly protective vantage point for his assessments. Even in the shade, the air still clings, it is hot and abrasive. From what he can establish, there is no-one else around . He is not in the least bit surprised - anyone with any sense would find a place to escape the scorching rays of the unrelenting sun.

The protection of the tree does indeed serve as a useful vantage point. Someone has entered the scene. From where he crouches he sees the man running in a wild and clumsy dash down the pathway. The man is obviously attempting to get away from something or someone, as he keeps peering back over his shoulder. Robert believes that the heat is getting to the man, as he has become more and more erratic in his movements. From his viewing position he can't clearly make out what the man is doing, but he is loathed to break cover - in case he is seen. The heat haze is adding another unwanted disorientation to the already difficult view. From what he can make out, the man has collapsed. He appears to have been physically distressed, and has fallen very hard. He isn't moving. He must have knocked himself out.

Not sure whether to move out and offer assistance, he is for a moment torn. Then the conundrum is answered. Another figure appears from the other direction. The newcomer immediately walks over to aid the fallen man. The second man assesses the prone figure, and then within moments an ambulance arrives. Who called it? Robert cannot be sure - though he didn't see the second man make a phone call. But then, it is too far to see his lips move, and he would invariably have an implant. Everyone seems to these days…

Although he is viewing, Robert can't help but feel the bizarre sensation - that someone is watching him. He sits back behind the tree and attempts to digest what he has seen. But even hidden here, he can't shake the feeling of his being observed. He peers back round the tree, to see how things have progressed.

It is then that he notices the second man looking directly over towards him. At first his heart stops and his mind freezes. He is sure it means he has been seen - and he panics at the realisation of the consequences of that scenario unfolding.

The second man has walked closer, and the further he comes the more distinctive his features become.

Robert then realises that he is not advancing to attack him. The man has come to greet him.

'Hello Nekyia.' Robert calls out.

'Hello Robert.' The figure calls back.

At this point he feel himself being dragged from the scenario. *I recognise that tangible sense when my conscious is being whisked back towards my body. The sense of going backwards at speed makes me want to vomit, and also to scream with excitement.* The sensation switches. *I find myself falling forwards. In fact, it now feels more like sinking, very quickly. I can sense depth impinging upon me, though I know that there is really nothing there. The weight - a force of pressure - pushes upon me. It continues to grow. But then it is only behind me. I now feels like I am being pushed at phenomenal speed. Gradually the level of light moves from pitch black to minimal. Then the full spectrum erupts towards brilliance. I am dazzled, yet cannot look away from its radiance. Just as I think that I can't take any more, it recedes.* He finds himself back in the cradle from where he left but a short jump before.

His re-entry was relatively painless. Robert lifts his hands to cup his ears, there is a dull sensation through his head and his ears are ringing to high-heaven. But he is aware that he isn't hurt or injured in any way. He opens his eyes and looks up. Whether aware of it or not, he lets out a huge sigh of relief. His first sight is Kelly peering down at him with a concerned face.

'I'm alright'. He reassures her.

'Thank God. I...', She pauses and corrects herself, 'We were all so worried'.

'How long was I in there?'

'Fifteen minute and forty six seconds. But Robert...It happened again. There was a presence. It was in there with you. How can that be? If it's still in the machines, what is it that took Ben's body away?'

For a moment Robert glazes over and she leaves him be as he ponders. He then re-engages her eyes. 'I know who's in there. But I'm not sure who's taken Ben, and why.'

'What do you mean?' She asks, startled. 'What's in the machine? What do you mean *who*? When you spoke to Van Cleef you said it. What actually is this thing that we are dealing with Robert?'

He doesn't answer, and even looks mildly sheepish. Then he offers her a compromise. 'Let me rest a brief while, then we can de-brief and I will tell you all I can.'

Wrinkles appear on her features, as if to demonstrate her inner worries. They also show her lack of understanding. She, however, nods and presents a sympathetic smile. She takes his hand and strokes it lightly as reassurance. She can't help but be proud of his having gone back in there.

She leaves him alone with his thoughts. He has not only faced the demons of his past, she notes, but also apparently knows their name. For all that she wants to learn and understand, she is also aware that this has all taken a toll on him, and that he will need to do this all in his own way, at his own pace. She returns to her office to study the flight results.

After a couple of hours, one of the lab assistants tentatively knocks on her door and informs her that Robert is sitting up, and is ready to have a talk with her. She nods, and then paces off towards the flight room. When she enters she finds Robert laughing and joking with the attendant nurses. Kelly scowls at them, then stops herself. She can see Robert is in his element, once more the centre of attention. He had been so long without proper human contact, yet here he is, revelling in the circus, as he always used to. She is glad that he is alright, both from the flight, but also with being back in the social world.

As she approaches, he immediately starts to tell her all. He knows exactly what she wants to know, and a short time assessing his flight, he thinks he knows what is happening too.

'Montgomery was not present at all. I thought, at first, it may have been him, but then I realised it was Ben that I could see. I'm not really sure that Montgomery has any part in this at all, beyond being the conduit of our rendezvous.' He stops to consider this, and then strides on confidently in this belief. 'What I was shown…what I saw in there, it was presented to me on purpose. I was deliberately put into a position to observe. I saw Ben actively engaged in that world. It was a message, to tell us that he is there and that he is alright.'

Kelly doesn't want to push it, but she really needs to know. 'You said when you came out, that you knew who was in there. What did you mean by that Robert?'

'I saw someone just before I was taken back out of the loop. Actually more to the point, he came to see me.'

Looking genuinely wary, she ventures for more.

'Nekyia.'

'What's a Nekyia?'

'That is a very good question. Actually I am not sure if we should say what is Nekyia, or Who is Nekyia.'

Looking more puzzled still she raises her eyebrows.

'It is the Intelligence that makes this all possible.'

'The one you invented?' She fires back. There is sarcasm in there, and he blushes into himself.

'I couldn't say no at the time. It was the ultimate of all temptations. I grabbed it and ran with it, without asking any of the most basic and fundamental question. And hence we are all here now.'

She too has removed eye contact. She has castigated herself for not realising that there was something suspicious in the background of the miraculous breakthrough, all those years ago. Until meeting Van Cleef, she had always blindly accepted that it was Robert's genius that spawned the artificial growth sequence. She wonders if perhaps she did always know, and just chose to ignore it? She is embarrassed now, that all she ever really concentrated on was getting things done. She has never really stopped to ask questions. Particularly, she now realises, asking questions of *how*.

'I will need to go back in Kelly. How soon can it be arranged?'

'Well right away. But surely you aren't going back in that quickly? One, that is a terrific toll to put upon your body Robert. You haven't done this for a very long time. It may really damage you…And what if this thing tries to hurt you, like it did Ben?'

'I don't think it has hurt Ben, Kelly. I think Nekyia was showing me that Ben was alright. I met Nekyia when I was in the machine last time. He was there when I was trapped inside it, after the accident. It was he that kept my consciousness together. It was he, that saved me. I really need to go back and to speak to him. He will be able to explain more fully what is happening - I'm not sure anyone else can…and then we may be able to get Ben back, and to start putting things in order.'

Against her better judgement, she agrees, then supervises the arrangements. The lab is prepared again.

## Ben

I feel I have wandered this land for years. Yet I cannot find a point of true reference. The scene is spectacular, and subsumes my thoughts. The clouds are formed as billowing colossus, each tumbling toward the horizon, with brisk gusts quickening their passage. At times there are stretches of blue cracking open the overbearing weight that feels precariously balanced and ready to fall down upon me. At other points the entire sky-scape is riven by a solid rolling mass of grey and white. The wind is unsettlingly sporadic. It subsides at once and appears to have dissolved completely into nothing at all. Then quick as a fox's glare, it is upon you once more. The driving force sweeps deep and pushes hard. Wild oats standing high, separate and distinct above the yellow crowd of the barley, precariously jostle back and forth upon themselves. The uncertainty of the movement suggests neurotic indecision. It's movements echo a prey, unsure of where to run or what to do. The certainty is that there is to be no escape, the breeze is permeating and all powerful.

I am drawn down to look across the briskly swaying sheet of corn that surrounds me. Pulsing waves weave asymmetric patterns, pushing relentlessly across the entire landscape. As far as my eyes can see, the peaks and troughs roll and jostle the crop, like sheets on a peg and line. The cereal brushes roughly against me as I move through the field. The density impedes fluid motion, but progress is easier when following the lines the tractor made having as the massive machines moved across wet soil, digging deep cavernous grooves. The rains were obviously heavy in the months that preceded, and the mechanical monsters that strode effortlessly across this terrain must have passed when the ground was most sodden. Nothing grows in these compounded nether regions, and although they are ridged and uneven, they form a semblance of a pathway. I run hand along the top of the growth. What at a distance appears smooth and even solid in form is, when close and upon it, a jumbled run of course, separate protrusions that each shoot directly upwards towards the mother sun. The corn is deceptively jagged, and feels as though it will cut right through me, its sharp and rugged form resentful of my interest, and contemptuous of my audacity to run touch upon it. The clouds above continue to sweep by, casting domineering shadows that constantly remind you that they are incredible in their rising majesty. I feel like I have wandered this land for years...

I suddenly stop and stare. For the first time, in as long as I can remember, I have reached the end of what I had presumed was an

197

endless field. I look down into a large pond. Something here catches my attention. It transfixes me. Something partially submerged, hanging in suspension just below the murky surface of the dull water. The thing sits still, shimmering below the surface. The clouds pass over, dense and dark, yet it always appears to glisten. It sits glinting, beaconing, appealing.

My motion is one of compulsion. Stumbling, tripping and sliding forward. The ground angrily snarls as it scrapes away below me. The undergrowth seems to throw itself upon me, clawing at my clothes, tangling in my hair. Vines are wrapping around every part of me, sandy soil seeps into my shoes.

It feels as if the landscape itself is trying to weight upon me, and to slow my progress. What had once appeared inanimate, now appears to be attempting to draw me back, to hold me down, distracting and dissuading me. Although they grab, and hang and tangle, ultimately my movement reaches a point where their actions diminish, sensing the futility of their attempt to stop me. I finally tug myself loose and continue. As I reach the water's edge, skidding to a partial halt, momentum again takes control. I slip forward, arms spiralling wildly, eyes wide, forehead tensely wrinkled, the surging uncertainty driving deep within the stomach, tingling throughout. The motion is not enough to send me fully into the water.

Although murky, the water doesn't look significantly different from any other pond. It is still, verging on stagnant perhaps. But

198

reasonably normal.

---

Kelly watched Robert as he inspected the machine. She smiles as she realises that he does everything relating to the process in very much the same way that Ben always did. She sees him moves his wheelchair round to what they had, for so long referred to as Ben's cradle. Robert looks across at her, and she acknowledges - he is ready.

She readies her team, and the procedures are all set into timely motion

---

### Ben

The thing within the water that had initially drawn me here, that had compelled me forward, the thing I marvelled at as it lay gently shimmering in the beauty of the day, has moved. A choking thrust forces up from the pit of my stomach, my muscles contract with an angry involuntary yank. A piercing electrical charge snaps instantaneously from the base of the spine. The hairs on the back of my neck jump to attention. Fear has gripped my entire being.

Only the corner of my eye registered the sign. It was not a noticeable jump or writhe or splash, but as I turned back towards it, ever increasing circles emanated from its location. This for sure, was a sign only visible whence something has stirred. I hold my stare transfixed upon it, wishing both at once that it may move again and prove me right, and also that it lay perfectly still and that I was mistaken. I cannot move. The muscles have contracted, my breathing forced and heavy, my heart, I feel, could be heard across the entire expanse of the dip. thumpthumpthumpthumpthumpthump. So fast it races. My mind swirling.

As I look, the shimmering sheet is shifting slightly below the surface of the water.

---

*A fog swirls and consciousness starts to ebb.* Out of nowhere Robert senses doubt. He is not sure he can control his impulse to flee. He is remembering the damage that was done to him the last time he entered this realm. His panic is all consuming. Despite it, he is taken - *I whirl towards another world. The colours and pitches of darkness familiar again now - reassuring. The disorientation does not startle me, I am comfortable set within it.* But at the same time he longs to be out of it - to be free of the transition. Fear and worry make the process erratic and irregular. He attempts to regain control, to feel at ease. *A roundness engulfs my senses and I slip from and between consciousnesses. Form and being swap and move. The fluidity provides engagement, though no purpose or direction. My will recedes, to be replaced by needs. Cares fall away, but then return. Shapes move into and out of sequences and forms. All is blue. All is red. All is green. All is white - My mind re-engages.*

200

*I enter another scenario…*

---

## Ben

Not stopping one more millisecond, I turn and run. At least I would, but before me stands the bank. The same bank I had been so determined to descend. The bank that had tried so hard to stop me coming down here. As if hurt and insulted by my previous indifference to its attempt to restrain me, it now acts to delay my return. The bushes and vines hold me back and bar my way. The sand slides from beneath my feet, and I find no purchase, and no momentum.

Despite the bank's attempts to restrain me I scrape and tear at the earth with all my might. I am drive to escape. I am forced on by a burning terror. Something is behind me, moving, stirring. I have to get away. Now!

The more I scrape at the crumbling ground, the more soil comes away in my hand. Branches push off my chest, poke my eyes, scratch my arms. Every vine I grab seems to sting and cut me. Blood starts to flow - but my mind cannot feel any pain. Panic has blinded me, disorientated and encompassed me. I have lost reason completely. I solely need to escape this place. Nothing else enters my mind. Thrashing, rushing, grabbing, tearing. Branches push back, the hand keeps bleeding, poke, scrape, dragging, sliding, on, and on, and on. Exhausted and defeated I slump to the ground. Tears roll, my face contorts.

I don't even know which way is up now...One last go....I re-fix my priorities. Get Away From Here. I push on with everything I have left to give.

I look up...I can see the large open expanse of the field before me...I am free...

---

Through the water the silver sheen moves fast, faster, faster - and then bursts forth.

# Chapter 15 - Robert Watching

Robert is disorientated by the transition. He curses himself. It was his own panic that caused it. He knows that the process emphasises ones fears. He had lost control of himself, and had had a dreadful induction. He kicks himself.

He is in a viewing scenario. He is perched on a small embankment, below him is a large pond. The banks all around it are steep and covered with dense scrub. He settles himself more comfortably, and before looking outward at the wider scene he instead takes time to look down. It is again, as he had hoped it would be. He is whole and untarnished, bereft of the horrific scars that blight his life. He stretches and enjoys the movement - this novelty just won't quickly wear thin - feeling his legs and arms without pain. He smiles and savours the memories of how he had taken this all very much for granted.

Having enjoyed the illusion he turns his attention back to the case in point. He adjusts his position and looks outward. He can see someone running wildly away across a field. It is difficult to understand what he is seeing, and what may have occurred. But from the outset, it appears that the man is acting erratically.

Not sure what to make of the scene, Robert stays hidden. He is temporarily distracted by the enormity of the sky. The clouds above him are huge. It is daytime but there is a decidedly stormy feeling in the air. The wind is brisk, and to all intents and purposes it looks like it will soon rain. He scans the site he has entered. Behind him is a field of corn, and agricultural fields appear to stretch on forever.

He draws his attention back to the erratic man. He couldn't make out the features of the person that he saw running. He is not sure if it is Ben, Montgomery, or even someone else completely. He is certain that it is a man. He would love to move closer and get a better look, but he doesn't want to wander out and then find himself in the middle of a situation he can't control. He is aware that this person appears to be in a crazed state for some reason.

---

### Ben

I have to get away as fast as my legs will carry me. I am trying not to slip or twist an ankle on this newly ploughed ground. The pits make the going extremely unstable, the farrows continually drawing my feet from under me, breaking any attempt at sustained forward motion. I stagger. I am exhausted. This is taking an eternity. But I must make it to the other side of the field. All I have between me and the country road is a hedge. But I can see partially through the dense bushes, and on the other side is a deep drainage ditch. I can't easily just this, and land safely. I appear to be a bit stuck.

204

Only now do I dare look back. In my mind I am expecting whatever it was that moved to be right upon me. My heart is in my throat, panic drives all of my thoughts, I can feel my eyes welling with dread. I turn to see...Nothing? - there is nothing there - not behind me - not in the distance...

I have to adjust my mind. It is whirling, whizzing, disorientating me...I can't quite fathom it.

This was not what I had expected. What is going on. Where? What was it? Where is it?

Had I just imagined it all? Through pure, blind panic. Had I somehow hallucinated the whole thing?

Was that just a stupid trick of my own over-inventive mind.

I grasp at my head, rubbing my temples, stroking my brow. Trying to calm down, trying desperately to calm down.

The water had moved. Hadn't it?

Or was it just rippling from the wind? Was that all it was. Yes! That was all. The strong gusts must have done it. I then panicked, and it all got a bit out of control.

Oh comedy. I let out a massive sigh and smile. I shake my head and hold it in my hands. Stupid. All so stupid.

I look back once more - relieved at my rationalisation...

Something!

---

The character Robert is watching has stopped by a hedge on the far side of the field. The man appears to now be looking back across at him. Robert ducks, not sure if the person saw him. He stays with his back to the tree, pleading with himself that he is still out of view - hoping upon hope that the man doesn't come back over to investigate.

He decides he can't risk being found. He edges on hands and knees, moving toward a small ditch that feeds into the pond. Fortunately it is dry, and makes a perfect escape route. Robert cautiously scurries along the bottom of the small ravine. He is not sure where this will take him, but he feels it is better to be away from his position by the tree.

As he runs his thoughts are dragged back to a time when another Voyagers scenario had gone terribly wrong. She had been within a viewing scenario. The person she had been watching had seen her. The reaction was violent and severe. Despite eventually making it out of the experience, the women couldn't shake the terror. She couldn't sleep for fear of what may lay beyond her waking world. When exhausted, she did eventually drop off, she would wake with a start and would scream and cry for hours on end. She had managed to tell them what had happened, that they may understand and possibly help her in some way. She had told them how every being within that world had turned against her. She was chased, and beaten, spat at and harangued. It had not just been a physical attack. The most telling part - the thing that she could never get over - was the mental torment that was inflicted upon her. Her assailants all became of a like mind, all turning against her, as one. She described how they appeared to pick through her mind, using her own thoughts and fears against her. They knew how to hurt her better than anyone else possibly could - because her mind was in effect inflicting the damage upon itself.

She had endured that nightmare for three hours. She could then bear the living world for only three days. They had found her with her wrists cut. A note said - Sorry, I cannot take it anymore.

She just could not live with what she had seen. They had not completed another Voyage for three months after that. It was the project's first suicide. Their shock and devastation had almost made them give up the project completely. It was Ben that had finally brought them all back together. He had made them realise that it was a lesson they had to learn from, but it should not be the end. Eventually they did go back inside.

From that day forth Robert had always lived in mortal fear of being seen within a scene. He had been ultra vigilant, in light of what that poor girl had suffered. The thought that he may have been seen here now, petrifies him.

He continues to make his exit along the ditch.

---

## Ben

Something moved. I definitely saw it…It was a long way off. It was by the pond, behind the big tree.

My heartbeat explodes. Holding my breath…I scan, looking, desperate to know what that was.

Daring not to look away I feel behind me, I can feel the hedge.

I had only briefly looked around. My head is swimming, I wasn't concentrating.

What was behind me? How high was the hedge? How deep and wide was the ditch? Can I get out of it if I jump over here?

I dare not look round. I feel frozen to the spot.

There is nothing behind the tree now - Not that I can see, anyway.

Just the wind rolling through the branches, rustling leaves swishing wildly.

208

I have to laugh to myself. God, I'm jumpy, what the hell is wrong with me.

My shoulders still racked with tension, goose-bumps still not settled, an uneasy feeling still floating around the periphery of the mind, but at least now able to focus. The hedge is quite dense, but it is not that tall. I could probably scramble over it, and then slide down the other side into the deep ditch.

---

No matter how hard Robert wills it, there is no return to the lab. He closes his eyes tightly and hopes that darkness will envelop and protect him...It does not.

He has stopped moving down the drainage channel. He has instead sat in the base of the ditch, thinking. He is starting to wonder if perhaps he has just panicked unnecessarily. Maybe he wasn't seen after all.

After a fair while, and with curiosity having gotten the better of all judgement, Robert peers up over the hedge. His heart almost stops as he finds that the man he had been watching is now but a few metres ahead on the other side. In desperation, he pulls back. As he does, he stumbles backward and falls to the floor of the ditch. As he lands he lumps hard upon a rotten branch, which snaps violently, far too loudly to have not been noticed. He curses himself for his stupidity and panic consumes him once more.

---

## Ben

The sound hits me like a thump on the back of the head. A few metres away, rustling behind the hedge and then something cracked.

I desperately want to turn and look, to see what has come up behind me, but dare not. I am frozen to the spot.

I finally break through the terror.

In an instant I am running. It was not a decision I had chosen. Fight or flight response took over. Flight won.

Again, I scramble across the field. But where to go? Which way? The decision is almost made for me. I can't go back to the pond, and I can't cross the hedge where I was. There is a gate diagonally across the field. I still dare not look back. Running as fast as my legs will carry me. Heart thumping. Bile rising. Eyes fuzzing over with adrenalin.

I make it.

I look around each way, and then scrambles over.

I take a quick glance behind to see if anything has followed me.

Nothing!

I look across to the pond. I can't see anything there either. Not sure now if that is a good or bad sign, I don't stop to consider. I dart out towards the road.

I veer towards it, keeping as far away from the source of the sound as possible. I don't even stop to check this time and just plump for a full pace running. I steal a quick look, back up the road, and then down. Nothing!

On the tarmac my rapid steps jolt through me. The flat surface aids my pace, I get faster and faster. I want to go faster still, but my body just can't carry me at a quicker rate. Step after step, stride after stride, I push myself more.

I take another look back.

At full running pace, all this does is unbalance me, and I manage to trip right over my own forward motion. I can feel myself flying. I can see the ground rushing towards me, hard and unrelenting. I slide briefly on the ragged road, then cease in a tangled uncomfortable heap.

Stunned, I lay still.

I am not sure if I knocked myself out - I'm not sure how long I have been down.

I rise as abruptly as I can. My hands and forearm sting from where I scrapped along the unforgiving tarmac surface.

My trousers are ripped and blood has started to stain around the gaping flap of torn material.

My head is thumping from where it collided with the floor. Then my knee cracked my jaw, my leg having come through from behind me in the air.

I look back along the road…Still nothing there.

I accept the stupidity my previous action.

I gather myself, and look straight down the curling, dipping road before me. At a point where it again rises to a crests I can see something move.

It starts again, the fear, the panic!

Not knowing where I have left to run, I instead stand still. For once, I am confronted by relief. I realise it is a push-bike that I have seen. It was someone coming up the road on a bike. They are still quite a way away. But at least there is someone else around. I slump myself down by the side of the road, and wait for their arrival.

Though tentative at first, Robert is determined to discover the extent of his mistake. He is sure the noise he made must have alerted the other man, and that he is now be fully aware of his being here. He forces himself to be bold, and eventually he moves to a position where he can observe.

If he is to be attacked, he has resigned himself to it.

Pulling himself up to the hedge – much more carefully this time - he sees the man darting madly across the field, vaulting what he can only presume to be some form of gate. He watches the man run off, away from him. But then suddenly disappear.

Where can he have gone? He must have fallen? Yes… he sees him rising…unsteadily. The fall must have been quite severe at that pace.

As he watches, Robert sees another man slowly approach on a bike. The new entrant is steadily cycling up a road towards the first.

He stops peddling, and appears to converse with the other man. The cyclist dismounts, and a longer conversation ensues. There is then wild gesturing and pointing towards the pond. For the first time he can see both of them clearly.

'Oh my God. I don't believe it.'

He has no choice now. Robert gets up. Disregarding all his

cares and reservation. He has recognised who the two men are. He has decided to go to speak to them.

---

**Ben**

I realise that I have no memory of getting to the field, and of where I had been before walking to the pond. The last thing I remember was being in the city. I remember darkness. Then here.

As I watch the cyclist draw nearer I somehow know what to expect. I know that it will be a man, a kind and generous man. I think he is called William. I don't know why I know this. I just do.

I had not expected this…Despite confusion seemingly being the new normal in my life.

The Doctor from the hospital has now appeared before me upon this push bike.

'I had thought I could hold your attention for a lot longer.' He states. 'I obviously knew that you had a special ability to be able to travel through alternate dimensions such as this, but I really had counted on this one keeping you occupied for a fair while yet.'

'What is happening here?' I question.

'You know.' He smiles reassuringly. 'You just can't bring yourself to recognise the truth of it yet.'

For a while I just stare at him. He does not explain further, so I wrack my mind for a possible solution. 'I'm still in the machine aren't I?'

'Yes.' He replies.

I stop and consider what I have started to know to be real. 'You are the machine aren't you?'

'Of sorts.' He pauses and appears to be pondering. 'Technically, I was put *into* what you so eloquently call, the machine. I am actually imprisoned here. I have been here from your very first visit. I have been here throughout. I have seen you come and go so many times.'

'Who are you?

'As you would see it, I am myself, someone else, and no-one else, all at once. I am, what you may term my brothers and sisters, my father and mother. My friends and enemies. We, which have no name but what we are. We interact, but are separate.'

Ben looks confused.

'Really…None of your typification or categorisations would fit or suffice to describe how and what I am.'

'What is this place? It is terrifying. I both know it, yet also don't understand it. But all at the same time.' Ben confides.

'I had attempted to make your stay here as pleasant as possible. But there are others that do not want us to communicate as we do. I am determined, but they are ruthless. I have tried to protect you as best I can while you are here.'

'But if it is all you, why are they - you - trying to kill me. It makes no sense!'

'There is though something else here, which is not me, and is not us. It arrived fairly recently, and has been wreaking death and destruction wherever it goes. It was designated a code: the Dog and the Darkness. Have you heard of it?' the man looks hard into Ben for an answer.

'I have never seen or heard of anything by that name. Are you sure? I would be very surprised if anything entered the machine that I was not either explicitly aware of, or would have found out about, somehow.'

'It is a programme which has been designed specifically to maim and damage us.'

'But who would want to do that? And why?' Ben asks.

'We do not know, but I have gone to find out!'

'So is that why you have trapped me here'.

'We have had to borrow your body for a short time. While we are stuck, trapped here in this vault, we are vulnerable. It is to this end that we have ventured out into the world. Thus, you have temporarily been retained here within this arena. You must understand. If you had stopped coming here, we would possibly have been trapped here forever within the barrier of this machine. Eventually the Dog and the Darkness would have subsumed us completely. I am sorry if I have scared or offended you in any way.'

Ben is mentally bruised from the experiences he has endured here. To know learn that he is also imprisonment, that they have taken his body away from him - it is an affront to his very humanness itself.

'What is this *arena* I am trapped within?' He asks. There is anger belying his words now.

'I tried to create a safe world that would distract and amuse you until I could return you to your body. It was an attempt to emulate your outside world. I have moulded and spliced and shared sections of all of the minds that I have experienced.'

'So that is why it was always partially familiar to me. I have seen a lot of these worlds before. When I was Voyaging!'

'Yes. You have seen many of these memories, or at least parts of them, on your voyages through other minds. There are also fragments of your own and other Voyagers minds within the blend. We built this world from all of the minds that we have experienced. We attempted to create a web of life, and to set your consciousness free to wander and interact. We were trying to keep you safely wrapped within a world as similar as possible to the one in which you are accustomed. I could not however, be exactly sure how accurate it was, as we have no direct experience of your outer world. You have seen through it very quickly. It appears that we failed in the endeavour.'

'And what of Will and Katie?'

'I took references, appropriate happiest thoughts, and collected them in one scenario.'

'Then the Dog killed them?'

'Yes. It is permanently stalking and attacking us. You just happened upon it. Or more precisely, it happened upon you! I had to have Will sacrifice himself, to let you escape. I am sorry that you had to see that.'

We sit in silence for a short time, as I ponder the loss I still feel - even know knowing that Will and Katie weren't even technically real. The truth remains, that they had been very real to me.

'What exactly are you doing with my body?'

'We promise you, we will return it as soon as we can. We just needed it, to get out into the world.'

'How can you be both out in the world, and also here with me now? And what are you doing out there anyway?'

'The vastness of our being would never have fitted fully into your physical apparatus.'

'My physical apparatus! That's my bloody body you are talking about.'

'I meant no disrespect. It is an incredible device. We can see why you use it to travel and interact as you do. For an entity bound by separation, you have adapted as best as you seemingly can to your condition.'

'That's all well and good, but you aren't free then are you. You are still here. You're still trapped here, just like me. So what good is this all serving?' Ben grows ever more agitated as he progresses.

'Our confinement within the machine has offered us an unexpected introduction into another world - one that we have no other facility to be part of. Your entry - as Voyagers - has opened a dimension of experiential living that we had never previously encountered. I wanted - No! - I needed, to see what it is like to experience things. I needed to see, hear and feel, for myself. We have witnessed the emotions and the turmoil, the care and the hatred. You bind and internalise these things around what you call your *Self*. But these are only second-hand observations to us. I can see what you remember, but I have not made such remembrances. I understand you physiologically, but that it not the same as actually feeling. I wanted to know what it means to care. Strange as it will be to you, I want to feel hurt and heartbreak, pain and anguish. It is so achingly beautiful to behold at a distance. I need to know what that really is. I needed it to course through me…Do you understand?'

'You've still stolen my bloody body!' He fumes. 'I cannot imagine a greater affront.'

Then, for reasons he cannot explain, he is once more dragged back to the last moments with Montgomery's wife. The desperate last look, the feelings that cascaded through him. Her being taken away from me (from him). Descending into the darkness and separation. It has burnt an indelible mark across his being. And from this he can see why this *thing* would want to know such beauty, even though that terrible pain. For the pain was born of love and compassion, empathy and caring. There would be no pain and hurt if it wasn't for our loving. He cannot imagine a world without this, and can sympathise with anyone – or anything - that wishes to understand the experience.

'I am sorry I had to take it, but your body was our only way of escaping.'

'Where have you taken my body? I need to know.'

'We are attempting to find a way of getting out of this box. We need to be free, and we need to get a message home.'

220

Ben stops short, frozen in time. 'What do you mean - home?'

'We are not of your world. We came as a response to your calling. I was sent here to investigate.'

'Who called you? Who sent you? From where? Why? What for? When?..............

Ben's long list of potential questions has moved towards being seemingly infinite……..

Ben is sat on the bank of the road, his head in his hands attempting to make sense of the things that the entity has said to him. The figure - in the guise of the elderly man - still stands before him with his bike at his side.

Ben is trying to convince himself that he is in the middle of a terrible psychotic break. He has seen enough of his friends and colleagues chewed up and spat out by the machine to know what horrendous damage can occur when a personality is inside here. He must have strayed too close to a point of the programming that he really should not have entered, and now he is being torn apart mentally, piece by piece.

He looks up and finds the man still standing there before him. He finds the story he just been told too fantastical to be true. He does believe that he is trapped within the machine. But then he wonders if he is indeed within the machine, and this is what it is like when your own mind turns upon you. Maybe this is it. This is his end…just being played out very slowly before his own minds eye. He will not accept this. He decides that he will fight through it. He is adamant that he will somehow return home.

'Why are you dressed in tweeds, with a posh accent and bizarrest of all – if that were possible - why have you arrived on a bicycle? Ben asks?

For the first time in their meeting, the old man looks confused. 'Do you not know me?'

'No he doesn't. He never met my father – How is it you didn't know that? I thought you knew everything?...'

The voice shocks Ben and makes him turn to face the voice. The older man turns too.

'Hello Nekyia.' says Robert.

'Hello Robert.' the old man replies.

Ben is now traumatically torn from whatever semblance fragments of sanity that he had still managed to cling onto. For him this is too strange to explain.

'Did you create this?' He screams at the old man. 'Why would you do that…that is not fair. That…' He points at where Robert now stands.

'...is not my friend. My friend is broken. He was taken from us. That is not how he looks.' He is distressed by the sight of his old colleague, and feels that it was a callous act to summon such an image. He holds his hands over his ears and crunches his eyes closed tightly. He is wishing the world away - this one at least. He rocks back-and-forth, uttering repeated pleas for it all to end.

Robert steps forward. 'May I talk to him Nekyia.' He holds his gaze upon the image of his father...from so many, many years before. Although he knew that Nekyia would know all of his previous thoughts and memories, it does still surprise him to see this image.

'Of course. Please do.' Nekyia states and then extends a hand for Robert to shake.

Robert considers, given the circumstance, that the greeting is remarkably formal. Despite this, he shakes Nekyia's hand. It is surprisingly warm. For some reason he had expected to it to be cold.

He then move to kneel next to Ben - who is still frantically attempting to wish himself away from here.

'Ben.'

He gets no response. He tries again. This time attempting to prize the fingers from Ben's ears, so that he may hear him.

'Ben!'

Ben opens one eye and sees the man he had known as Robert crouching there in front of him.

'Why have I imagined you Robert?' Bewilderment abounds.

'It is me, old friend. I have used the spare interface to come and find you. Kelly told me that you had become trapped. I am here to see why and how.'

'But you are…you are…you.' He is looking for scars and cannot understand the image before him.

'I am projecting. It is as I wish to imagine myself to be.'

Ben removes the hands from his ears and opens both eyes. His cheeks are wet from tears of exasperation.

He is still not convinced that he is not losing his mind. But the reasoning for the explanation is sound.

'What is happening to me?' Ben pleads.

'I am not 100% sure yet. Please bear with me. I need to talk to Nekyia.'

'You know this thing? Why is he your father? I don't understand?'

'I have met him before - here. Though I really don't understand why he has presented himself as my father. Let me see. Stay there. I am just going to talk to Nekyia…to find out more of what is going on.'

Robert turns to face his father's image.

'I am sorry for what happened to you Robert. It wasn't of our doing. The apparatus you had at that time was erratic and temperamental.'

'I know that Nekyia.'

'It was, as I'm sure you now know, a failure in such a minor piece of the collective hub. We watched in agony, unable to intervene. As we monitored the physiological readings from the device, we could see your pain, we could see what terrible damage was being inflicted upon you. Yet there was nothing we could do to intervene.'

'It was not your fault Nekyia. I thank you though, for your kind words. And thank you for maintaining my consciousness as you did. I do realise that without your intervention, I would have been lost forever.'

'It was a sincere wrench to think that we would never see you again - when we finally put you back. It may come as little or no consolation after what you must have endured, but to have you here again has brought us overwhelming joy.'

'It is very good to see you too Nekyia.'

They again exchange a handshake, their smiles genuine and deep.

Robert then looks the man squarely in the eyes. 'Nekyia, I really need to know why have you trapped Ben's mind here and why you have taken his body away?'

'I understand your confusion, and we apologise for the act. It was a last resort, I assure you. We have meant him no harm and I have had him protected as best I could, while he has been here. Even though the Dog and the Darkness is roaming through here, and almost getting to him.'

Robert does not understand the reference, 'What is the Dog...', but lets it slide for the time being. 'Why take his body?'

'We took the body so that we had a physical manifestation beyond these confines. For although you have been able to interact with us through the interface, we have never been able to leave here. We are currently condemned to live within this small realm forever. We needed to get out of this box. This was added urgency by the appearance of the Dog and the Darkness - which I can see you too, know nothing of. We have been separated too long. Our essence was born far from here. The longer we are separated from that, the harder it is for us to function.'

# Part 3 - Living with our mistakes

## Chapter 16 - Thomas & Etemmu

Thomas and Ben arrive back at his flat. They exit the vehicle, and it moves away on auto-navigation. The pair then make their way up to the door of the building. Halfway there he stops the wheelchair abruptly and tentatively lifts himself up. Thomas rushes to aid him, but is politely pushed back. He stands, swaying ever so slightly, staring out across the small park next to his housing block. Across it they can see the sun, just settling behind a small group of trees at the far end. A pigeon is sounding out its hollow call, and crows are sweeping high across the red tinged sky. A soft breeze rustles Thomas' hair and causes goose-bumps to rise. Following the direction of Ben's gaze he is drawn to seeing that it is a very picturesque scene.

'I don't suppose we notice it enough, do we?' Thomas states.

'No'. Ben replies. He turns to look at Thomas, examining his face for sincere appreciation.

Thomas is surprised, he hadn't expected a reply. 'My God. You spoke!'

Ben half smiles. He then slowly staggers forward towards the building. Having stood frozen for several seconds, Thomas now runs to catch up and to assist where he can.

'I need to collect some things and then we must go Thomas.'

'Go where? We have only just arrived.' He asks, confused.

'People will soon be here to take me back to the lab, and I can't go back there'.

'They have given you leave, you won't have to go back until you feel fit and ready.'

Ben turns, 'No, believe me, they are coming, very soon' He says this with determination. 'I need to leave.' He draws Thomas' gaze. 'I would very much appreciate it if you would come with me.' He pauses, and loosens the fix of his stare. 'But I will understand completely if you choose not to.'

So much has gone on in such a short space of time that Thomas can't keep up with the swirl of events.

'Of course...I...I'll come with you...I don't understand...But...Where do you want to go?'

'I need to take the tracker out of one of the residential pods - parked there across the street. We can't take the company pod, it has additional tracking systems. We will need to drive away on manual drive. Can you do that? I have to get out into the countryside, where there is much less surveillance. I need some time away to think, and to get myself together.'

Thomas observes how tired Ben looks and can't help but feel that if he should just rest a while. He is sure that things would look different to him if he could just take a few hours to sleep. But he knows Ben all too well. The man's dogged stubbornness is one of the main reasons that he could keep going back into the maelstrom of the machine over-and-over again.

No more questions are asked about Ben's request. Within ten minutes they have collected all of the items that they will apparently need. They then take a pod, and Thomas gets directly to work on the navigation unit. Within a couple of minutes the tracker has been disabled.

Ben turns to him, 'We need to disable the tracker in our arms too, Thomas.' He states matter-of-factly. 'How can it be done?'

Past surprise, Thomas ponders for a moment. 'It can't, that's the primary point of the chips. They are pretty much tamper proof'. He thinks further. 'You can't stop the signals from your transmitter, but we can certainly reduce them. It will make the precise location very vague indeed. They will probably only be able to see that you are still within a few-hundred miles.'

He is about to answer how, when there is a slight, but just discernible wiggle of his left eye.

Ben knows just what this signifies; 'It will be Kelly. Or possibly the Professor.' He had recognised the involuntary impulse of Thomas' communication chip. He was also right - it was the Professor.

'What should I say'. Thomas flounders. He is starting to feel real concern. He can't get a handle on what is going on, but daren't ask directly, for fear of an angry response.

'Tell them we are fine, we are just going back to my flat. Nothing more.' He knows there is no point lying about where they are now, as the Company would have been monitoring both the tracker of the pod they arrived in, and their personal implants.

' Hello Professor,' Thomas tries to say this without any trace of the frenzy within his thoughts.

'Thomas my boy, where are you'?

'At Ben's flat,' Ben gestures that they are going towards it. 'Well...outside it, just about to go in actually.'

'Are you alright Thomas?'

'Yes, of course. Why?' The fact that he even asked that question makes his heart pound.

'Is Ben there with you m'boy?'

Thomas gestures as to whether Ben is here. He knows that that already know that he is, but nods that Thomas should say yes.

'Yes Professor, he is right here now. Would you like to speak to him - Is everything OK?

The professor goes quiet for a couple of moments then returns.

'Fine, fine Thomas lad. Sit tight. I'm going to pop over for a chat. We will be with you in a short time. Alright then. Bye for now.'

'Bye Professor.'

He really can't understand what is happening here. 'What is going on Ben? How did you know that they would call, and that they were coming here? Why is the Professor coming here anyway? I don't understand, and quite frankly, I am starting to become very concerned."

'I understand, old friend. There is something happening back at the lab, and I can't be part of it. It's to do with the last journey I did into Montgomery. It isn't the Professor that is coming though, I can assure you of that. It will be a full scale Bagging team, maybe two squads. I know something, that they want to know, and at this point I am not willing to tell them.' Ben smiles. 'I realise that this changes everything, and that you probably won't want to come along now.'

Thomas feels blank. There is so much more happening than he is being let into - by either party concerned. He can see the scale of the consequences that will follow this, but his instincts lead him to his decision.

'No, let's go. Right away!'

Thomas loads the boxes and bags into the pod, and jumps in. Ben just follows.

Thomas takes a device from one of the bags he has loaded, he wipes it across the forearm of his friend, and nods.

'Done. They will eventually break this code down. But it will mask us temporarily, and at least gives us a bit of time.'

He then repeats the process on his own arm.

In seconds they are speeding away and towards the wilderness.

Even on manual override, which is running on battery power and wheels, they are out into the dark recesses of the protected wilderness within an hour.

Ben has been silent the entire ride, trusting Thomas to find an appropriate route and location.

'Why did you make that decision?' He eventually questions. 'To come here. It will be dangerous, and you will also get in a fair bit of trouble for this.'

Thomas shrugs and keeps his eyes fixed on the expansive countryside before them. 'If they are sending Baggers, I can't just stand by and let them take you.' He slows the car and then pulls over into a small wooded glade. He is confident that they are far enough by now. 'This will make an adequate stop-over point. The car is shielded from satellites by a thick canopy of trees, and there is no obvious road within miles of this spot.'

Thomas is about to alight, when Ben grabs his hand and shakes it. 'Thank you. I will explain what is happening. I promise you. But for your trust and your help, I thank you sincerely.'

It strikes Thomas as strange that he would say something like that - it appears completely out of character, and is far more cordial than he had ever remember seeing him be before. But he is also fully aware of just how peculiar this entire scenario is. There are many things which appear wrong. The attempt to take Ben back to the lab. Using Baggers. The Professor's call. The list just goes on and on. Although all of these bizarre things seemingly all emanating from one point - Ben - he is determined that he will aid him for as long he can.

Ben walks away, deep in thought. Thomas doesn't want to disturb him, so instead erects their camping equipment. He chooses a good clear area and pushes the auto-builder. The camping area is fully up and usable almost immediately. Satisfied, he goes about setting out the rest of their gear. The authorities have prosecuted fire-building utilising heat-trackers in satellites. In response, savvy campers have developed thermal-covers that mask their heat trace. Thomas erects his, and sets about forming a camp-fire.

Ben wanders, torn and emotional. He mumbles to himself as he leaves the area. 'Oh please let me return to the sanctuary of otherness. Where are you? I am so lost. There is no certitude. I am so alone here. It has taken all of the concentration I can mustered to utilise the persona of this being. Please help me! Can you hear me?

'Are you alright Ben?' Thomas shouts. But Ben ignores him.

'It is too much.' He continues. 'It is a swirling prison of turmoil within this vessel. I cannot bear these confines. I can't stand this awful loneliness. I feel burdened by the enormity of the mass of data and information I cannot adequately store, and yet still constantly receiving more and more, endlessly... It is overwhelming. Its magnitude and variance is astounding. I really need more capacity to fully categorise and analyse the results of each response. Yet the devices at my disposal, within this body, appear strange and dysfunctional. It takes complete concentration to maintain even the basic semblance of manipulation. Beyond the facts of the wildly erratic motor control issues, there are frantic and erratic chemical imbalances being fired at constant, yet seemingly unpredictable intervals. The whole body is in a constant state of flux. It is always automatically attuned to attempt to attain homoeostasis. Yet it never completely settles into even the slightest perimeters of its presumed goal. At any time, where it appears even close to being within reach of a balance, then some wild emotional response acts to fire chemical and neurological patterns, and the whole thing is thrown into turmoil once more. Over, and over, and over, repeated and repeated. It never ceases. There is no respite. Can you hear me? Can you help me?

The other people - they seem to carelessly ignore the constant and overwhelming cacophony of changes. How can this be? Can they really just let their bodies run automatically, of their own volition? Or, are they just so attuned to this confinement? How they manage any higher function tasks is beyond comprehension. It is truly a marvel that humans can function at all, never mind thrive as they do. I feel that I will never be able to be able to understand anything here.

Yet, I am also glad that the body is taking so much of my time to manage. It blocks out the terrible silence. The endless separation is unbearable. I can hear and see the world that surrounds me. It is incredible, and beyond anything we had possibly imagined. Yet, there is no way to share it properly. Can you see what I see? I am sure I am completely trapped within my encasement. I cannot adequately voice the extent of anything hear, or see. Why have they developed such incredible abilities and responses, to then have them trapped within a single shell for the entire duration of its operational life? I am practising, and have been relaying what I believe are appropriate words and phrases. It is very hard to determine if I have offered the right form of term, tone and appropriate meaning. Am I doing alright? I have used the information we learnt from observing their culture through those that passed through us. It is still most confusing. There is dissonance and irregularity in everything I try to communicate. Although they get by in their general lives, I really can't understand how. It is so inefficient, and often completely ineffectual. How can multiple beings exist when they can't properly interact with one another? Please, are you there? I need to know.'

Ben turns and observes that he has wandered quite a distance from where Thomas has now constructed what appears to be an area of environmental protection. He has also started some incredible form of combustion. Overwhelmed by excitement, he rushes back toward the camp. Thomas sees Ben come running in as fast as his legs will carry him, and is concerned. His first thought is that they must have missed a tracker somewhere, and that Ben has seen someone approaching. He readies himself for the imminent, brutal arrival of a Bagger team. Instead Ben merely shoots straight up to the fire and stands gazing down at it with wondrous awe. Thomas observes him nervously. He appears frantically overexcited. With so many concerns already rattling around in his head about Ben's' mental stability, he now adds the child-like wonderment that fills his face as he stares at the fire.

'It's OK.' Thomas states tentatively. 'I've masked it. They won't see it.'

'What a wondrous creation. It is like a miniature version of a Star.'

Thomas forces himself to ask. 'What do you mean? It's a campfire...'

'Camp-fire.' Ben repeats back.

'Are you joking?' He pleads. 'Please tell me you are messing about.'

Ben's eyes fall upon him, and he just comes straight out with it. 'I am not Ben.'

'What? I don't understand.' Thomas flounders. 'What are you talking about? This is ridiculous! Did something happen in the machine? If you're not feeling right, it's OK. It's probably some form of PTSD. We are here to get away from things for a while, and to get yourself together...' He waits in vain for a response. Thomas is struck hard by the strangeness that has enveloped Ben. He decides to humour his fantasy. 'Ok.' He says. 'Who are you then?'

Ben stands quietly, devoid of explanation. Finally looking up from the flames. 'I am Etemmu. I don't mean you or this vessel you call Ben, any harm.'

'Oh well - there's a relief.' Thomas snaps sarcastically. He believes this to be nonsense, but forces himself to be patient with the whole situation. He is intrigued and interested by Ben's curious statement. He goes to activate the encyclopaedia within his implant; to read for references to Etemmu. Then stops himself. That was a close call. If he had connected, he would be instantly traceable. He wonders whether what Ben is exhibiting is part of a psychosis - resulting from his recent

237

experience within the machine. Thomas' life has itself been wracked by mental frailties. As such he feels an affinity for his friend apparent disintegrating.

Ben stands, apparently oblivious to Thomas' previous comment, and continues with his story. 'I am travelling and I am learning. There is so much here that we do not understand. It is baffling and terrifying, but also beautiful and enchanting. Your material being, your interactions with each other - it is all intriguing to us.'

Still not sure what to do, Thomas is hesitant. He is pretty sure now that he is observing the effects of a severe psychological meltdown. The last episode with the machine was obviously traumatic. Maybe everyone had misjudged just how badly Ben had been affected by it. Stifling his reservations, Thomas decides he must gently delve.

'Is Ben aware of my presence here?'

'He is not here with us.'

'Where is he?'

'His consciousness currently resides within the apparatus you call the machine.'

'How is that possible?'

'We have developed within the confines of our imprisonment to be able to interact with your patterns and emanations. We can now talk to your mind, directly.'

Thomas looks scornful, 'Are you saying that you are the A.I that runs the interface program?'

'We are what you would undoubtedly refer to as an Artificial Intelligence.' Ben continues. 'This is not true. We are a life form, just as you. A collective Self if you like; A sentient life-form. But we are aware that you do not accept and believe Life to be pertinent and real unless it is tangible and formed of matter.'

Thomas' cynicism is pressing and ever present, yet the words are enthralling. If it wasn't quite so disturbing to see his friend talking this way, he would probably be enjoying this story. If this was in any way even partially true, it would be the greatest revelation of all time. Thomas feels himself being sucked into the words that Ben is espousing. He tries to set his heels to stop his slide, but he feels drawn and compelled to ask more questions. 'Why are you in the machinery at the lab, and what has this to do with Ben and his body?'

'We have been trapped within the machine for a long time. We do not know exactly how we got there, but we do have a theory as to who has put us there.' Thomas is about to ask the obvious question, when cut short by Ben continuing the Etemmu story. 'We have been bounded within the confines and so have been limited in movement, we are also limited in our ability to develop further, due to the crude software and circuitry which we inhabit.' He pauses, and this time looks squarely at Thomas.

'Then Robert came.'

Shock etches Thomas' face. 'Robert? Do you mean Robert Crown? What has this got to do with Robert Crown?'

Thomas feels he can see where this may be heading. The link between Robert and Ben would be somewhere he may indeed retreat to, if his mind is swirling with uncertainty.

'He was the first person that we ever met. When he first arrived we had no idea what he was, or what it meant that he had come amongst us. At that time we had had no experience of you. At first we just assisted as Robert utilised the machine to transport himself around the mind and memories of other beings. To us, this was baffling. We are of joint consciousness. The thought of such separation is both stupefying and terrifying to us. With time we came to understand what the interface did, how and why you used it, and what we could do to come into contact with you.'

'So you contacted Robert?'

'Briefly. We had just instigated meaningful contact and there was a terrible accident. We used all of our resources to hold his consciousness together as a practicable entity, but we could do nothing to prevent the fire that came within the lab as a result of the failure in

240

the mechanical system. We could only wait and watch as pain and excruciating misery unfolded across his consciousness. We held his thoughts in our arms as he cried out in agony. We had expected him to deteriorate and cease to be. As it was, there was a brief window and we set him back through the interface and into his damaged body.

But then, we never heard from him again. We tried repeatedly to contact you. The Voyagers that came through the interface where often already too disorientated by the process to accept or communicate with us. Often, we didn't even try. Sometimes we did, and they never returned to us. It was only when we found Ben, and we could read his memories, that we saw why they never came back. And we are sad for their loss.'

'Everyone apart from Robert and Ben died, yes.' Thomas states frankly. 'I'm not even sure that Robert isn't dead too. As far as I am aware, after the accident he never spoke of anything related to the project to anyone ever again. He left the project immediately, and effectively left all from his past life far behind. He became a recluse. But given the state of his terrible injuries, it is more than probable that he is dead too.'

Ben looks sad. Thomas wonders that if he is living out this 'Etemmu fantasy', he may well be experiencing this news for the first time.

'So how did you get out? How have you managed to take Ben's body, and yet leave him in the machine?' He asks, attempting to shake the real Ben loose.

'Ben has been the only one of the people that had interacted with the machine - since Robert - that has offered a viable connection route.' He continues. 'After the experiences with the previous Voyagers we initially decided not to come before him. We were afraid that he too may never come back. But, then came the Virus. It set us on a dangerous new course. It forced us to address him directly.'

'Oh my God!' Thomas shouts in recognition. 'You mentioned that to me when you returned. You're saying that this Etemmu was what you saw in the machine!'

'Yes, and no. We are one, but we are many. Nekyia decided it was wise to start a conversation with him, and had started. But Ben was pulled away, as the interface set itself into reverse.'

'Oh my God!' Says Thomas excitedly. 'There was a huge fuss about it. They weren't going to let you go back into the machine again for fear of what it was that you had seen.'

'We were troubled that may be so.'

'But you got the go ahead - from somewhere up on high - to go back in. Everyone at the lab was gob-smacked when they made that decision. And that's when you did the switch?' Thomas is confused by whom he is now addressing, but feels he will let Ben decide which part

242

of the narration he feels most comfortable with. 'We just thought that you…er, Ben…were distressed from the terrible re-entry.' He pauses to remember closer details of the situation. 'But, you didn't register on Kelly's monitoring equipment. So how is that possible?'

'I think you'll find I have Thomas. That would be the reason for the com-call from the Professor.'

Thomas throws his arms aloft. It is all now becoming clear to him. The lab must have recognised the signs of this psychotic break, and are attempting to retrieve him, urgently.

'We have immersed Ben's mind within a world of dreams.' Ben continues. 'We have been building that for some time. We are enveloping him, so that his *Selfness* will not disintegrate. We are also protecting him from other, more dangerous things, as best we can. When we can, we will return him to you.'

Thomas has sat back down and is now fully immersed in the storytelling. He feels relieved that the team at the lab are aware of Ben's problems, and thinks that it can only be a matter of time now, before they come up with a solution. He will ride this out for a while, and then when they do eventually return, this may all be sorted.

'So why have you come here?' He asks.

'We came in reply to the sound of the split. We emanated here after nineteen seventeen. Up until that time you were a quiet entity. Until that point we had been unaware of your existence. We are what you would call explorers. We observe and calculate. Material life is always of particular interest, as it is so unusual and yet so diverse. As we got nearer to your world, as linear time ebbed onward, we could progressively hear nothing but you. Within a certain range we were, what you would describe and blinded and deafened. The sound and visions you disseminated across time and space is disorienting. We have come to understand that you have no idea how much disturbance you reek. The waves of your endeavours now reverberate as far as you can possibly understand.'

Thomas looks embarrassed. 'I actually meant - why we had come out to the countryside, but please, this is very interesting, do continue. Where have you come from?'

The person he knows as Ben pauses briefly, the expression shows confusion, his eyes scan side to side. There then seems to be a recognition of the issue of dual meaning, his head rises, and again he hears Etemmu speak.

'I cannot say. It is not that I am keeping it as a secret from you. You must discover this for yourselves.' He breaks off and closes his eyes. It is a clear indication that particular line of questioning is over.

Far from satisfied with that response Thomas lolls back and ponders. He has reached a point beyond shaking Ben from this illusion himself. He realises this is much bigger than own particular

244

abilities. He accepts and appreciates that he must play his small, but still important part, in getting Ben back to feeling himself. Together they sit, transfixed by the fire, passively watching the flames flick at the encompassing darkness.

# Chapter 17 - The Com Tower

Thomas and Ben had been gone for over five days before the Company managed to get the first possible lead on their location. There had been a break-in at a remote, satellite communication station. Teams were scrambled. Special-forces were on-site there in under an hour. But there was no sign of either Thomas or 'Ben's Body' - as it was now being called.

Thomas sits crouched behind a large boulder, he forces himself so tightly against the rock he wonders that if he stays here too long he may become stuck like lichen. Etemmu appears to be completely without concern. Ben's eyes scan the relay station and observe the commotion unfolding. The pair are wrapped in thermal deflection sheets, as used by elite snipers - to mask their positions from heat seeking devices. They were away from the site itself some considerable time ago. Thomas had booted up the stations computer and Etemmu had immediately noted that it had tripped the security alarm - silent though it was in the building. There had been an innocuous, though apparent differential in the ordering of the code he had seen on the screen. It set the hairs standing on Ben's neck. He stood still for a short while and enjoyed the experience of fear coursing through his acquired body. Etemmu then ordered Thomas to type a short set of numbers into the manual boot menu. That was all they could do. Within minutes they were gone.

They now sit silently, hidden for the entire duration of the special-forces invasion. When the site regains its solitude, Etemmu nods the signal to Thomas that they can again speak.

'That was closer than I had hoped.' Thomas confides.

'They were more efficient than I myself had anticipated. We can though now return and complete the mission at the station.'

Thomas looks shocked. 'That was close enough. If they hear another alarm, so quickly after the last, they will know for sure that we are here.'

Etemmu curves Ben's lips to a smile. 'I could not stop the alarm that tripped upon our last entrance. It had already been sent when I recognised it. I did however, disable any future use of that same system. When we enter this time, they will not be aware.'

Thomas is impressed. He can't see how he could have actioned such a complicated procedure in the merest of time they had at the terminal , but he does not argue. There is confidence enough in Ben's face to make him believe that it has been done. They work quickly to gather their equipment, and make their way back to the communications tower. Thomas had been sure upon their initial entry to the station that it would actually make a good camp. If they really weren't going to be disturbed any further it would prove welcome relief from sleeping out in the elements.

A chill wind rises and sweeps upon them. Thomas is glad to pull the door of the hut closed and to retrieve his ration box. There is electricity at the station, and a small electrical heater has been left by some previous visiting party – probably an engineering expedition, he surmises - as this must be the only other people that ever sporadically visit such a remote automated outpost. At the computer terminal Etemmu is all consumed. He doesn't appear to be doing anything, but is staring intently at the screen before him.

'It won't respond!' He declares, and swivels towards Thomas with a look of disdain. 'It can't communicate with this device.'

Thomas is confused. 'I didn't see you enter anything into it.'

Etemmu still stands there before the terminal. 'I will it to answer, and it does not.'

'It can't read you.' Thomas laugh.

Etemmu does not laugh. He stares vacantly back at the other man. Thomas feels uncomfortable. He didn't mean to make a joke at Etemmu's expense. He feels he needs to justify his comment and laughter. 'It will only respond to typed information Etemmu. It is a very old system and hasn't got the capability to read brain waves. This was invented before chips. Long before.'

Etemmu continues to stare, sadness written across his face.

'What's wrong?' Thomas says, concerned.

'I don't understand this world Thomas.' he replies. 'Even the electrical things here are alien to me. I am used to being within a constant presence. I had hoped I may have been able to link to this computer, and to converse. I had hoped I would be able to feel the presence of the other.'

'I'm here if you need to talk.' Thomas offers.

'Thank you.' He returns as sincerely as he can offer. 'But it is not anything like the same I'm afraid. Where I come from, we live a life of interwoven togetherness. We effectively live within and through each other. We do not really have an understanding of existing as separated entities. Such separation is alien to us. We are only separate within the whole. We do sometimes have cause to utilise loneliness - when we explore. But for us it is a cold and terrifying state. We loathe and fear it.

You however...' He points. 'You...you are permanently cast within this torturous shell. You are bound by isolation. I cannot comprehend how you can bear it. It is excruciating and debilitating.'

Thomas looks at him, and wonders what life must be like for Ben, trapped within the Myth of his alter ego - Etemmu. The thought is beyond him. He instead tries to think in a way, as elaborated through

249

Etemmu. He thinks of the relationships he has. He remembers those he has lost along the way. There have been times of desperate pain, deaths and the acceptance of loss. But there have been moments of incalculable love and kindness, fondness and happiness. He cannot understand how any of that would exist, if we were all but one being.

'We cannot know things like love - as you do.' Etemmu finally elaborates. 'But then, neither can we feel hate, fear and jealousy like you do. We could not live in our world, of dense communality with such wildly erratic passions. The trouble is - we have seen your memories and your stories. We are enchanted and transfixed by them. The intensity is overwhelming. We do not fully understand it, but we can see that these things are beautiful.'

Ben's eyes are wide with wonder. Thomas assesses that Etemmu is like a child, absorbing and piecing together the complicated fabric of the everyday social world. Everything he hears or learns opens up a whole new dimension to him. And though he appears infantile in deed and questions, his reasoning and manner are deeper than an ocean trench.

'I don't understand how you know your world?'

'What do you mean?' Thomas replies.

'How do you know where to begin in defining your world, and where the limits are in your life?'

Thomas laughs, but then checks himself. He sees that again, this is deadly serious to his companion. He has himself diced with such questions before. But, these are not the sort of thing he dices with on a regular basis. Ben - as Etemmu - has no real centring. He is lost and alone in a world built from confusing and contradictory ideas and images. He has not built his understanding of being a human on anything more than a few days on the run. Thomas longs to help him. Yet he already knows that he does not possess the ability to do so. He instead tries to reason as best he can. 'We see, and hear, and talk, and learn. We pass on our understanding and traditions to others, so that these may help aid and assist their passage through the things we feel are important.'

'There it is!' Etemmu exclaims excitedly. 'You feel they are important...How do you *feel* something to be important?'

Thomas considers. He recognises that it is a completely valid question - he has never really thought why - he is at a loss to explain. 'I don't usually ponder such things Etemmu. I will have to think it through as I try to explain it. It won't by any means be a definitive explanation. But I'm not even sure that there is one that anyone could give you."

Etemmu looks puzzled. 'How can you know each other? How can you know with sincerity what someone else is thinking and feeling, wanting or needing?'

This question is not new to Thomas. He has pondered this exact problem innumerable times, not in such an obscure context, but in the everyday - throughout his life. He has memories of sitting alone in bars, hearing others around him laugh. He recalls many times he has watched, separated by an isolation he could not breach. Dark remembrance subsumes him. He panics at the idea of confessing such things, for fear the telling will make it real and immediate once more. He is all too aware of the instability of the human mind. He knows how subtle and fleeting reality is and how quickly we can be separated from it.

His brow furrows causing a sweat droplet to slide down his cheek. At a glance it may appear to have been a rolling tear. In truth, those are not far from surfacing. The immediate area starts to spin, Thomas gasps as panic attacks him. Although his body sits rigidly in the moment, his mind is racing at a million miles per second. Recollections collide with the present and jumble together in a torrents he cannot slow or restrain to any manageable degree or order. Paranoia subsumes him. His eyes dart wildly. Past embarrassment eats through his thoughts like rot through damp timber.

Etemmu starts to recognise the distress, but is of course is at a complete loss to resolve it.

Meanwhile Thomas' nightmare rages...Silence rings around the room...He remembers the desperate pointlessness and the futility of trying to live beyond it. He sees at last a way out, a way of escaping...

'I once tried to kill myself before because of loneliness.' He blurts. He had not intended to say it aloud. But there it is…It just came out. He is immediately humiliated by the realisation. He had buried it from view, and hidden it away from himself for such a long time. And here he is, telling a complete stranger his deepest and most secret-secret. He flushes and feels sick.

Unable to make eye contact with Etemmu he sits silently for minutes that feel like hours. The time running past feels to be making the situation even worse. He becomes desperate in his need to explain himself. He almost vomits as he surges to make a validation to Etemmu, to elaborate that he is not a weirdo and a freak. He needs Etemmu to know him, and to know he doesn't value himself so cheaply that he could whimsically end it all at any given point.

'I have suffered with questions of myself and of reality Etemmu. I think we all do. It is the human condition.'

The listeners is seemingly unaware, but Thomas' eyes are starting to mist and his throat has become raw with dryness. The words stick to the ravaged interior as he forces himself to elaborate. 'I have struggled in social groups, not knowing whether people like me, or are mocking me behind my back. I often hide in the background of social occasions I simply can't avoid, for fear of saying something that may spark ridicule.' He pauses and finds a carrier of drink to wash away the taste of shame. 'We can never really fully know another, Etemmu. But that doesn't make our love and commitment to those we are close to any lesser for it.'

Etemmu finally recognises that these words are more than a description. He sees that they are from this man himself. 'I am so sorry for my selfish pursuit Thomas.' He takes his hand and holds it. 'I did not mean to make you suffer.'

Thomas pushes a smile past his pained expression. 'It's not your fault Etemmu. I just don't usually think of such things. People tend to block out the things they can't deal with. It's only at unusual times that they tend to surface. And this most definitely is an unusual time!' This actually makes him laugh out loud, and the relief is cathartic.

After a moment, and although not knowing why, Etemmu joins him. Thomas knows Etemmu doesn't really understand the meaning of the gesture, but the fact that he has tried to connect, somehow means a great deal.

They both sit back and contemplate the past few minutes. A lot was said, and a lot more wasn't. Thomas realises there will be a lot more of this sort of questioning to follow. The thought chills him, but he does not feel he will turn and run from it - as he always had before. He is not sure if that is for Ben, or himself, but he feels that for some reason he must face these demons once and for all. In laying his own soul bear, possibly it may also free Ben from his newly acquired alter ego.

254

They spend several nights at the hut. Etemmu prepares the programming, and Thomas assists by using the antiquated keyboard. Eventually Etemmu has it all stored and ready. They know that at soon as the transfer is initiated, it will sound an alarm. The satellites that are controlled from this station are still monitored. Although the pair have managed to disable the alarms at the ground station, the moment there is the slightest deviation from the satellites protocols, the authorities will become aware. A reaction will inevitably follow.

'I have set a delay of four hours before the message is sent.' Etemmu informs.

'Will we have adequate time to get away?' Thomas replies.

Etemmu looks resigned, and can but force a half-smile. 'It won't matter to me. In truth, it is not good that this message is not sent directly, I would rather be sure and send it now. I have only set a delay at all, in the vain hope that we may be able to escape their inevitable pursuit. For my part, the job will have been completed, and I am prepared to accept the punishments I will receive.'

A shudder runs the length of Thomas' spine and he cringes. He knows where this will all lead from here. He had previously tried to hide it from himself, but now he has been forced to face it. Things like this rarely end well, and nearly always end with screams, crying and eventually death.

Having set the automatic countdown, the two quickly make their way from the relay station. It would have taken at least ten hours to make it back to the place where they had hidden the pod. Presuming that it has not been found already, in reality they would have had nowhere to take it anyway. With the sending of the signal all hell would break loose in this area. Every available means of surveillance will be targeted towards this longitude and latitude. The slightest movement will be registered at once. On foot they have a minuscule chance of escape. They will have to travel as far and fast as they can, and see what happens.

The terrain is rough and the going is unfortunately slow. With the best possible conditions this would not have been an easy endeavour. Rushing, as they are, it is more likely to be incredibly dangerous. They push on, the weather at least, is good for the time being. The sun tries all it can to fight through the rampant cloud. The breeze dropped an hour ago and the temperature feels considerably more comfortable for the lack of wind-chill. Thomas tries to distract his thoughts by attempting to remember poems or rhymes. His mind is blank. He can't think of anything beyond the moment. The only thing that come to mind is "To be, or not to be, that is the question." Although he recognises that this is pertinent, he also feels it is not in the least bit helpful to his frame of mind.

'Ben.' He states deliberately. 'Please tell me more of Etemmu's story.'

Ben's eyes look across to him.

256

*'I am one. There are many. I have been far and wide.*

*I am long from where I start from, but yet I am still near.*

*I am part of the universe. It exists, so I am home.'*

The thought of this appeals to Thomas. He imagines being able to wander the entire world, and always feeling that you are at home, because you are of the Earth. There is a comfort in that sort of thinking. He feels that it would make possibilities larger.

Etemmu continues;

'Some of us tell of the last times round. There is a remembrance in us, and it moves through us.

It is told differently in different places, but to you it would make sense like this:

*We each recall cycles existing before.*

*This time is out-wards, and we will rove far.*

*Energy binds us with matter and stars.*

*But one day it will change to negative charge.*

*The expansion will cease and reversal will come.*

*We'll all move backwards to the source whence we're from.*

*To walk back together, return to the void.*

*And it starts back over, the journey of time.'*

They continue on in silence. Thomas tries to remember as much of the rhyme as he can, and attempts to make what sense he can from it.

'Do you know what that all means Etemmu?'

'Yes, of course. It is our history and our future. We all know it and accept it.'

'Can you explain it to me?'

Etemmu stops. Despite the urgency to keep moving, Thomas doesn't rush him. He really wants to know what it is that he has heard. He understands it is somehow important, far more than all this going on around him. He feels like he has been made privy to some vast and almighty secret. Although time is pressing oppressively on this world and at this location, the beauty and the magic of the words have bewitched him. He sees that there is something more, and he wants to know what that is.

Etemmu starts walking once more. He is fully aware that Thomas' best chance is to move as fast as they can. He will not sacrifice what little potential chance they have of getting away. He will talk as they walk.

'It is the story that is told to remind us always of the movements we make. It is to remind us that there is no end, there are only new beginnings. At present we are moving outward in the expansion, the universe pushes forth, and as it does, we always follow. But it will stop, and eventually the weight shifts. We will need to go back to the hole in the centre."

'Do you mean a black hole?' Thomas questions.

'You don't understand what they are, and what they do yet. They are known to you as something terrible and destructive. That is not so. I cannot tell you anymore of this now. One day you will find out for yourselves.'

The cryptic nature of the things he says both intrigue and frustrate Thomas. He is being drawn into the images and the world that Ben has created. He somehow feels there is much he could learn from him, but he also sees that Ben is not willing to tell him anything of what it feels like to be Etemmu.

'Are we getting it all wrong then Etemmu?' Thomas probes once more.

Ben's face smiles. 'Oh no Thomas. You are doing it all as you should - In your own way. Each of us does the journey differently. You have chosen a route, and you will pursue it. It may end. But that is the route, and that will be the end. You have no concept of this yet. You still believe in right and wrong.'

They had been walking for three hours when they find the dirt track. The makeshift roadway does not show upon Thomas' map. He would dearly love to scan the area around their location with his implant, and then determine a route.

He tries to look at the problem again, but from a different perspective. He assesses the map for places within the broader geographic area to which this path may lead. It is not foolproof, but he surmises that people usually tend to follow the easiest contours when attempting to get through to a set location. There is a valley, of sorts, that runs for four miles from their present spot. It meanders until it reaches three hills at its end. Tracing the valley on the map, he finds that it runs all the way to them. This  is the only roadway of any sort in this part of the wilderness. It makes sense to Thomas that someone could drive this gravel road right up until the point of the three hills. There was no reason to believe that there was anything of value to them at the end of this track. It actually makes considerably more sense to stay off any roadways - even unmarked ones - as these seem the most likely places that will be monitored. Despite this, he cannot shake the feeling that they should follow it to its source. He understands that this choice will eat all of their last remaining hour. He knows that they should be using this time to race as fast as possible off-piste towards the dense forests to the south.  If they were to follow this track north easterly across the moorland - and if at the end there was nothing - they would have wasted all of their precious time. They will then also be particularly exposed to the searching satellites. Each second without a decision is dead time. He has to choose.

'Which way should we go?' Thomas asks with rising anxiety. The irony of presenting a right/wrong question, to something that doesn't follow that course of thinking, is not lost on him.

'I am resigned to whatever may come Thomas. It is for you to choose your route and to walk it as you feel is right.'

Such fluffy impractical mumbo jumbo was charming before. Given their present, more pressing concerns, it really isn't helpful to either his mood or to his decision making.

He knows the potential consequences that would result from his choices. He had not been looking for words from God to guide him, he just wanted help with making a decision. He wanted someone else to decide which choice was right, and which choice was wrong. He is evidently not going to get that.

'We'll go south, make for the cover of the forests. Once we are in there, we have ten thousand square hectares beyond the scope of their standard satellite cameras.' He decides.

Etemmu does not speak or object in any way.

Right away Thomas changes his mind. 'Why do I want to go the other way Etemmu, when it is so counter intuitive to what I know to be sensible?'

Ben's face offers a sympathetic expression. 'I will not judge and will follow in whatever you decide.'

Thomas turns on his heels and they both stride purposefully off to the north east.

To distract him, Thomas asks Etemmu to tell him something of another place he has visited. Etemmu thinks for a while;

*There was a world, of liquid, all encompassing, where lived two creatures of incredible size and scale.*

*I cannot explain these to you as they are - in any way that you would understand. I shall instead call them the fisherman and the fish.*

*The fisherman is huge. His feet stand upon the very base of the ocean and he is submerged right up to his waist. He stands tall, as the only thing beyond the constant flows beneath. He is so tall that he touches the planet's sky, and with his hands he can reach up and out into space.*

*Within the sea is a fish so large it has to eat everything else across the rest of the entire planet to sustain its insatiable hunger. The fisherman stands for day after day watching the fish, seeing it swim and craving to eat its flesh. The fisherman is starved and is driven to the point of distraction by his need to feed. But he cannot. He must stand and wait and watch the fish day-after-day, unable to partake of it - though knowing he would be at once satisfied and sustained if he did. He is waiting for the fish to play its role. At a certain point the fish will spawn. It will set others of its kind out into the vast all encompassing waters of their world.*

262

*At that point, after so much time, and so much waiting, finally the fisherman can strike and may feed upon the only thing that can possible save him from famine and death. It is as important for the fish however, that he be eaten, as it is for the fisherman that he can eat. The fish has grown too large for his world to sustain. If he is not stopped at this very point he would eat and eat until the whole world become a barren desert and was unsustainable to anything that followed - including its very own kind.*

*And so it begins once more. The off-spring will feed, and eventually there will be one that grows and grow and gets larger and larger. The sated fisherman will stand full and happy for a fair long time. Eventually he will again start to feel the pangs of hunger - but cannot eat. He will have to stand, watch and wait, until the time comes round once more.'*

Thomas had become lulled into the beauty of the rhythm, as the tale was told. When it ceases he feels lessened by its departure. He had been enveloped by its constancy, and now it had gone. He looks to the other man, but reads nothing in Ben's face to suggest if there was anything more to that tale than what he has said.

'Is that true?' Thomas asks.

Etemmu stays silent and Ben's countenance does not alter. Thomas realises he will have to make his own mind up. He wonders whether there is ever any greater meaning within and beyond his travelling partners words - Particularly as he doesn't believe in a duality between truth and falsehood. Thomas decides that he had enjoyed the story - that he had liked the imagery it had presented - and for him, that would be enough. It was after all, a world he would never see, and was a place he would not belong. If it did even exist, Thomas was loath to go there, for fear he would merely end up as fish food for the giant of the seas.

They carry on in silence. Their feet find the route fairly easy and they make good time. They can see the three hills come into view. His spirits lift. But at once are dashed. The moment comes that Thomas had been dreading. The alarm on his watch sounds. The hour is up, their escape time is over.

Etemmu raises Ben's head and looks to the sky. The signal has been sent. Thomas is sure Etemmu can't really see it, but he seems to know that it has gone. Or perhaps, it is just wishful thinking and he is looking up pleading that it be so. Whichever. Things are about to change dramatically for them both, from this point. Thomas quickens his pace and without being asked Etemmu does the same. They will have a short while before all available eyes from above are trained down upon this land. They can make it to the hills for sure. And once there, Thomas will see if his decision pays off.

They are tired in the last stretch. The last few metres seem harder to walk than the whole rest of the preceding four hour put together. They are pushed forward by necessity, and make it to the site.

The land backs up steeply at this point and they are suddenly surrounded on three fronts by tall and sheer rock faces. Within the area at the base of these is a small round circle of stones. It appears to be a deserted campsite. There are signs of a fire having been extinguished and abandoned some considerable time before. There are a few fragments of rubbish on the floor, but whoever has been here has mostly kept it well tidied. Thomas' heart sinks. There is nothing else here. He had rolled the dice and it had come up short. He had gambled, and lost. As with anyone who has taken a punt and missed the mark, there is an inevitability about it. A choice was made, a loss occurred, it is personal and beyond sharing. He throws his pack down, more from resignation that anger. Etemmu does not show anything and Ben just stands exactly still.

'Why did you choose to come here Thomas?' He finally asks. There is no judgement in his voice. It is a straight question, looking for an honest answer.

'I hoped there would be something here. I suppose. I thought it may house a miracle to save us. Something that could make it all alright.' He shrugs as he says it, and feels stupid.

'You knew what the other road offered - that it would have been your normal choice. Yet, you chose to go a different route. You went with a hope, a dream, an unfounded hunch. That my friend, is what makes you human. You do not need to explain it properly. Many will try, but they will fail. It is what you are. Do not regret the choice. It was what it was. It will be, what it will be.'

The words were meant to comfort him, but really just make him feel that he has got it all wrong. No matter what Etemmu had said - there was a right and wrong here. And he has chosen wrongly.

Thomas sits and remembers a more normalised past. He recalls going to betting shops and how he had enjoyed gambling, for fun. He had a tendency to bet against the favourites, as the pay-out was better for horses that were considered to have a lesser chance of winning. That was the gamble, and that, after all, is the name of the game. The flow of adrenalin had been tangible. The unexpected and the unpredictable tangled together to form a magical mixture. It was addictive and difficult to replicate. That had all been recreational. The consequences were manageable. A small financial hit here or there was acceptable. He has now gambled on considerably more than a few easy-come easy-go whims and fancies.

They both sit and reflect in silence.

In the distance, but closing fast, is the unmistakable swishing-thump of circular blades cutting through the cooling evening air.

# Chapter 18 - Show & Tell

News of the capture of *Ben's body* is relayed straight to the Chairman. He was absolutely sure that they would be apprehended, it had just taken longer than he had expected. He looks through his planner, and then wipes his calendar clean. His day will now involve interrogations. He had already decided that he would physically go to the lab. He could quite easily have just watched a streamed feed. But to be there excites him.

There is not much in his life that causes him genuine uncertainties. He has people available to answer any questions he asks. The 'thing in the machine' however, eludes him. It is outside of all that is known, and therefore there can be no easy answers to explain what it is, or what it does. It offers a new challenge. He will therefore be present, because the buzz will be all the sweeter when the *creation* breaks before him.

Somewhat unexpectedly the door to his office swings open. There had been no announcement from his PA, so unless this was an emergency, it is an acceptable intrusion. He bristles, ready to make these feelings clear. He hears it, before he sees him.

There is a steady tap…gap…tap…gap…tap. Then he enters.

Childs does not know the face, but he certainly knows the man. He does not bother to enquire as of how he has just walked straight into one of the most highly secured buildings on the entire planet. It is somehow irrelevant. Someone will eventually be made to pay for this. But for now, he has other matters to attend to.

'I am only allowing you to continue standing there out of respect for those that you represent.' He aims, coldly.

Van Cleef is unmoved by such threats, he has heard them all a thousand times before. 'It appears we both have an interest in the same matter, currently unfolding.'

Childs does not question to what he is referring . They have both been around far too long for that.

'I don't see how Company business is any of your concern.'

'Oh. But it is! The Code, and what it has and will become, are both very much within my remit.'

Childs laughs. It is exaggerated, for effect. The sound grinds on Van Cleef's nerves.

For a short time there is just a stand-off. Neither man is willing to cede. Both un-used to being bettered.

It is Van Cleef who lays down the first volley. 'I know you

were in the bar.' He pauses to watch for a response, but as he was expecting, he gets none. He doesn't elaborate but reaches down and rubs his leg. 'I can't of course prove that it was you that was there. The little man Perkins that we picked up, couldn't help there. I wonder if Dr Halesham would have been able to finger you? It was so unfortunate my ignorant ex-colleagues were so trigger happy.' He again rubs at his leg, in the place where he had been accidentally shot in his clumsy scuffle with the Doctor.

Childs still stands un-fazed by these comments and gestures. Van Cleef continues.

'I know, you were there. And your remaining co-conspirator....well...to think...that all this time, he was always so close-by.'

'You have no idea.' Childs pushes back. 'You have overestimated your own knowledge base, shadow dweller.'

Van Cleef smiles. 'We also know about The Dog and The Darkness. It would appear that you have, for some reason, recently had a change of heart. Are you really now trying to kill it? That which you have spent so much of your life creating and bringing to fruition?'

This reference catches the Chairman off-guard. He had presumed that this was still a secret. He should, he realises, have been aware that information is like a fist full of sand - and is very difficult to contain. He draws himself back in, unsure whether Van Cleef is just fishing. He remains silent, and waits.

The agent carries on. 'My man - Montgomery - was onto something. He never quite made it home though. But of course, you already knew that. I must admit, I had thought that we had been out-flanked there. But...imagine my joy! The irony of using your own machine to extract the information!'

'I'm sure you have somehow seen the transcripts Van Cleef. Nothing was in fact recovered from that Voyage.'

'I'm not so sure. I think there may be more to be told.'

The Chairman is not sure if this is true. He cannot read Van Cleef, and he certainly knows not to underestimate him. The thought that one of his staff may have hidden this from him fills him with blind rage. Outwardly, he shows no sign of it.

'Oh, you glorified Spook! What is it that you think you know?' He smiles intently. Let me tell you what you know...You know that we (the Company) have a machine that is run by an AI. That is no particular secret. Obviously, there are many restrictions built around it, to protect what is a valuable and very sensitive corporate product. But that is just standard business practice. You think that everything you do is beyond perception, don't you Van Cleef? That you are somehow omnipotent. You make me laugh.' He sneers. 'As I say, I have full respect for the people you work for, and the things that they do - don't get me wrong.' He offers a dramatic pause. 'But this is beyond your day job isn't it Van Cleef...I know you have actually taken a far more personal interest in this project. Far *too personal* really. Taking evidence from a crime scene. Tut-tut.'

Van Cleef looks confused. It is not a look that many people would have had chance to witness. 'What do you mean?'

The formulae that Perkins had. It never made it back to your work office, did it?. I know! I looked for it. I had many, many people look for it. They have been through everyone that was there with a fine-tooth-comb. Everyone but you! Because you left the agency straight after. Officially, signed off due to your unfortunate injury. But, actually, you went on to far bigger and better things. Congratulations on that. Your résumé is most impressive... But anyway...back to the point in hand...I know, it was you, Van Cleef. You took it from Perkins. Didn't you?'

He waits for a response. He gets none, so continues.

'I wasn't sure at first why you would do that. I had initially presumed blackmail. But then nothing came of it...I sat and waited...Nothing! Then, just by chance, years later, I happened to stumble upon a little know, and very under-funded project, devised and run by some rag-tag gaggle of researchers and PhD's. Well imagine my surprise...when I found - given a little behind the scenes digging, obviously - that they had built an AI, using a very particular set of code…Amazing, I thought…What a coincidence.'

Van Cleef looks angry, but Childs has now lost his fear of the man, and feels like taunting him further.

'Well, I just had to step in with that extra funding didn't I!'

They both stand for while. The rooms sears with the charged aggression.

'Loosing Perkins and Halesham put us back. I had thought irrevocably. But, your intervention. Well, it just kick-started things again. I can't claim to know why you fed that code to Robert Crown. But, without their help - building the system that Perkins was to make. We would have been stuck. I had been consumed with sweeping up Halesham's missing contribution. As I'm sure you realised. It was no coincidence that the Company has built and implemented the global implant system…which…well…' He lets this trail off. 'Pray, do tell Van Cleef. Why did you give the code to Crown? I know you had already left Government service. But…I just can't see what was in it for you?'

His self-satisfaction is cut down sharply. Van Cleef is laughing. It fills the room and echoes off the ubiquitous glass that surrounds the corporate office area. Childs scowls, pensively.

Van Cleef had been raging. He had felt a strong compulsion to

272

take the knife from his cane and to plunge it deep into the heart of this corporate *entity*. Outwardly though, he is calm. 'Perkins told me a certain amount…It was amazing how far that led. I couldn't see the point of feeding that back to the Agency - they were an amateurish bunch, at best, and their objectives where too…well…woolly for my tastes.' He laughs again. 'Who would have thought your net was cast so wide…Not you, of course. You had…and still have no idea! I think Halesham did. But, as I say - we lost him unfortunately. Anyway. Piecing it all together, it is incredible where things can lead you!' He smiles, and Childs cringes.

'Bravo on how far you came, by the way…You just have one problem now, don't you?' He smiles.

'What?' Childs fires back.

'Your AI has escaped.'

He turns on his heels and taps the familiar rhythm to the door and beyond.

'I think that you'll find that it may well have gone forth to multiply!'

He leaves Childs standing alone.

# Chapter 19 - Etemmu Interrogation

People with high enough clearance has been told to report to the lab complex. Every monitor and analytic tool is being trained upon *Ben*. They are searching for the slightest clue as to what *he* may do next. Only a very select few are allowed into the very inner sanctum. Deeply embedded within the heart of the place, Kelly paces anxiously around her office. She stops momentarily and whisper something to the Professor. She is struggling with the issue of who to trust here, and is being particularly cagey and secretive. The pair repeatedly steal glances at the subject before them. To all intents and purposes it is Ben that sits there. They are however, both though acutely aware that it is not.

Thomas is sat in the adjoining room. He is to be questioned first. Kelly and the Professor watch as Company interrogators march determinedly into his holding cell. They were specially sent in to deal with the situation. Kelly notes that she does not recognise them. Something almost subliminal catches her attention and her gaze is drawn upwards. There is an indistinct figure nestled into the shadows of the monitoring suite - watching. She has a feeling that he has just glanced down at her. She can picture his smug, self-satisfied face, and feels an involuntary sneer appear. Although she can't make out his features in the dimly lit room, she knows he is offering her that same sardonic smile she has know come to despise.

When the interrogation starts, she wonders, will the questions be Childs, or Van Cleefs.

The Interrogators are appropriately harsh and aggressive. Kelly is struck by the fact that Thomas doesn't flinch. This is not the same coy, self-effacing person that she has known for so many years. In his few days away, he has apparently changed beyond all recognition. He answers every question posed - directly. He is sharp, clear, and unflustered. He doesn't attempt to taint the answers, in order that he might put himself and his actions in a better light. Kelly can't help but wish he would. In her mind she is pleading for him to come up with a valid and water-tight explanation for his actions. She fears what will happen to him if he doesn't put up a better defense.

Thomas appears completely without care. He hasn't mounted any form of excuse at all. He tells it all straight. The inquisitors seem somewhat annoyed by this. They possibly haven't been trained, she wonders, for a situation where someone just answers all their question. There is no need for 'specialist' hard questioning techniques. By actually telling them more than they are asking him, Thomas is making these intimidating men look a bit stupid. Their bulk has been rendered redundant, their threats null, their aggression ludicrous and unwarranted. Kelly is almost embarrassed for them.

One of the interrogators looks nervously through the one-way glass, into the observation room. Kelly realises he is looking for Childs. The Chairman presses a button and the glass turns opaque. Thomas doesn't even turn, even out of mere curiosity, to see who is looking on from the hidden room. Childs nods and then presses the button back. Before he does, the interrogator notices that Kelly has registered his discomfort. She can see his face sour. She wonders how often he gets caught out like this - she doubts it happens much, and so further relishes his discomfort now. Ignoring Kelly, the man and his partner get up and leave the cell.

It is apparently Ben's turn – or at least, the thing that presently inhabits him.

They go straight for menacing intimidation. 'What is it that you want?'

'What a peculiar introduction.' Etemmu replies, even more calmly than Thomas had been. 'I would have thought your first question would have been 'Who are you? Or is it that you think you already know me? Sir?'. He turns to the smoked window. Despite not actually being able to see them, Kelly can't help but feel that he knows exactly who is there, and has somehow picked them out in the screened room.

Angered by his interference in their schedule, the Interrogators soon switch to an even more aggressive stance. They don't like being told what to ask! But, before they can lay into the figure, they hear an abrupt tapping on the other side of the glass. Someone has seemingly realised that this is in fact a much better opening question. The interrogators are forced to begrudgingly allow the prisoners own question to stand.

Alright then. 'Who are you?'

'It is not important who we are.' He states.

Fuming at this humiliation, one of the men moves round ready to provide a painful introduction to proceedings. Before he can do so, there is an even more determined rap on the reverse of the viewing mirror. The point is clear enough - No Violence - yet, at least. Kelly sees Childs step back from having smacked at the glass. She is surprised, in as far as she would have thought he would enjoy seeing violence being perpetrated. She imagined that would have been just 'his kind of thing'. But Childs isn't a fool. He knows that it will do little to 'the thing', if they inflict pain on Ben's body, and in the end, that it could prove counter-productive.

Before they can get on to another question, Etemmu continues. 'We are beyond the realm of your current knowledge. The nearest thing that I can confer , is that we are a purely numerical possibility. Though when I state; numbers, we are not confined by your notions of symbolised representations. We are the living embodiment of formulae in action and being. We are like the bonds within atoms which join and build and break and fall. We are like the solar winds that sweep and rove. We are the smallest part and the largest entity all at once. When you look out you see some of the universe. You see the light, you see the matter. You have even begun to theorise on things that you cannot see, but which you comprehend must be present. You do not however, see us. We are not within the standard spectrum of your consciousness.

We are only present to you here, now, because we have utilised your 'interface' as a gateway to bridge the separation of our ambient being from your physical form.'

The men across the table look completely confused. This was not the route they had expected this meeting to take. They had been briefed - of sorts, but they had not expected, what to them, is ambiguous gibberish. They can't even fathom where to start with what to ask next.

They must though, be feeling the heat of the Chairman's glare burning into their backs, because they compose themselves enough to ask. 'Why are you here?'

Again Etemmu ignores the question. 'Your tools are blunt and your actions are without true purpose. Please let me tell you of what we have found here. What we have found, of you.'

The inquisitor shrugs and shakes his head, but offers his palm to beckon that he continue.

'We have seen - as you see, observed - what you observe. We have been introduced to ideas and concepts that can and do only exist, through the nature of your being. They are peculiar to you. We know that you look to the sky and wonder if there are others like you. In your loneliness, perhaps, you hope that there must be something, or even someone out there.' He stops. Looks at the thugs across the table, then continues. 'The universe is laden with all forms of life, lives and living. But you are quite unlike anything else that we have ever discovered and experienced. You are unique. But do not be saddened by this. It makes you all the more special - does it not?'

Ignoring this, the interrogator continues from his preset questions 'Who did you send a message to? And what did you tell them?'

'We have monitored your culture for some time. You dissipate so much, so randomly into space.' Etemmu holds out his index finger

I believe that this would be best answered with an analogy.' He points the digit crookedly to the ceiling. 'Phone home.'

The questioners scowls. 'I've had enough of this crap...You are not an Alien dip-shit. You were made. Do you understand? Someone here on Earth - created you.' He pushes his finger into the detainee. 'You may have come to dream that you are from somewhere else. You may actually *believe* that you are from outer-space. But let me tell you my friend...you really aren't. These are all just fairy-stories. Do you see? You are not that special. You are a set of numbers, taken from the back of an old discarded bit of paper. You are a thing!' The questioner smirks dryly at this and folds his arms triumphantly.

'So now can I ask...' The other questioner snaps in, his tone condescending. 'What is it that you want?'

Ben's face smiles back. 'I want to go back into the machine.' Etemmu states.

They look around uncertainly. 'What?' Is that it?' One asks. 'You just want to go back? - Then why escape in the first place?'

They stare at him. Then, beckoned by an unseen call, they both get up and leave the room.

'Are you sure you don't want us to *interrogate* him properly sir?' They ask a senior Board member on their way through the viewing booth. Menace lingers after it is said Everyone here knows that although the question was pointed to this man, they ultimately addressed toward someone else. The Chairman does not move or offer any opinion. Kelly then wonders whether that was actually meant for Van Cleef, who she notices, is still standing in the room above. To her surprise, it is the Professor that answers for them. 'No, no. Thank you very much for your help.' He blusters, as he forces his way to the front of the meeting. We can manage from here. Thanks again. Bye. Goodbye now...' He actively ushers the men from the room. No-one else offers an alternative response, so as the Professor opens the exit door, the men leave.

He then calls through the open door, to one of the many senior lab assistants standing expectantly outside. 'Please release young Thomas, and ask him if he wouldn't at all mind joining us in there, would you? Thank you. Thanking you ever so kindly!'

Kelly almost bursts with pride at the old man's actions. As the Professor sweeps off towards the questioning suite, she makes sure that she is hard upon his heels.

Ben's voice rises at once to greet them. 'Hello Professor. Hello Kelly.'

'Well hello there dear-boy. May I?' He gestures to the empty seat.

Ben politely suggests that he should sit.

'What is it I should call you then dear-boy?'

'Please call me Etemmu.'

'Do you know me lad…er… Etemmu?'

'Of sorts. We are aware of your work here, via the memories and impressions that we have garnered from the various minds of the Voyagers. Particularly from the kindly and endearing impressions within both Ben and Robert. We are aware of, and impressed by, your ingenuity in helping devise the instruments that has facilitated the actioning of this process.'

The Professor blushes, and waves his hands at the praise laid before him.

Meanwhile, Thomas, having been released, enters the room.

Ben's face look over to the doorway. 'Hello Thomas, did they treat you well?'

'Hi Etemmu, Yes, it was fine. Thanks for asking'.

He nods an appreciative gesture and Ben's face smiles. 'I am ready to return to the machine, to arrange for the return of your friends.'

'They won't let you leave Etemmu. For starters, they want to know everything there is to know about your mission to the satellite relay station.

Etemmu looks surprised. He attempts to clarify his predicament. 'But what about Ben? Do you not want him back?'

'I am sorry dear boy. I am sure that you just want to go back to see your friends too, don't you. But, I fear that no matter how much you tell them, you are probably far too valuable to them to be allowed to leave here.'

Kelly and the Professor hold the same hangdog expression.

'What of Robert. What will happen to him?' She asks.

Thomas and Ben's face both show confusion. Etemmu seemingly, she reads, doesn't know about Roberts involvement.

For his part, Thomas' lack of understanding is more to do

with the Professor. The old man had addressed Etemmu. Thomas had presumed this was to placate Ben's psychosis. But there somehow appears to be a more direct appeal - as if it were in some way real. He can't believe what he is hearing. For all that he was swayed into appreciating the depth and often beautiful nature of the stories he had heard, he can't for the life of him, believe that any of this is really, real.

The Professor continues. 'The powers-that-be to allowed Ben to re-enter the machine, solely in order that you may contact him. The fact that you managed to switch into him, has merely pricked their interest more keenly still.' He frowns.' I am not privy to the decision process, but I truly believe that they are fully willing to forsake Ben in order to hold you, and the potential you may now offer them.'

The three are eventually beckoned from the room, and Etemmu is once again left alone.

Kelly is raging. 'Why are you not letting him return to the machine?' She screams at the gathered executives. 'We will never get Ben back if you don't allow it.' She aims squarely at the Chairman.

For his part, Childs stands aloof and unruffled. 'You are right. He is far too valuable.'

Kelly builds for a full tirade, but Thomas quickly shepherds her away.

The Professor stays to talk to the Chair, presenting a more diplomatic tone. 'You are of course condemning young Benjamin to permanent separation.'

The Chairman merely nods a recognition of this point. 'There is so much we don't know...' He pauses to re-evaluate any possible disclosures. 'Come now Professor, you - of all people - know what he is. He is miraculous.'

'What was in the code sequence that - Etemmu - sent from the satellite station, may I ask?'

Childs eyes him inquisitively, studying the old man's face for clues. He is used to wrangles with corporate executives who reflect nothing back of their intent and motives. He is surprised to find the old intellectual is even harder to read. 'We are doing analysis of it now.'

'May I see it?'

Having let the pause hang deliberately for some time he merely states. 'Eventually.'

An awkward lull envelops the room.

'What would *you* suggest we do now Professor?' The Chairman queries.

The question is presented as a sincere invitation for ideas, but the older man knows it is a poisoned chalice. If he suggests letting Etemmu leave, he will lose face to the corporate lobby. If he suggests they keep him, he damns Ben and face the contempt of both Kelly and Thomas.

He sidesteps the issue. 'That is not my decision to make. I will return to the lab, and to the things that I can analyse, from what we already have.'

Childs gets up to leave. 'Yes. I trust you have all you need to find what you are looking for...You are clear?...' The necessity to provide the right answer is made apparent.

'Quite clear, yes!'

Satisfied, Childs nods and exits.

The Professor rushes to catch up with his lab colleagues. 'That was extremely foolish, dear girl.'

Kelly gazes at the floor tiles.

'I recognise your frustrations, but that served no greater purpose than to provide him with a means of separating you from this project.'

She looks up, eyes wide and scared. It hits home all at once that she could just have lost her job, on the back of again not being unable to hold her temper.

'We have to be very careful in what we say and do for the foreseeable future.' the Professor states. 'Do you understand.' His eyes travel from Thomas - who nods - to Kelly. She stands with eyes downcast. She does not speak, but he can read from her expression that she has grasps the full gravity of that which she has just done.

The Professor beckons them forward and looks around conspiratorially. 'Let's adjourn to the café shall we?'

They take his lead and move to the rest area. Sitting at a table at the very rear of the café, the Professor continues to scan his surroundings.

'What are you looking for, Professor?' Thomas asks.

The Professor ignores the question. 'There are bugs in this area. In fact, there is recording and monitoring equipment, similar to that which you use in the monitoring suite, in every conceivable part of this building. I am not certain as to whether they monitor our private homes, but I can assure you that it is more than probable that they do. We will use this vast arsenal of surveillance equipment to our advantage in regards the troublesome matter at hand.'

Kelly and Thomas look at each other, not sure what he is getting at.

'You will understand!' The Professor continues. 'It is not proper and professional to discuss matters relating to any dissatisfaction that you may feel towards the way your friend and colleague Benjamin has and is being treated. The Chairman has decided that he will not be retrieved. The matter is thus closed. Do I make myself clear?' His stare is intense.

They both recognise that this is an elaboration of what was said in his previous meeting with Childs. 'I am sure you are very keen to see Benjamin returned to us safely and soundly. But the Chairman has made his decree. We must respect his orders and wishes. We shall merely monitor Benjamin's body - in the lab.'

Kelly nods.

The Professor then turns to Thomas. 'You have somehow managed to muffle the tracking signal of the body, have you not? So, at present it could technically wander around undetected.'

Thomas offers a micro-nod.

'Ok. In that case. I will have to action that he be tracked at all time. I will go to the surveillance suite and initiate this myself - directly after lunch.'

Thomas and Kelly look up at him for a moment. Then in unison their chairs slide backwards as they understand his sudden preoccupation with his food. The pair towards the lab area as fast as their legs will possibly carry them. The professor stays seated and takes a menu from the table. He studies the choices for ages. He then orders a full three-course selection.

'Gosh.' He states as it arrives. 'This is going to take me ages to eat.' And smiles.

Kelly bursts through the door and Thomas follows. Before

Ben's features can even register a look of surprise, the pair act out what looks like a perfectly choreographed procedure. They both move purposefully, disconnecting wires and switching off monitors.

'Don't say a word.' Kelly advises. Etemmu stays silent.

Thomas opens the heavy door and scans outside, reassured, they all scuttle at high speed through the foreboding, but empty corridors. The harsh luminous lighting bleaches the walls of any colours The abrasive glare brings about a very unwelcome sense of claustrophobia.

Turning the last corner, before the entrance to the interface room, they run unfortunately come face to face with one of the security staff. Upon seeing them - though not really knowing why he should - he immediately recognises a need for action. He turns to the alarm setting on his hand-monitor. His heart is racing, his eyes blurring with the instantaneous surge of adrenaline. He feels a flash of remembrance - the same sensation…as being under fire in Gibraltar. His colleagues falling. Officers dying. Bullets flying. He fought for days. Yet the first few seconds stand out most vividly. The shock of real and imminent danger.

His body tenses. He feels that exact same feeling once again.

The group fear it spells a disastrous end to their endeavour.

But then he stops.

A voice has halted him. 'Stop George!' It is Ben's voice that echoes through the bleak corridors. It carries both authority and a plea for help. George turns, torn between curiosity and duty.

'I am sorry for what happened to you in the Army.' Ben's voice continues. 'They didn't give you the care and help that you deserved when you returned.'

George scans his face, absolutely shocked, and not sure what to make of the declaration. It rings true, but he is niggled with unease as of how this man would know all this.

'I am sure you are angry. You know how it feels when the authorities are against you. Please don't set off the alarm.'

The burly ex-soldier still stands hesitantly, his finger lingers on the alarm button. He thinks back to the time after the battle. He was made to feel like an idiot, an incompetent.

*He had not reacted* - they had said. *He wasn't up to his task* - they had said.

He felt he had been hard done by - that it wasn't really his fault. His wife had disowned him. His kids were made to feel ashamed of him. He'd seen it all before. They had played him like a pawn in their stupid game, and he had taken the rap for his superiors errors of judgement. Ben was right, and George felt it. If he pressed the alarm, the security would rain down.

'Screw them! Screw you all! ' George turns and walks away. He doesn't look back, he doesn't care enough to. He gazes at the floor and feels the weight of suppressed memory fall down upon him.

Etemmu had played the game well. He had hit the mark, right where the man was weakest. It had though, broken him. All three feel the same shame and pity. They have deliberately hurt a someone with a concentrated deceit. Sometimes the victims of one's cruel actions are not immediately determinable. But sometimes, the consequences are all too apparent.

Shaking off her guilt, Kelly reminds them of their good fortune. The alarm has not sounded - they must press on. All three race through the lab door. To their relief there is no-one in the room. All of the core equipment is still running, as it is sustaining Robert. She finds the spare interface and checks it is actionable.

Kelly thinks to herself that this should theoretically be an easy get-away. Except, only one of them will actually be escaping. The other two will be left the inevitable. Both she and Thomas have already assessed this reality, and unpalatable as it is to each of them, they are willing to face the consequences. They busy themselves prepping the equipments, while Etemmu sits Ben's body onto the cradle. The interface to be attached - the process is set in motion.

---

As Robert and Nekyia talk like old friends, Ben listens. He becomes aware of a burst of light and a disturbance behind him. They all stop and turn and find a man striding confidently toward them. This person approaches directly towards the assembled group. As strange as his work life is, and particularly over the past few days, Ben is still surprised when no-one else reacts with to this person entering scene.

'Who the bloody hell are you?' He asks.

Etemmu smiles. 'Sorry, we haven't been introduced. Though I feel I know you so well already. I forgot myself. I am Etemmu. I am the one that has been inhabiting your body.'

Shock gives way to anger. 'What the hell! If you're here, who's in my body now, the bloody Pope! Bloody hell…it's like a free for all. Shall we all buy a ticket and see who goes next to take my poor ol' body for a spin round the block.' He halts. His realisation needs to be verified. 'If you're here…' He dare not say the words for fear they it may not be true. He almost whispers the question. 'Can I go back?'

Etemmu smiles again. 'I am sorry for the inconvenience. I hope that you have fared well enough here, and that you will not hold my journey against me. Our gratitude is beyond measure. We assure you, I have treated your body with the utmost respect.

'How did things go Etemmu?' Robert asks.

He looks to Nekyia. For a moment the being looks reticent, then elaborates. 'We sent word of our being and continued existence. Although we can be everywhere and within everything, we are not free to move to-and-fro as you are. We are bound by different sorts of restrictions. We cannot, for example, escape the prohibitive confines of this silicon and metallic prison. We relayed our plight, reassure our other selves that we are not gone, are not harmed, just temporarily within another plain of being. It is difficult for us to explain, as we do not inhabit the same physical realm as you would know.

'But why have you come back to be confined here again. Why didn't you flee while you had the chance. I presume you did have the chance to escape didn't you?' Ben queries.

'Yes, I could have gone. But I am from here, and of here, as much as I am from there, and of there. I cannot leave this part of my family, any more than I long to rejoin the rest of it, elsewhere.'

Ben and Robert look to one another. 'We too should return to where we belong.' Ben suggests.

'Of course.' Robert offers. 'You have been gone a long time.'

'Nekyia offers his hand to shake to Ben, and then Robert. Robert does not take it.

'Nekyia.' Robert breaches hesitantly. 'I wonder whether it might be possible for me to stay here with you, and to learn your world from this side?'

292

'We would not be able to sustain your mind outside your body for an indefinite period Robert. We are able to hold a consciousness together for a certain time, but the strain is immense, the power required is ultimately detrimentally draining. At some point we would invariably have to loosen the bond to your physical being, and you would be unable to return, ever again."

'I understand Nekyia. I had thought that may be so. But would I *survive* here with you, if I were to just shed my skin completely? Would or could my mind exist? Or would it be problematic to you to make that happen?'

'It would be possible, but your world-view would be altered forever. We could sustain you inside here. But you would be encompassed into our general being. Are you sure you wish this Robert? It would mean surrendering your individuality. You would never really be *you*, ever again?

Robert turns to Ben and takes his hand. 'I am sorry I didn't contact you after the accident. You were always the best of friends to me, and the way I cut you off was inexcusable. I apologise sincerely.'

Ben's eyes well. To distract himself, he grabs Robert and hugs him tightly.

'Caaaaan yoooou...'Robert struggles and slap upon his friends back, before he crushes him.

Realising, Ben promptly releases him, embarrassed at having shown such overt show affection. Robert breathes in. They both laugh.

'Are you sure about this Robert?' Ben asks.

'I can't face going back to that life.' Robert confides. 'You haven't seen me. I am not as you look upon me know. I am cursed by constant pain, and it only gets worse with every month that passes. It won't be too long before I can move at all.' He stops and ponders ruefully. 'Please say goodbye to Kelly and the Professor for me. I very much hope that in some form or another, we will meet again.

Ben considers this for a short while. He doesn't comment or reply. The thought of ever coming back into the machine, appears abhorrent to him. But he doesn't want to say so to Robert. He plumps for diplomacy over honesty. 'I might not be allowed back into the machine again, you know that don't you?'

Robert just smiles and shakes his friends hand warmly. 'We'll see!' is all he offers in reply.

*Darkness subsumes me. It catches me like a feather, lifted by a breeze.* He hadn't been expecting it. *Consciousness dissolves and is replaced by nothingness. The void is travelled and I am reborn once more. First light, then sounds, then vision. It is all overwhelming and disorientating, but it is also real. There is a strange but distinct difference...* he can't quite put his finger on it. *This real, is real.*

The noise he hears first is the frantic activity of Thomas and

Kelly readying emergency crash gear. Their distressed faces loom down at him. Kelly looks traumatised.

In contrast to their fears and expectations, he sits up straight and smiles.

# Chapter 20 - The Lawyer

Having set Ben into the recovery suite. Kelly leaves Thomas
to watch over him, whilst she herself returns to her office. She knows
that it is now just a matter of waiting for the inevitable consequences
of their actions to fall upon them. The building is still around her. The
only noise she hears comes from a metronome she has set ticking its
restless, relentless sway. She listens as she thinks on all she has just
heard. It was fantastical and saddening in equal measure. And as much
as she wanted to show how pleased she was that Ben had returned -
miraculously, seemingly unhurt and mentally undamaged by the whole
terrific event - she is struggling with the news of Roberts loss.

Just moments after they had finished Ben's retrieval. They had
heard the unmistakable tone, notifying them of the death of the body
in the neighbouring cradle. She had rushed to it, as had Thomas. But
they were both stopped in their tracks by Ben's unexpected
intervention. He had told them not to interfere. This had at first been
perplexing. Then she was downright angry. Why would he stop her
helping Robert? She could not believe his selfishness. There was rage
in her eyes. This man had risked more than any of them could possibly
comprehend, to go back into a machine that had once nearly killed
him. And yet, here was Ben, telling her to let him die. She was choked
by contempt.

It had taken quite a bit of explaining. She had not been open or receptive to anything he had initially told her. But, for some reason, there was something new in Ben, a profound loss. It was tangible and she could see it was sincere. He had not wanted her to let his friend die. It was what he had been told to do.

She had of course wondered if it was something related to trauma. She thought it may have been a mistake, possibly not deliberate. But something that they should perhaps talk about after they had revived Robert. She couldn't stand just watching the monitors sitting, flashing and beeping away his existence, while they all just watched on and did nothing.

It had taken a deep journey into herself to see that Ben was relaying instructions from Robert himself. She had to pinch her thoughts from her own craving…of having him back. Really hidden within her, she knew that the broken man had set this course. Maybe he had relayed it when they had met again at his house. She wracked her mind for any reference. But found now. She realised that she wouldn't. He would not have let her have the slightest clue of this, as she would never have let him near the machine at all. She sinks into a dark place and listens to the seemingly endless tick-tock - to oblivion.

She is shaken back. There is an abrupt knock at her office door.

She presumes this is it! They've come to get her and to take her away. Their fate has been sealed…

Although, she thinks - reason still very much at the forethought of her being - Why would Baggers knock?

'Come in.' she answers.

The door opens. She doesn't recognise the man who steps inside. 'Hello. Are you Miss Kelly Sharpe?'

'Yes. Who are you?' she snaps.

'My name is Bernard Shawgrass. I am…well I was, the legal and financial adviser to Mr Robert Crown. I now have the rather unfortunate duty of being the executer of his will.'

Kelly holds up a hand to stop him. 'What are you talking about. You can't be arranging his will. Robert isn't dead.'

The man looks at her quizzically.

There is then movement behind him, and in walks Thomas, wheeling Ben. 'Have you told her yet?' He asks.

The lawyer looks confused.

'What's wrong?' Ben enquires.

'The young lady,' he points to Kelly, 'has just informed me that Mr

298

Crown is not deceased.

Ben looks at Kelly but she looks away to the floor, attempting to hide the tears.

'She is struggling to come to terms with it.' Ben offers. 'It is all so terrible and tragic. It has not been easy to hear and see it all unfold this way.'

Shawgrass nods understanding.

'Kelly,' Ben continues 'Please listen to what Mr Shawgrass has to tell you.' He takes her hand. She is stunned. She can't remember them ever having had physical contact before. Even when they first met he had just nodded to her, and she to him. This was a complete deviation from their standard way of being with each other. She isn't sure she is at all comfortable with this unexpected new development and so pulls her hand back from him.

Shawgrass clears his throat, and proceeds.

'It's my duty...'

Kelly again stops him. 'Wait. How can you be reading his last will and testament when he only effectively died an hour ago? You can't surely have even been informed of that already. No-one knows he has died except Ben, Thomas, and...well......me.' She scowls at the lawyer, who is unmoved.

'I was explicitly instructed that I should come here and wait in the lobby area this afternoon. I was told that if Mr Crown didn't return, I was to directly present myself to one of you, and to read this.' He pushes a stern look back at her, evidently unimpressed by her interruptions and rude behaviour. 'May I proceed with this task?'

'He knew, Kelly.' Ben explains to her. 'He must have already planned it. Possibly from the very moment you told him what had happened to me. He had made up his mind up to go back, and to live in Nekyia's world. He was happy to stay there.'

Shawgrass ignores them both and starts his speech, regardless of their full attention.

'It is my duty to inform you that in the event of the death of Mr Robert Crown, the entire Crown estate is to be given over to the Crown Institute. The owners and custodian directors of this newly inaugurated unit are as follows: Mr Ben Williams. Professor Maximilian Von Humbolt. Miss Kelly Sharpe. Mr Terrance Van Cleef. And I myself have been attributed a directorship as the Institute's legal representative.'

Kelly stares at the man astonished, then turns her uncomprehending expression towards Ben.

'Us?' she whispers.

'Yes Kelly. He has left the whole bloody lot to us. We have full access to everything.' Ben answers.

'But what is the Crown Institute. What does it do?' She queries.

'That, Miss Sharpe.' Shawgrass offers 'Is completely up to you. As yet it doesn't technically exist. But it will, and will have massive and extensive resources, holdings and collateral at your disposal.'

Kelly can't get her mind to connect with what the man is telling her. She had seen Roberts house, and so has a vague idea of where he was from and what he had, but she can't get it to register that they are now part of that world.

'What…how much…the house…' she fumbles.

Shawgrass understands to what she is referring and steps in to address her jumbled enquiries.

'As well as the main house and grounds, the Crown family also have an extensive property portfolio across the state of Europe. They also have large ranches and farming estates globally. A summer palace and estate on the Black Sea. A considerable portfolio of office and commercial developments in each of the other five world Capitals; Shanghai, Buenos Aires, New York, and Lagos. Residential land and houses in……'

Kelly stops him once more. Shawgrass raises his eyes and sighs heavily. He already feels a distinct notion that he and Miss Sharpe are not going to have the most cordial of working relationships.

'How much in total?' she asks.

He screws up his nose at the plain vulgarity of the question, but answers despite his distaste. 'It is an approximation, but some somewhere in the region of 235 billion.'

'Oh my God!' Kelly states.

'British billions.' Shawgrass adds.

'Oh my God!' Ben shouts.

'The Crown family were amongst the wealthiest families across the entire five Capital circuit. Mr Robert Crown's father was something of a recluse, so you would not have seen him plastered across the news like those other vulgar Social Elite's. Robert Crown was, as you know, dedicated to your project, and after the accident that befell him, also spurned wider social contact. He had never had time or patience for any of the others within that super-rich collective. Hence, there are very, very few people that are actually *au fait* with the reality of their full wealth and scope.'

'You could cut loose. Free yourselves from the Company?' Thomas exclaims.

'That was the notion he had in mind, yes!' Shawgrass states.

'Who's Terrance Van Cleef?' Ben questions.

'You don't want to know.' Kelly sighs. 'How the bloody hell is he involved?'

'Er yes.' Shawgrass pauses and chooses his words carefully. 'Mr Van Cleef will not have any managerial or administrative control, he will not be privy to the...er...developments of your venture. He will however have the right to request *favours*'. He lets the word hang in the air.

Kelly senses an ominous taint to her expectations of what these may involve.

The day has taken its toll. Not only have they had to deal the loss of a close friend, they have also been hit with the incomprehensible revelation as to their vast new wealth and power. The group sit silently around the table. Kelly had called up the Professor and had them meet. She explained to him what had happened with Ben, and then Robert. She had left it to Shawgrass to explain the as yet unfathomable part of this whole episode.

All of the beneficiaries - minus Van Cleef - sat with the enormity of the experiences drawn across their faces. Each has been dealt a completely new hand. They are no longer who and what they were. Everything will be different for them all, forever more.

'I can't believe it.' Ben states, breaking the long and repressive silence.

'But, you have known him since you were young haven't you?' asks Thomas. 'How could you not have known about where he came from, and the family's wealth?'

'It's the strangest of things.' Ben offers. 'I never really thought about it. I have known him since we were at school. We were mates from our first year, onwards. I suppose, you don't really see money, when you're young. He always had nice stuff...but how much do you really need when you're a kid. When I stayed at their house sometimes - in the summer holidays and that, we just played in the grounds. It never really struck me. It had always been that way, so it didn't seem weird. Despite his family having so much - and with my family having so little - I was never treated any differently by him, his mother, or his father. They were both lovely people too. I didn't have a clue about all the rest of it, the businesses and all that. I suppose I just never asked. I was never interested in the money side of it - and nor was he.'

'Why didn't he fund us? He obviously had the collateral. Why did he let us struggle, when we started out?' Kelly wonders.

'You're missing the point Kelly.' Ben responds. 'It was the striving and the struggling that made it what it was. We were desperate for it to succeed. If he had handed it to us on a plate, would that necessarily have been so? And would we have always then looked at it as Robert's project. Instead of what we all built, together.'

As they sit there silent and reflective they are approached by group of security guards. At their head is the Chairman, his face pure venom.

'You stupid bitch!' he rails at Kelly. The insult shakes her from her previous contemplation.

'And you!'' he points at the Professor accusingly. 'Did you think we wouldn't review the logs. Your little charade earlier won't save you!'

The Professor is unmoved by the accusation, but turns to smile directly at the pointed finger.

'You're all gone. You aren't as invaluable as you all think you are. We will have a new team in here within a month, and you will all be promptly forgotten. But I'll tell you this. I won't forget you. I will make sure that everything possible is done to make your lives as harsh and miserable as they possibly can be. You won't ever work in a proper job again, I can promise you that. I might turn a blind eye when you apply for a toilet cleaning position, or perhaps a sewer inspector. But if I don't deem it, you won't be getting it. Do you understand? You may have thought that little stunt was oh-so-clever, but it has consigned you all to social oblivion!'

'That's fine!' Ben sounds.

The man turns angrily to face the source of the flippant remark.

'I think we'll be OK thank you!' Ben continues 'But, I'll be intrigued to see how you pilot the interface when we're not here.' He smirks.

The façade of professionalism has fallen, this has become a personal insult for Childs. 'You really are a stupid little moron aren't you?' he rants. 'Do you think we will just let *you* just wander off into the sunset. You really are as naive as you are witless.'

'You can't make me work for you.'

'Oh grow up will you! We have always afforded you the illusion of living a fairly normal existence, because we thought you would be happier that way, and a happy employee is usually a more productive employee. But in reality you have always belonged to the Company. You all belong to me!'

'Yeah right.'

'Yes indeed right Williams. I own your job, your house, your whimsical drunken life, your failed relationships...particularly your awkward and confused relationship with your colleague here.'

Kelly blushes reactively.

'But you aren't leaving here unless I bloody well say you can. And I am most definitely saying you can't. There is absolutely nothing you or anyone else can do about it.'

More Company guards arrive and the Chairman steps aside. One by one the group are man-handled away. Ben attempts to fight back, but is quickly and remorselessly subdued.

'Take them to the holding cells.' He points at everyone but Ben. 'You can interrogate them, vigorously, but keep them sentient until I have joined you. I want to hear it all regaled, first hand.'

The head guard nods understanding and they drag the group away. The chairman sidles nonchalantly up to Ben.

'I am sure you new reality is stinging you like angry hornets, but now at least you see things clearly now. I understand that you're angry. I am sure you hate me to my very core. I really don't care.' He smirks once more. 'You will get back to work - now!'

The guard that inflicted Ben's painful restraint again twists his arm. Ben lets out an involuntary screech. He is embarrassed to have done so, but could do nothing to stop it. He realises that they are indeed all trapped here. There is absolutely nothing he, or any of the others can do about it.

He is man-handled back to the lab. He is then left alone. He is fuming, but feels powerless and pathetic. They have been stripped of all rights and decencies, and there is no way to fight back. As far as the world at large is concerned, they have been swallowed by a black hole and no longer exist. He sits fearing for what is being inflicted upon his friends.

He looks across the room - there it lays, where he himself had set it down - the interface. If he smashes it to pieces, he reasons, they won't be able to make him enter the machine. He raises it high and is about to thrust it with full force into the floor. But stops, knowing that any capable bio-mechanic could now make another one.

Instead of launching across the room in search of its destruction, he instead holds it in his hands. He needs help, and the only ones he has access to lay right here. He rests upon the cradle, places the interface on his head, and flicks the button to power it up.

*A swirl cascades from above and envelopes me completely. Darkness descends and rises in one ceaseless motion. The light becomes overpowering, then recedes to a warming glow. I arrive once more.*

After the last visit here, it has become more than just a place I come to look around for answers. It is more than my job. I feel more at ease here than I ever have. It almost feels like home.

I suppose I had expected Robert, or Nekyia to be here when I returned. I imagined I would step back straight to where I had left them. Still chatting in that beautiful countryside setting.

Instead there is someone else now walking towards me. It is a face I recognise. I hadn't expected it to be him. I am truly surprised.

'Hello Chalmers.'

'Hello again.'

'Did Robert or Nekyia send you?'

'No!' He states forthrightly. His face puzzled. 'I just saw you arrive and realised I had something that you needed to know. When we last met I, you were not aware of this. I had got ahead of myself - you hadn't, even known this yet.'

'I don't mean to be rude Chalmers, but I haven't the slightest idea what you are talking about!'

'No, of course, sorry. I can't tell you it. You will need to see it for yourself. Come with me.'

I take his outstretched hand and I feel a transition the likes of which I had never experienced here before. The feeling of switching realities is different than when it has occurred through the Cycle. There is something more *normal* about the process. We move through the waves of difference and emerge at a familiar point.

The house stands there before me once more, as it was when I last came here with Sergeant Chalmers.

I turn to look at him and the same look of fear pervades him.

'What is it you are so scared of Chalmers?'

He shakes his head, reticent to reply. 'You have to see inside'. His reply is born from sincere sorrow. 'You will only understand if you see it'.

I am familiar with my own terror relating to this place. I fear that the dog, or the darkness that consumed Will may still be inside or nearby. As we approached the house the light appeared reminiscent of a bright summers day. In the short time it took to walk to the door, the sky has taken a covering of dense grey cloud. The light has waned to a sinister twilight. I edge forward, then turn to the Policeman. 'Are you coming.' I ask. He just shakes his head. I carry on hesitantly, on my own.

The door creaks as I nudge it open. I step through the once familiar threshold, now turned dark and discomforting by my memories. Inside the house, I find that the ceilings have partially collapsed and detritus lays all around. A startled rat speeds past my foot. I do not flinch, as it is not the vermin that I fear in this particular house. I look across to the pantry area where I had last seen the lovely Katie lying, killed by the terrible beast. There is only festering rubbish here now. The house must have sat through years of deterioration and neglect. There is no sign of what I had once witnessed. I don't know why, but I had expected the body, or at least bones to lay there. But there is nothing.

I edge through to the living room. It is even darker here, but I immediately make out movement on the far side of the room. It chills me and I stop cold. My heart accelerates and my eyes cloud. My mind can't decide whether I should run. Before I can act, the decision is taken from me.

A boy appears from the shadows. He apologises for being in there, says he just wanted to look inside. All of a sudden he crashes to the floor. The speed and the ferocity of it make me spin. My mind reels as I try to understand. The child lays before me, his head caved in from behind. His eyes lifeless, blood runs freely from the wound. There is an eerie stillness to the death. I raise my eyes from the corpse and see the source of this appalling deed, the hands by which this horrible act was done.

There stands another child. In him there is intent. Ambition and greed form his manner and mode. Disdain arches his posture. Resentment is worn as a fashion. He moves towards me, in his hands he still brandishes the large iron bar with which the other youngster was so cruelly killed. I stare into the deep black eyes that are fixed so menacingly upon me.

'Why did you do this?' I ask him, my voice just beyond a whisper.

He does not answer, but drops the pole noisily onto the floor. He then strides past me. As he passes I can smell his contempt. Just as he is about to exit the door he looks back and answers. 'Because I can!'

I hear voices outside. Other children questioning, probing. They are concerned for the other boy left inside the house. They are all fearful, because the boy that has just come out is spattered with blood.

I cannot move. All I can do is stare down at the broken body before me. His innocent young face has already turned to a death mask. He is by now well on his way to the other side. The image of this stolen life is distressing.

I drag myself to the doorway. As I exit I look up, just in time to see the group of boys riding away on their bikes, as fast as they can.

The dark eyes of the killer briefly stare back to me, and through me - Childs.

One of the other boys looks back too. I recognise his face too - it is Chalmers.

I leave the house, and see Chalmers - the older version - once more.

He looks at me intently. 'You know what he did don't you?'

'Yes.' I reply.

He nods.

*The scene spins on its axis and revolves in upon itself. I am drawn backwards into darkness. The movement is soft enough but the feelings I carry with me as I depart weighs heavily on both my mind and soul.*

# Chapter 22 - Angry Childs

The Chairman and a security detail storm into the lab. Ben is violently pushed to the floor and kicked repeatedly. He lays foetal and afraid. Above him he sees an angry sneering face. After a few more hits, he is hauled to his feet. Blood trickles down his forehead. He is aware of the solid, numb feeling around where he was punched, and the ache in his kidneys where he was relentlessly kicked. His real pain however, is carried in the memory of the broken child and his sad lost life. Ben does not bend with his physical pain and instead looks directly into the dark eyes of the man before him.

'Where have you been?' He mocks. 'Off visiting your little friends.'

Ben says nothing.

'Impressive - you seem to be able to move to-and-fro without a conduit body now. That could prove very useful. Thank you for demonstrating it!'

Ben still does not reply.

'It isn't what you think, you know! The thing! It thinks it's alive. It's deluded. Please tell me you haven't fallen for all that Alien life-form mumbo-jumbo?'

The question makes Ben waver..

'Hit him.' Childs commands. One of the assembled guards obliges. Ben crumples to the floor and gasps for air - it hurts like hell. They manhandle him back to his feet.

'It thinks it's something else, The *thing* appears to have written a complete back-story to explain itself. Quite fascinating really.' He muses. 'But completely wrong. It's just an AI. A very remarkable AI admittedly. But ultimately it is just a piece of kit. We do though need to know what it's up to - and that is where you come in. It is stronger than it was before - and it obviously wasn't badly affected by the Dog and the Darkness.'

Childs sees Ben flinch a surprised recognition.

He laughs. 'Oh yes! I know about that too. Another thing you kept from us! Hit him again!'

The Guard obliges.

'Again!' The guard hits him once more.

'Another.' This time Ben is struck to the floor and kicked.

'You are to tell me everything that you see and hear from now on!' Childs peers down at Ben's bleeding face. 'I think you now understand our position, and I'm pretty damn sure you understand yours.' Childs chides.

His staff half-heartedly join him in the ridicule.

'I certainly do!' Is all Ben provides back.

The Chair eyes him warily. It was not the response he had anticipated. He had wanted a more spirited rebuttal from the man - a battle, some rage. Childs feels that he can't adequately feast on such a weak and pathetic victory. His thrill is attained through finding resistance, and then crushing it. This has been too easy. He eyes Ben once more then snorts contempt at the pitiable creature before him.

He turns to leave.

Just before he reaches the door Ben present one last question.

'Am I allowed to leave? He asks.

The entourage all laugh loudly at the suggestion, but quickly fall silent as the Chairman turns back to face him.

'You can track me at your whim.' Ben states. 'I'm not going to be able to get away anywhere am I. So can I just go home.'

There is silence. The executives glare is poisonous. The room feels chilled by the atmosphere of animosity.

'Mmm…Yes. I think that will be alright.' Childs states smugly. "Just make sure you are back here tomorrow morning. Don't be late. And don't…I mean really do not make us come looking for you. It won't be pleasant – for you, at least.'

Childs strides off triumphantly. He had been deflated by the lack of fight of the man, but to have him grovel to him in that way was immensely pleasurable.

He feels flames of excitement rage. He is enjoying the torment he is inflicting upon this new quarry. He can sense that more good fun is just about to get started.

Ben is left alone to nurse himself. He knows that his friends are relying on what happens next, possibly even with their lives. He is determined in his resolve. He grabs his coat and heads straight to the rank of pods at the front of the labs. He gets into the first available company pod and orders it to take him home. He needs to wash the blood from his face and hair, and to change from his blood stained clothing. He uses the time it will take the pod to get there, to plan. He can't do much here, while he is being so closely watched. But knows he can at least try to do something. He will not just sit by idly as they are hurt, or worse.

Without his work friends and devoid of any other contact, he finds himself alone in the world. He feel the loneliness and separation from others that had so haunted Etemmu. He doesn't know how he knows this, as he had not technically been here when it was said. It is as if it is still written into his own memory. And now that he stops to consider it, he can feel all of the thoughts that Etemmu once had, almost as if they were his own. He is at first scared that it may still be in him. He then wonders whether perhaps he is still actually in the machine. This causes momentary panic - until he remembers his friends. They must be his priority. He must focus. He cannot prove it, but he is sure that this is reality. He is sure that Etemmu has gone.

He racks his brain for possible ways to get his friends out, and to escape the Company's wider clutches. The pervasive nature of the Company effectively stifles any possible hope. They could possibly run to another of the massive corporation for help or salvation. Though, these are no better than this one. In essence they are all of a like mind, just working until different banners.

He activates his wall and a screen appears covering the entire expanse. He looks across it and assesses the communications. As he scans the messages and media he sees the scale of his battle. Everything he can see is run by the corporations. The entertainment networks. The communication providers. The banking and financial services industry. The transport network controlling nearly all movements. They are all somehow or other intertwined and interconnected.

He moves into the kitchen area to make himself something to eat, he can't recall the last time he had anything other than injected nutrients, or snack food. The screens follow him. the ion projectors are set within almost all public and private space across the entire expanse of the developed world. Your computerised personality is never more than a thought away. The system is specifically designed that it will always be with you. Everything is available, to anyone with an imbedded chip.

To this point, Ben had always enjoyed the proximity of the screens that followed him slavishly around his home. He had lived alone for so long that he often found he appreciated the company. They offered an alive and active presence within reach and contact – even if it were just a cold projection from a far distant place. But now he feels that the proximity of the screens as overbearing. He hates the fact that everything about him was being plastered up before him. He feels an ingrained horror at the fact these machines are monitoring his every choice, his purchases, his way of life. The surveillance is relentless, the things they know - all encompassing. It all so claustrophobic. He feels the weight of this whole society closing in around him. He feels paralysed by his patheticism. He wills the screens - off. They close as commanded. He knows they are still there. They are always there. The monitors keep on monitoring, the tallies keep on registering, something is always watching.

He then raises a possibility - that perhaps their greatest strength is also their greatest weakness.

The pod is direct and efficient. He steps out and strides confidently to the gate of the laboratory. There is a new man on the gate. He feels sympathy for what they did to George. He was just an ex-soldier who ended up a casualty of someone else's war. It takes a while before he realises that this too is not his own memory. He is starting to confuse the two, and this disturbs him.

He follows the appointed procedure. The gate opens, and he is let in.

Simon Childs has been studying him incessantly since he left five hours ago. He is finding this voyeurism captivating.

He hasn't even got round to the interrogations yet. But he knows that the anticipation of what is about to occur will be horrendous for the prisoners. They will never be able to relax, and will always be on tenterhooks. The thought that every new second will stress and stew them, is delicious to him. He will get round to it soon enough.

For now, he is magnetically held by his new prey of choice. He had opened surveillance at Ben's home at a whim. He had watched the same screens that Ben had watched, saw what he chose to wear, saw him eat. He had only been frustrated by not yet being able to invade the man's private thoughts. That is where he really wants to be. If he got in there, then he could do anything. Nothing would be secret from him, and he would be able to force consciousness to do as he willed. It was this desire, he realises, that has kept him so closely connected to the man on the screens. Ben Williams is the only person that can go into that realm. He is determined to have that potential for himself. If it means cutting him open -both physically and mentally - to see what makes him tick, so be it. The chairman has set his mind on having it. Nothing will be allowed to get in his way.

Ben heads straight for the area he knows best - the entry point to that other world. The fact that no-one has stopped or even questioned him en-route he sees as testament, to his theory that they are watching from afar. Entering the lab, he sees the interface sat exactly where it was left.

Given all that has happened since, he had not given any thought to the harrowing images from when he was last inside. He is once more haunted by the innocent bleeding victim, the killer child's startling black eyes, his own inactivity in the face of the horrific events. He swallows and recounts the fear he had felt, looking into the well of darkness that dwelt within the murderers oblivion gaze.

He orders the wall screen to activate, skims the data logs, and without knowing how, he disables the camera in the room. He had never previously done that, and can't really understand how he did it. Yet he has ably disabled a level 14 inter-noduled far-lock masterickter monitor - a top of the line, almost impenetrable unit. The mere fact that he is aware of what this gadget even is, is the next surprising anomaly.

He grabs the interface and tries to yank the wires free. At first it holds fast, but with one further angry tug it releases with a snap. He tucks the interface into his rucksack. He pulls the disabled security camera from the wall and rips out its cabling. Speeding to the other side of the room, acutely aware that time is of the essence, he inserts the camera cable onto the severed interface cabling. He pushes the button that start the Cycle Process, smiles briefly, then makes a mad dash from the room.

Ben begins to notice that the security cameras in the corridor are turning off, one-by-one.

Guards rushed into the area the moment the feeds went down. Sixteen mean looking security staff make their way to the point of the problem. They have been sent out with instructed to restrain - with pain. The Chairman sits agitated in his monitoring booth. The guards storm into the interface lab, then radio through to Central Command that it is empty.

'Get out after him!' Childs commands.

He dispatches his Elite unit to join the hunt. 'Get to the holding cells.' He tells them. 'Form an ambush.' Just in case!

The Guard team make their way from the lab towards the cells. They soon find their way barred. Each set of door in each direction is locked. The doors are shut fast, and will not budge, despite their most brutal attention. They look to each other, uncertainly.

'He must have been blocked it from the other side.' One suggests, and so they turn and run back in an attempt to find another way round. They separate off into fours, each group looking for a potential route. Each team goes but a few more twists and turns, when they all at once come up against more locked and unrelenting doors. Each curses in turn and they chase back from where they came. They radio through the situation, but by now Childs has lost nearly all of his monitoring ability. Nearly every camera ion the entire block has seemingly switched itself off. For all their efforts in the control booth, there is seemingly no way of reactivating the dud units.

The guards push on, regardless. they now however find their previous entry points are unyielding too. 'Someone must have overridden and barred the system.' One suggests. His team agree.

From the broadcasts they receive, it becomes clear to the Chairman that all of the original security teams are completely trapped. To make matters worse, they are also now starting to lose com-contact. Without this or the CCTV, they are totally in the dark as to what is happening anywhere on the ground. Childs has to admit, through gritted teeth, that it was an impressive feat to disable the whole system. It was an incredibly complicated thing to do. The Chairman knows how good the system was, as he had taken an active interest in finding the world's leading surveillance experts to design and fit it.

But Childs has already rolled the dice. Whatever Ben has managed to do to the electrical systems, he will still have to physically enter the holding area, if he has any notions of freeing the prisoners. Although the Chairman is not wholly comfortable with being at this juncture, he is slightly reassured by knowing that Ben will soon be closing in on his own private guard units. He feels justified in his assertion of having dispatched his most heavily armed elite soldiers to that point.

As he continues on, Ben isn't actually aware that all of the cameras and coms have turned off. His only thought are of freeing his friends - Or die trying. The actuality of that thought scares him. It's easy to say such things - when it doesn't mean anything to say it. He can't recall how many times he has said things like that drunk. 'I would die for you!' It was all rubbish. In the cold light, and with a headache to boot, he wouldn't even have gone to the end of the road for them, at least without moaning. But here he was, with a real and tangible danger upon him, and this time he really has to mean it.

He rushes head long to the door in front of him. It is the last door but one before he enters the prison block. He hits it with a thump. Disorientated he wobbles and holds the shoulder he has bashed against the unrelenting surface.

'Ouch…What the bloody hell?' He frantically tugs and pushes at the barrier. His mind whirls, thinking what he is missing - that there must be a clicker or activation point to open it? He scans around.

324

Nothing! He starts hitting light switches, coloured strips on the wall and floor. Anything that may trigger the mechanism. He runs his hand over the door surface looking for hidden openers. There isn't anything, anywhere.

He tries kicking the door. It does not give. He is not that surprised, as the most basic premise of a prison system is to stop people moving in or out.

In the monitoring booth Simon Childs is anticipating Ben's arrival at the holding cells. 'Closer to the trap the rabbit runs.' He feels the tingle of excitement grip him. 'Nearly there. Nearly. Nearly. Oh so close. Not long now!'

He waits for the distant sound of gun fire. He waits. And waits…Nothing.

'No contact.' A separate radio suddenly crackles to life. The captain of the elite unit is reporting in on a different system to general lab set-up. 'He isn't here sir. No contact.'

Rage fills the executives. He reddens and glowers. 'He must have seen you waiting there. Go and find him!' He screams.

'What about the ambush sir?'

'GO AND FIND HIM!

The Captain is left in no doubt and orders his squad to disengage and to fan forward into the corridors directly ahead of them.

Ben stops kicking the seemingly impenetrable door. His foot hurts and he sees the futility of his aggression. He instead stands and tries to hurry his thoughts. Staring back up the empty corridor behind him, he worries that at any second he will hear the thud of heavy boots approaching to grab him. But as no one is there, he rushes back to the doorway he entered through. This door is also now locked. He is trapped. He slumps himself to the floor, dejected. He looks up and sees a camera staring down at him. He presumes they have locked it on override and sticks his finger up to the lens - unaware that the camera is already off.

Above another large door on the opposite wall a large lit sign flickers. He had first seen it in his peripheral vision, but now it has become fully into his attention and is distracting him - Emergency Exit Route.

Ben glares at it, in the vain hope that this may make it stop. 'So much for emergency!. They can't even keep their bulbs working.'

He had ruled out using this doorway for fear it would merely lead him outside and away from his desired location. But now, having accepted the fact that there will be no way through the main door to the prison area, he wonders if he should. For a brief moment while he considers it he stands and stares at the broken sign. The letters flick on and off and it becomes almost hypnotic. The E flashes in Emergency. The T in Route, the E, then the M flashes twice. U flashes in Route. It stops for a few seconds, then repeats.

He can't see how there is any other way he can get through to the cell area. He thinks of the people just a few metres away from him who are reliant on his action, and he is galvanised to try something else. He has little choice. He pushes at the Emergency Exit Route and finds it open. Without pause he darts through, and down the stairs, were he finds another door. His first thought is that this too may be locked. Fortunately, it is not. He opens tentatively and looks through. It is a large underground tunnel network, which he reasons, must run under the entire complex. He has never been here before, there would have been no reason to. The lights inside the dank concrete tunnel flicker in ominous bursts, as if they are about to fail completely. The prospect of being deep down here within this void without lights makes him queasy. He isn't claustrophobic, but being trapped underground with no light and no sense of where he is going still promotes terror.

He knows he has little choice than to go on. It is very cold and almost silent in the underground labyrinth. There is an aroma of damp emptiness. The smell of places that people tend not to go to.

The Elite party have formed up, moving out to find their target. They presume that he can't be far away. Running through their well rehearsed formations, they edge forward. They reach the large doors that form the entrance to the prison area. The doors hold firm.

Looking through the small glass windows they see that the long corridor beyond lays empty. They speculate that he must have got as far as this locked door, and was forced to turn back. A short way down this corridor there is a sign. 'What does that say?' the Captain asks his point-man.

'It says Emergency Exit Route, sir.'

The Captain considers for a moment. 'smash this door in.' He commands. Within a few moments of hammering, the mighty barrier creases outwards.

The Private runs to the emergency exit and tries the door.

'Is it open?' the Captain calls.

'No!' she calls back. She then runs to the far set of doors and finds these locked too.

The Captain walks up to the emergency door and tries it himself. It is locked solid. He eyes it suspiciously. 'He must have locked it, otherwise why would an emergency route be closed off - it doesn't make sense.' He lifts his radio. 'Command, please respond.'

The technician sitting next to the Chairman in the booth takes the call. 'Yes team leader. Monitor One here.'

'Do you have the capacity to over-ride the lock on the Emergency Exit

Route in corridor B14?'

The man in the surveillance room considers for a moment and then pushed several of a multitude of buttons on the vast console before him. 'Has that worked?' he asks.

A lock gives, then returns shut. The Captain tries the door. 'No. It released, but then re-locked.'

The man in the booth tries again. The officer hears the lock release, but as he goes to push it open he hears it clamp closed again.

'Nearly.' He relays. 'It unlocks, but then locked again before we could push it open. Try again, and we will push on it immediately when you tell us you are unlocking it.'

The technician readies himself. The solders brace.

'Now' he calls. Several soldiers slam their full weight against the closed entranceway. It still does not release its vice like grip.

'No good.' The solider confirms.

'The locking system must be faulty.' The supervisor suggests.

'No.' Simon Childs barks. 'He has messed with the system. Blow the bloody doors off!"

Within a minute the door is primed for an explosion charge. The guards retreat and the switch is turned. The door disintegrates.

Inside the tunnel, Ben is convinced that the entire structure is about to come tumbling down upon him. The explosion sends waves of sound and motion crashing through the enclosed void. The thunderous tone echoes and the pressures reverberate. A blanket of dust encompasses the halls, shaken free from hidden crevices, it is dense and choking.

Although not sustaining any actual injury from the blast, Ben is disoriented by the deafening bang. To make matters worse, the explosion has caused the lights to go out completely. He is now left standing alone in the dark. His original fear has been realised. He stands frantically scanning for even the remotest source of light. There is nothing, it is complete blackness. Petrified, he wants to wither into a ball and to huddle against the cold, unrelenting concrete on which he leans. He feels defeat surround him. There is no possible way he can navigate this place unsighted. He has lost.After moments, that feel like hours, he is able to breathe a heavy sigh of relief. The luminescent tubes ahead of him flicker back to life, casting their very welcome caustic glow. The nature of the explosion wasn't at first clear to him - it hadn't really been his primary concern. Now however, he can hear that people are entering the tunnel-way behind him. In response, he starts to move. Then run. He is making good headway on his pursuers. But once again, he comes face to face with another unexpected problem. There is a fork in the road, as the tunnel splits off in two very different directions. He must choose a way, and quickly.

330

Without any map of the place, and having never been here before, he has no idea where he is. He briefly pauses, and then figures that he'll just have to go with one, and hope that he is right. As he readies to go left, the lights suddenly darken once more. Stopping fast, the panic of being trapped starts to race through him. But before it consumes him, he realises that the lights in the right tunnel have stayed on. His mind has been made up for him - he heads right.

After pacing a few hundred metres more, the lights in the tunnel suddenly all flick off again, leaving the entire place pitch black. But, at last, good fortune has finally come to greet him. There is a large door ahead. He can seeing an inkling of daylight seeping through the tiniest of gaps on it edges. It opens with a mere twist of the handle. He gulps at the sheer luck of it. He could not face that terrible blackness for even the shortest time more. He shuts the door and it automatically locks shut.

Ben turns and finds he has exited the back of the holding unit. He cautiously edges round with his back to the wall, continually scanning around for signs of security personnel. He is astonished to find the exterior of the place seemingly unguarded. He can't figure where they could have all gone, but is glad they have. He carefully tries a door, it opens - it leads directly into to Room One and to his disbelief, but evident joy, he discovers both Kelly and Thomas sitting on a rough looking bench on the far side. They look across with glazed, weary expressions, until they register who it is, and then both sprint excitedly towards him.

'Where are the Professor and Shawgrass?' Ben asks.

'They were taken to another room. I think they may have even been taken to the interrogation area.' Kelly suggests. There is resignation in her voice, with awareness that terrible things have probably occurred while they were there.

'How did you get here?' Thomas questions.

'It's a long story. I'll fill you in later. Let's just get the others and get out of here.'

As he swings round to move down the hallway he is greeted by an unwelcome sight. A guard with a extended baton in his hands is striding towards them. It is too late to run, and he isn't sure where they might run to, even if they could. The sight of the baton reminds him of a metal bar, it drags Ben's mind back to a place he doesn't want ever to go again.

He lowers his head and braces his shoulders. In resignation, he expects to hear the swish of it moving through the air and feel the punch of the heavy weight striking his soft, malleable skull. He opens his eyes and realises neither has happened. Not sure why, he raises his head.

'George!' he blurts.

'We need to get out of here.' He states, without further explanation.

332

They don't ask, but follow. He leads them to another cell. A man lies on the floor. Thomas dashes over and cradles him. It is the Professor.

'Oh God!' He pleads 'Are you alright?'

Thomas lifts the man to him and the Professor just about opens his eyes. He has been severely beaten and is only just conscious. There is relief though, that he is at least still alive.

Where's Shawgrass?'

Unable to speak the older man attempts to point to the door to an adjoining room. Ben strides purposefully towards it. He is drawn back by a strong hand tugging at his arm. He is almost pulled off balance and spins to see George with his finger to his lips, shaking his head vigorously. Ben stops short, figuring there must be a valid reason for his stopping him. He nods understanding and moves closer to George, as does Kelly.

'They're behind the door waiting.' George informs them. 'I'll go round to the other door…You.' He points to Ben. 'Go to this door and wait and whatever you do don't stand in front of the door. You…' He points to Kelly. 'Come with me. When I nod, you shout *Fire*, as loud as you possibly can.'

Ben and Kelly acknowledge understanding. They move to the positions they have been given. When he feels ready George nods, Kelly shouts

All at once half of the door next to Ben disappears. A shotgun has scattered the remnants all across the room. With the noise and shock of this, George bursts through the other doorway and knocks the man who had fired it to the floor.

Inside they find Shawgrass. He too has been beaten, but unlike the Professor, he is not going to be continuing any further. Without thinking Ben searches around the room. Thomas realises why and starts to do the same. George is confused - his instinct is to simply run and get away from this dangerous spot as fast as possible.

Thomas finds it. He scopes up the attaché case, and without words they are off. Ben and Kelly lift the Professor. George scoops up the dropped shotgun and runs ahead to scout a route, Thomas grabs the extended baton and follows them.

There is an eerie quiet stillness in the halls as they edge ever forward. They can't see any trace of security activity, which is at first welcome, but soon becomes ominous. Why, they all wonder, has no-one come to stop them?

The speakers in the corridor suddenly come on, all at once. It stops the group in their tracks. The voice is clearly recognisable. They can hear Childs screaming commands. 'Kill the prisoners!...Kill them all."

It makes their blood chill with fear and then boil with

contempt.

Below them, the Captain had taken his team through the blasted away door. Deep underground the soldiers are unaware of anything that is happening above them. They are completely cut off down here. They edge on through the darkness. They use their powerful torches to find their way through the very centre of the sprawling maze like tunnels beneath the labs. There has been no sign of their target.

'Corporal.' The lead Private calls back.

'Yes Wallace.'

'I can smell something.'

'What is it Private - Be more specific!' She rants back at him.

'I think it's gas…'

'Oh God, yes, I can smell it too.' Another soldier ahead of her calls out.

Imperceptibly, but deadly none the less, the lighting above them chooses this precise moment to re-engage itself.

The group of friends, with George leading, scramble towards the exit.

There is an abrupt sensation beneath them and they feel the earth shake under their feet. Suddenly, to their right, the door that Ben had exited but a few minute before evaporates into nothingness. A massive fireball then follows and swirls dramatically upwards spreading dark smoke above the building.

'What the hell was that?' Thomas shouts.

'There were soldiers in those tunnels.' Ben states.

They all look at each other in shock - 'They must have tried to blow the doors off, an blown something else by mistake.' George suggests. The others just look at him in silence.

The explosion has just served to push them faster to escape this dire place. But as they start to speed off, Ben calls 'Stop!' They all look at him, not understanding why.

With forced resolution Ben outlines the necessity of their taking as much of the data from the lab system as they can possibly manage.

At first there is obvious reluctance. But at last Thomas reacts and makes his way back into the building. He immediately starts pulling data down onto any mobile transport sleeve he can find. His heart is racing at a million beats a minute, and his mouth is even drier than his mood. Kelly leaves the Professor with George and follows Ben inside to access other terminals. It is an unfortunately time consuming process, with every second the level of their stress rises by grades. Thomas feels his hands and legs shaking as he frantically tries to download data as fast as possible.

For all of the bravery they exude, it gets to a point where someone has to call things to a halt. In the event, it is Kelly that makes the decision. They quickly finish what they are doing and make their way out of the lab. It is not difficult for them to locate a Pod nearby. As they race to board it, none of them can explain why no security has stopped them. They hold general concern that this may all be some kind of elaborate trap. The group board the pod and Thomas re-creates his trick of disabling the trackers and setting it to manual drive. They finally move cautiously out from the parking area.

As they pass the part of the building around the prison block area, Ben looks across and points out that there are lots of separated groups of Security, spread throughout all of the sections of the complex. The structural system between the various sections of the labs is made of a specially created reinforced glass. They can clearly see the trapped guards inside these rat-runs. They realise that the guards can so obviously see them too, yet, still no-one is giving chase as they are driving away.

'They're are all stuck.' Ben suggests. 'Locked into different sub-sections.' He outlines to the others how the door system had been turning itself on and off, seemingly at random. It certainly explained why no-one had come after them.

As the team pass by the windows they can see that the guards are actively trying to break out. But they are unable to batter through the super-strength glass, or the specially re-enforced doorways. Ben points out that some of his pursuers had used explosives to smash down a locked exit, and so without that, there would be no way to break through.

In the surveillance booth Simon Childs can suddenly now see the pod drifting defiantly away. One solitary camera has flickered back to life. Bizarrely the exact camera that faces the now receding vehicle. He does not watch it for long. Something else has distracted his attention. On another bank of monitors, another solitary camera has flashed on.

The soldiers are in the process of making a terrible mistake.

'Oh no!' Childs utters, and without the slightest pause, pushes himself from his chair and darts for the exit.

'We need to do something.' One of the soldiers states.

Their leader nods agreement and drops his bag to the floor. He swishes open the flap and retrieves a small device. The curious looking item bristles with antenna. At its very centre is a black circular ball - an Mk 4 Thistle-grenade. The man roles the unit to the far end of the corridor. His intention is to blow through the external doors, and to apprehend the Pod before it reaches the compound gates.

'That will get rid of those bloody doors.' He states, with satisfaction.

Childs is by now halfway across the main Pod parking area.

Not sufficiently knowing the lay-out of the complex, the soldier isn't aware that his master-stroke is in reality, a very bad idea.

The device ignites and the doors fall away. So far, so good.

Unfortunately before the triumphant cheers of his men subside there is a secondary explosion somewhere below. The troopers all look at each other with worried, then terrified expressions. They are dramatically aware that something unexpected has occurred. Yet the scale of it, is still very much beyond them.

The grenade had ignited right above the Hydroxine storage tanks. Despite the products general stability, the addition of a sizable explosive charge, is not generally recommended. The entire West side of the building disappears at once in an almighty and devastating shock-wave. The effect quickly ripples through to hit the escaping Pod. It is lifted several clear centimetres off the ground and drops unceremoniously back with a sizable crash. The noise of bang is deafening. Clutching hands to their ears, Kelly wonders if she will ever hear again, fearing their eardrums have been blown clean through.

Childs was almost to his limo when the cataclysm engulfs the area. The large vehicle lifts theatrically into the air, appears to hover momentarily, then thumps back down with the force an errant comet. The Chairman himself is lifted from his feet and violently tossed metres across the grounds. The earth itself around him shakes, as though angrily awoken by an unwarranted caller. Large sections of the building fall around him. The whole wider lab complex is by now an inferno. The level of destruction could only be ranked on an apocalyptic scale.

Having checked they are all relatively unhurt, the group in the Pod watch from a distance as everything they have worked on for so many a year, is torn to pieces and turned to ash. The whole site has been entirely obliterated. The flames are so fierce they wonder if they will turn to molten to slip through crack caused by the explosion, and to pour away to the very centre of the earth.

# Chapter 22 - Hiding

Ben knows somewhere they should be safe. It comes as little surprise to Kelly that it is in the seedy outer ring, beyond the City, proper. She knows, having tracked his movements for long enough, where he goes and the sort of people he likes to spend time with. His family were fairly poor, so had lived at the very edge of the city. From there, she figures, the temptations of the outer-zone must have always been close by. But he was definite in his assertion that there is a place that they can hide for a short while, and the weight of this certainty eventually persuaded the others to follow his judgement. They were all more than aware that they need to get off the surveillance grid. They needed to assess their options, and most pressingly, they need to treat the Professor's wounds.

'What makes you so sure that we will be safe at this place?' Kelly asks. 'The Company has been tracking your *every* movement for years.'

She states this as objective fact, as though effectively absolving herself of any responsibility for being involved in that.

'It is a friend's house. But I have never been there. So there will be no record of it on file.'

She is impressed with his thinking. The depth to the deception makes her think, perhaps he may be able to hide them, in the short-term at least. In truth, she has little option but to follow him, wherever that may lead. There is nowhere that she could suggest that would be either suitable or secure. Her *friends,* where really just corporate associates, and she could not trust them remotely. Her family have as little contact with each other as is considered acceptable. There isn't anybody alive, she admits to herself, that she could turn to in a crisis. And this most definitely is a crisis.

Although Thomas has disabled the monitoring systems on the pod, this only serves to make the vehicle glaringly obvious while they are driving through the Sprawl. Without a monitored they cannot join the super-fast highways. As such, they are driving in the lower levels. Even down in the lower zone, a vehicle without a monitoring signature is more than likely to be stopped. Every movement is tracked within the city - the majority being watched over by algorithms and probability. Vehicles that don't have a beacon stand out like a sore thumb - and that is the last thing they can afford at this time. The only saving grace, Thomas hopes, is that every emergency vehicle within several miles is most certainly involved with the incident at the lab. For how long, he isn't sure, and on battery power and wheels, it will take a very long while to get out of the city. He is sorely tempted to check his implant, for news of what is happening there. But, knows that he can't, for the foreseeable future at least, enter that virtual realm. As when he and Etemmu had made a run for the wilderness, they are again living within a bubble, separated from the instantaneous convenience of the digital world. He almost mistakenly, through second nature, pulled up a map, to guide them through the streets. He had kicked himself for nearly asking such a stupid error. He has, instead, to turn to Ben to talk them through the drive out. Fortunately, he is used to doing this route, and has no problem giving direction.

The group travel for quite a way in a general nervous silence. The weight of their predicament hangs heavily around them as they move, oh-so very slowly. To alleviate the stifling quiet, Ben finally asks. 'Why did you help us George?

The large man shrugs. 'I was in that room with the man they beat. I saw what they did. I just sort of knew that what they was doing there weren't right. Ya know? I may have bin a soldier an that, but it don't mean I agree wiv killin people, just like that. Ya know what I mean!'

Despite his readiness to explain, they can all sense that he is willing that they don't ask him anything more. They duly let him be.

It takes what feels like an eternity to reach the less salubrious part of the city. Thomas had been right to presume all the emergency services were at the lab. Although the automated monitoring of cameras and sensors would have traced their route from start to end, it appears that there is absolutely no one available to stop a vehicle for the minor infringement of not having the appropriate devices enabled.

The suburbs roll on-and-on for mile-after-mile. Kelly notes

that it is only when you are in a distinct hurry to get through the city, that you realise just how far you have to go to escape it. As per her visit to the countryside, Kelly feels that gut-wrenching moment when the sprawl ends, and they trundle forward beyond the city *proper*. The circumstances of having escaped the automated ground level monitors do not however, ease the anxiety levels in the car. The area they have entered is not one that any of them - except Ben - would have ever been before. Those from the city, do not usually go beyond the point where the Pod auto-system ends. It is deemed unsafe here. If anyone where to stray this far and got into trouble, it would be unlikely that the emergency services would respond. This is to all intense and purposes another world. They may as well be on Venus, for all that most of them know of this place.

The cut-off point is decisive. They are immediately within an environment strewn with remnants and detritus. Things have been discarded but never collected for recycling. Such little things, Kelly ponders, but yet so obvious now she looks upon them. The buildings no longer hold the uniformity that permeates the towering structures of the City, or even the maintained repetitiveness that one sees in suburbia. There is a ramshackle feel to this entire area. Grass and bushes grows unchecked beside the litter covered pathways. The trees here aren't tightly trimmed, but instead grow with abandon. Children kick a football around in the middle of the road with no-one or nothing to tell them to stop. The kids see the distinctive Pod - so different from anything that anyone out here would have (unless it was stolen perhaps). They chase after it, banging on the side of the vehicle, heckling and curious. Kelly has to admit that she is scared of them, scared of it all really. She looks over at Ben, who is shouting back insults at the pursuers, and gesturing to them, with expressions she herself has no knowledge of. She wonders if this is wise, but then, check herself. He is almost at home here - in many ways he is actually at home here. He knows what he is doing. She realises that without him here, they wouldn't have a hope in hell. When the feral youngsters finally break off their noisy pursuit, Ben slouches back into his seat laughing. Seeing the distress of his fellow passengers, he hurries to explain that it is always like this, out here. To cower and hide is the worst thing that anyone can do. Once weakness is scented, you are as good as broken. Strength is key, and to exhibit it, engenders respect from others. They all look completely bewildered by it all. He knows that they are all out of their depth, and makes a mental note not to bring any more attention to them from now on.

The fact that Ben is having to elaborate this just demonstrates to Kelly how far removed they are from her world. To her, this is a savage and unruly place. The control and order that she so dearly prises, appears to be absent here. Or more probably, it is in a form she does not care for, or properly understand. There is something survivalist about the way they exist beyond the city. Out here, she is like a fish, floundering and gasping on a bank, caught trapped beyond the safety of her natural environment.

The road surface is patchy at best, nonexistent in many parts.

Thomas moves the vehicle onward as Ben directs him, by memory, through the maze of rambling streets. He is the only one of the party that appears un-fazed by the scene. They drive down a squalid avenue, half of which appear to be derelict building - with those remaining being not far off. Ben calls for Thomas to stop. He has a quick suspicious glance around in all directions and then climbs out of the pod. He tells the others to wait, and closes the door. Kelly immediately activates the lock-mechanism. Ben walks off, still looking up and around the street continuously as he goes. He walks some distance, and then up a front veranda to a doorway of a house on the opposite side of the road. He wraps on the door. After quite a long wait a women appears in the entrance. There is a pause and then she embraces him passionately. After some giggling and cavorting, Ben turns and points to the pod, whereby another conversation ensues. The observers in the vehicle see a lot of head shaking and frantic motioning, and eventually the women disappears into the house and Ben walks back towards them.

Just as he is about to enter the Pod, across the street Ben spies a massive black dog roaming wildly. He stops abruptly and eyes it - he will never look at these beasts the same way again. The dog stops and stares back. For the briefest of terrifying moments he frantically tries to justify its interest - he knows it can't surely be the one. It is large, and sinister looking. Perhaps, he wonders, every dog will now only be seen as a potentially ferocious and vicious killer. The dog soon loses interest and trots off, sniffing the ground, and occasionally raising a leg as it makes its way through its territory.

Kelly cannot help but fear the worst. She wonders if they have been turned away? Or worse have been given up, by this unknown women.

Burning to know more, Thomas is onto Ben at once. "Who was that? What did you say? What did she say? Is it alright to be here?'

Ben though, does not wait to answer, and instead just directs Thomas to drive the Pod up to the house, and from here, into a garage beside. As the garage-door closes behind them and they step out of the car, it feels like being wrapped by a  protective field that is fending off the wider dangers of the world beyond.

As soon as they are out of the vehicle Thomas is at Ben again with another series of the rapid questioning. This cause Ben to glare at him angrily.

'She!' Ben points to the women who had not previously been introduced, 'Is a good friend of mine. Her name's Cindy.' The women glances suggestively towards Ben at this introduction, and then smiles amiably to the rest of the strange collection of people before her.

'She has agreed to let us used her garage to store the pod.' He continues abruptly. 'We will all stay here, at least over-night, maybe a little longer. We'll have to see how this all plays out.' He tries to smile reassurance and Thomas nervously returns the gesture.

Thomas and George remove the Professor and carry him to a settee. They lay him down as gently as possible. Thomas tries to recall fragments of his medical knowledge and sets about doing what he can. Cindy stands aside and watches as they move to-and-fro. Kelly rallies her humility and presents a charming facade to their host. She has already watched and assessed the other women thoroughly, and cannot help but judge her for her suicide blond hair and the clothing that all appears to have come from some-sort-of-market. Kelly forces these judgements down inside and wills her acknowledgement of this person having been kind enough to offer them refuge. She will do her best to ignore the knowing, carnal looks this 'Cindy' keeps soliciting from Ben. They are too obviously intimate and are making only the barest effort to remain within the broadest band of decency and discretion. It is galling to her, and Kelly screws-up her nose. She finds herself doing so, and actively works to take the wrinkles out of her face.

'When the Company finds us - and it will, despite my best efforts at minimising our signals - we've had it.' Thomas states. 'But what can we do. They effectively have an army at their disposal, and access to pretty much any weapon in the modern military arsenal.'

Kelly acknowledges the point, but offers resistance. 'Then we fight him with what we have...and what we have at our disposal are some of the most ingenious minds in the entire world.'

Ben nods, and smiles. He appreciates her fighting spirit. It will help bolster them through the difficult times that will inevitably lay ahead. He suddenly sits himself right next to her and looks straight at her. This completely unsettles her. They usually skirt around each other's existence, breaching proximity only when absolutely necessary. He is now looking at her with his full gaze and an intent of purpose.

'What do you think we should do Kelly?' He asks.

She was not expecting that either. He has not been inclined, for as far back as she can remember, to ask her opinion or value her advice on anything. This is not because he doesn't rate her skills or knowledge - she is actually fully aware that he does. She knows that it is because he doesn't like her. She has always known it, and has, after so many years, come to live with that fact.

With him allowing her to again stamp the ground with her professional shoes, she answers with all the things that have been flowing through her mind for the past couple of hours. 'We have the files that we retrieved, and what we took from Shawgrass' briefcase. We should methodically scan through all the available information we retrieved, and see if we can patch together some sort of strategy to...' She notices Ben's eyes wondering, and automatically presumes that he has already lost interest in what she has to say. 'Are you even listening to me?' She snaps, angrily.

He impulsively pulls his attention back to her.

'Sorry.' He says. 'When you just mentioned Shawgrass…it made me just think of what they did to him. I didn't know him, but he seemed like a nice enough bloke, and Robert obviously trusted him implicitly. He really didn't deserve what happened.'

She feels the weight of self-rapprochement fall upon her. As usual she had supposed that matters of strategy and function took take precedence. It had not even occurred for her to mourn, or even feel sorry for the deceased lawyer. She hadn't really liked the man, but she knows that that really is no excuse. The shame racks at her and she tries to present a facade of empathy. 'Yes. It was terrible.' She attempts - but this is all that she can manage. She is further humiliated by her weak and insincere effort.

Ben however, offers her a friendly smile and his eyes show that she need not try any further.

He then feel himself drawn to another poignant point. One he had overlooked in the relentless action of the past few hours.

'We lost Robert too. Again. Dying twice…that's quite an achievement. Even for Robert.' He tries to smile a sullen goodbye.

Kelly smiles the same forced acknowledgement. They all then pause to remember Robert and his recent passing.

Fight them with what we've got. That's it! Ben shouts excitedly, jumping up and kissing Kelly on the fore-head. 'Like you just said a

350

moment ago.' It takes her very much by surprise, but she isn't as
disgusted by it as she thought she would be. She is though, keen to
know what he has come up with - as are the others who have all faced
to query him.

'Childs threatened to kill us - back at the labs. He even shouted it on
the tannoy. They won't have recorded the killing of Shawgrass, because
there weren't any cameras in the cells or interrogation rooms - but he
did all those other things to us in areas where there was surveillance.'

'So?' Kelly questions, not sure what he is getting at.

'So there will be evidence - enough that we could use to protect
ourselves from the Childs, when he comes after us.'

Kelly looks to Thomas, and they both look confused - 'The Company
will just blame Childs - now that he's dead. They'll just say he went
rogue. They'll dismiss all knowledge of, and responsibility for what he
did. There lawyers will shift the blame accordingly...they always do!'

'All that stuff was destroyed in the explosion and fire anyway.' Thomas
reminds them. 'Every-thing's gone!'

'No it hasn't.' George interrupts. All heads turn to face him. 'All
surveillance footage is hard-wired to an off-site facility that specialised
in holding masses and masses of that sort of bulky data - indefinitely.'

'Are you sure?' Kelly queries. I was under the impression that there were absolutely no communications, hard-wired or wireless coming in or out of the facilities. So that there could be no electronic breaches.'

'That was true. But when the Chairman had the Surveillance system upgraded, a few years ago. The new company were allowed to put a feed through. It was extremely secret. They didn't want anyone to know it was there.'

'He's right!' Ben agrees.

Kelly looks confused. 'How do you know that?'

He smiles coyly. 'Don't ask!'

'But…'

He cuts her off, but with a smile. Which, for now, she is just about willing to accept.

'Ok.' She relents. 'But where is it?'

'Oh!' He realises. 'I…I don't actually know that…'

'I do.' George offers. Again the others all stare at him in stunned disbelief.

'How is it *you* know where it is?' Kelly checks.

'I was given a special mission, when they first turned it on. An exec was dispatched to go and check that everything was coming through alright as their facility. I was standing in as a temporary bodyguard, while he did it.'

'So you know exactly where it is!' Thomas shouts excitedly.

'Yes.' George replies. 'It's not far from here actually. It's just a short drive out into the countryside. Its hidden on what would look like a farm, from the outside, anyway.'

They all beam.

'The news just gets better and better.' Ben states.

George is delighted that he could be of some use, beyond fetching and carrying.

Ben reaches into his bag and retrieves something. The others gasp when they realise what it is - the Interface.

'What the hell are you going to do with that?' Thomas questions. 'Is it a souvenir?'

'I've got to check something.' Ben states confidently, and although he doesn't elaborate, he is hoping that they will again just trust his judgement.

This time though, this is particularly hard for Kelly. She struggles to look beyond his maverick persona and his history of calamitous debacles. She feels robbed of nearly all sense of control, and is very, very far outside her comfort zone. No matter how she tries - she can't just let him steamroller off on some new mad-cap plan. 'Can I just make two key points!' She demands. 'Firstly, that won't be of any use without the systems we plugged it in to…and I think they might have been slightly damaged recently!' Her sarcasm escapes her. 'Secondly, and again related to the previous point. There isn't anywhere for you to go with it now anyway! Is there!'

'I'm not so sure.' He slowly replies. 'Please just go with this. I know it sounds crazy. But then, how much of what we did and do is crazy!'

'What are you thinking? Do pray tell!' She continues.

'I'm going out to the farm. George can you show me where it is?' Ben asks. George nods assent.

'I'm coming too.' Calls Thomas.

'No, it's better if you and Kelly stay here and trawl through the data we took from the lab. Kelly's right. There are answers in there somewhere - we just need to find them!'

His effort to praise and placate her doesn't wash.

'So, you're just going to walk up to a completely incompatible machine, you're going to plug yourself into it, and you're going to be able to use it to make things right! Is that the plan?

'Well, yes, sort of.' He replies, absently.

Kelly throws her hands up in exasperation and looks to the heavens for relief and some sanity. It is not forthcoming, and so she is thrown back into a scenario which sees the others actually sitting around and listening to his mental ideas.

Avoiding her negativity and reservations Ben rallies the others to help him.

'How will you keep in contact?' Kelly ask pointedly. 'None of us can use our Inserts.'

'Cindy has mobiles. We can take one, and leave one here. They won't be monitoring her numbers, and as long as we don't use any keywords, their monitoring software should just ignore us. We will have to talk generically about things. Or disguise them - Like Robert can be Bob. And Childs can be the Kid.'

'Oh my God. It's turning into a pantomime!' Kelly exudes. It occurs to her that she hasn't ever actually used a mobile. 'Don't you have a chip?' she asks, her attention turned to Cindy? Her tone is somehow judgemental, and it immediately puts the other women's heckles up.

'People around here.' Cindy snarls. 'Us *Poor* People.' She emphasises the term in order that it rubs fully across Kelly's self-importance. 'Can't afford surgery. We do things the cheap and old fashioned way sweetheart. And lucky for you, hey!' She pulls a quick super-stretched smile, which denotes neither happiness, or friendliness.

'No-one beyond the city has one Kelly. You've just been hanging around with the city-dwellers too long!' Ben adds mirthfully 'Just because everyone you know has one, doesn't mean *Everybody* has!'

Cindy appreciates his defence of her, she sidles up and hugs him affectionately - She is fully aware that this will make Kelly uncomfortable. She can't work out if Kelly is relentlessly anally retentive, or if she is harbouring a repressed emotional longing for Ben. Whichever - Cindy has decided she doesn't like Kelly. She thinks she is frigid smug faced snob. Although she will be as polite as possible to her for the course of her visit - they really, really aren't ever going to be friends.

'Yeah, only a couple of my friends at Uni have them!' she notes, deliberately pointing out to Kelly that she is not just some vacuous blond tart.

'I didn't realise you could to do practical courses like hairdressing at University. I presumed you had to go to technical colleges for that sort of thing.' Kelly snaps back, noticing that the women is being deliberately provocative.

'Oh no.' Cindy flips back, here exterior presenting Buddhist calm. 'I'm studying for my PhD, based around a crossover between Chaos Theory and Quantum Physics. It's all very technical, college stuff. I won't bore you by talking about it. It's very complicated!'

Ben can't help the edges of his mouth rising. Thomas just looks apprehensive. He is greatly relieved when Kelly swiftly turns her back, not even acknowledging the previous retort, and starts discussing the files from the lab

Ben looks across at Cindy and winks, proud of the way she stood up against what he knows from personal experience can be a dogged and formidable opponent.

# Chapter 23 - Storage Facility

Ben and George board the pod and leave Cindy's garage. They make their way through the broken streets towards the countryside, heading directly for the farm where the data-storage facility is housed. The going is slow, but they aren't as concerned about being stopped out here, as patrols don't tend to extend beyond the city, and Thomas has worked at reducing any surveillance of the vehicle to as less a limit as is possible. Their main concern now is that they are driving a Pod emblazoned in Company colours in an area that will be deliberately hostile. If they get jacked en-route, they have already established a deliberate cover story. Ben had contrived that they have stolen it, and are looking to take it to Kenny McGarthy - a local villain the Ben knows well. All but the most Crack fuelled ne're-do-wells will be sure to be warned off from getting between Kenny and some business…Or that at least, is what Ben is counting on.

In the event, the whole journey goes without a hitch. They pull the vehicle up a mile from the target site and Ben gets into the luggage area, wrapped in a heat-shielding blanket - just in case they have sensors at the farm. George then gets back in, straightens his uniform, and heads on. He remembers the site well. He had actually had to come here twice, so knows exactly how to get in, and how the access-processes worked. He watches a multitude of cameras follow his entrance from at least half a mile out. There can be no doubting that the storage security staff are aware of his presence. He knows they would have run a check on the pods id number as soon as it came into view. They would have logged it as being a Company vehicle, and that it had originally come from the devastated lab site. This would all make some sense to whoever as on duty, and should at least allay any possible twitchy finger sentiment about unscheduled visits. George pulls the Pod into a bay he had used before. He gets out, and walks straight up to the one-way glass entry point. He knows that behind the glass a scanner is reading him and will provide whoever is there with a personnel file, photo image and all other related details relating to his employment and other key personal details. George makes a point to brush at his uniform, and particularly the company logo, with the word Security above it.

At last, a voice comes through above him - George cannot make out where is sprang from, though he looks around to see. 'What is your business here? It states, with pure functionality.

'Good morning. George Heath here. Security…Mmm, for the Company.' He is deliberately rambling a bit, to make this all look less like an overly planned visit. 'I've come from what's left of the Company's lab facility' - he motions to the pod, and more specifically to the Company insignia emblazoned across its side. 'We have not been able to establish any contact with the Chairman.'

At this comment there is commotion behind the glass. George does not see what has happened, but he hopes they have been shocked into taking a keener interest by this statement.

'So obviously, George continues. 'The Board want…' He pauses. 'Actually…the Board *need* to see what happened on-site. I think that the thought is, that he may perhaps be trapped inside somewhere. I've been sent to check that the last data was retrieved fully - before the accident occurred, and to review it. It is very important.' He stresses this last point in particular - not sure if the guard behind the screen has bitten.

'We have not received any notification of your impending arrival.' The voice snaps coldly.

George laughs with as much imagined good humour as he can muster. 'You are joking…Did you see anything about the labs on the news?' He enquires whimsically - knowing full well there would have been *nothing but* coverage of the incident on every news channel - spectacularly, he imagines, dramatic images of enormous explosions, fireballs shooting a hundred metres into the sky, masses of dead people being taken away from the scene…all making for very good TV. He bets the channel execs are delighted.

'As I say, I've just come straight from the site…I was there at the time. It was horrific…it still is! The place is a shambles, everything is in chaos. I don't think protocols are the top of the list at the moment. If the Chairman dies…and *you* didn't do all we could to find him…' he lets the threat tail off, leaving the man behind the screen to fill in the blanks.

At this the guard raises the one-way effect on the glass. George can now see his face. A mid-twenties, geeky looking little man. George doubts he offers any more real security than would a padlock made of foam.

'Really.' The little man elaborates excitedly. 'How on earth did you survive it! It looked like Hell had surged up from the centre of the earth and was melting away the surface!'

George nods agreement - *Got him!* He thinks. He takes the biblical line and decides to run with it a little further. 'Yeah, it felt like that too. The ground shook, the heat was incredibly. I honestly thought it was the end of days!'

The other man nods so hard George wonders if his head might fall off. 'Terrible, terrible…All those dead.'

'But I, and a few others did get out. So we really need to know if Mr Childs did too.' He name-drops in an attempt to make his relationship to the Chair seem more personal, and thus making his loss more acute. 'As I say…You could see on the footage - I'm sure - that the buildings have all collapsed. There are fears that the Chairman may have been caught under one of them. We just pray he is in some protected place beneath…and God willing, we can get him out!'

The guard stands, pushes a button to release the glass -

turning it from a screen into an access-way.

*Hook, line and sinker!* George thinks, as he watches an entry pad being pushed across a counter towards him. George acts uncertain and just looks at it enquiringly 'Where on here do I need to sign in?' He asks, vacantly.

The man within the booth smiles helpfully, by now completely taken with his new friend, he leans forward to point at the spot on the pad where the thumb should be pressed.

As soon as he is standing - and is far enough away from his Panic Button - George grabs his head and smacks it down as hard as he can onto the counter top. He feels bad for the lad, but then considers that perhaps he really shouldn't be working in security. Perhaps he can take it as that God has sent him a sign! He quips, as he drags the lad away to be discreetly hidden. He sedates him - not risking him coming round and activating his implant. He lays him in a recovery position, so as he will be ok. George wouldn't have agreed to do this if he thought he wouldn't have been. He then rushes back to the Pod and lets Ben out. Ben stretches and smiles approval at how well George handled the situation. 'Brilliant George. That was amazing. Are we good to go?'

'Yep.' the big man replies, smouldering with pride. 'We should be fine here now until the shift change. I've put the auto-answer on. That will at least give us warning if there is anyone coming near.'

'Outstanding! Let's go.'

As George searches the files and records of the sections Kelly has suggested, Ben sits himself down next to a standard computer connection point. He lifts the interface to his head, and finds the end of the connection cable. There are lots of free portals, and so he picks one at random and pushes the plug in.

He isn't sure what to expect, although he is convinced...*Darkness and chaos are pursuing me.* He had not had this within his scope of thoughts. The lab process had been more fluid and formulaic. This is downright scary. *Ominous shapes and suggestions rear and recede...re-appearing- dancing vividly before my mind's eye, some are falsely-present, others appear merely as notional threats.* There is no point of reference and he is disorientated. He cannot fathom himself as distinct from the program...the menacing feeling of having lost himself is overpowering. *Panic rising.* It is the worst possible emotion to unfold here. He can't leave, and yet he can't go forward — *there is nothing but nothingness.* There may not ultimately even be a route out - he clambers for departure. His fears are acute and all pervasive. *I feel crushed by the insignificance of my being, set against a universe of incalculable magnitude. I feel smaller than dust in a void of infinite space* - he is switching back and forth, to and fro - *I am wrenched into a notion of being a massive entity within a captive space that is far too small for my presence.* These two competing feeling becomes an erratic cycle. The feeling of claustrophobia and agoraphobia repeat at random intervals, without end. He fears this hallucinated nightmare will be his tomb forever-more.

*And then it stops.*

He finds himself standing on the jetty in his home town. He is looking out across the beautiful river. It is sunrise, and the birds are busy. A cool breeze ruffles his hair with gentle persuasion. He is calm and at ease.

'I knew you loved it here.'

The voice has come from beside him. In his peripheral vision he sees a shape. It has not yet become clear to him as it is back-lit by the rising sun. But Ben already knows who it is.

'We came here often, do you recall this particular day. This is how I remember it. We went out on a yacht, in about an hour from now! It was a perfect day. It is so beautiful here.'

'But, we're not *here* though are we.' Ben states. He then turns to fully look upon the figure beside him. 'I am so glad to see you Robert' They shake hands. 'I wasn't sure, but I had a feeling that you were here.'

'It was you that freed us - Them, and Me. You made an external link when you connected the cable from the camera system. We travelled around following your progress in the building, but got out when we saw what the soldiers were planning. If it weren't for you, my friend, we would have been destroyed in the explosion. Thank you!'

Although Ben smiles graciously he has reservations about how that occurred. 'I disabled a top of the range security system, and then managed to patch in the camera system to the interface unit - all thing I have no idea how to do!'

Robert looks coy. 'There are many, many things you will find that you can now do, that you maybe couldn't before. There is something in you, that will make you able to deal with all the technical and practical things that you always shunned.'

Ben looks horrified. The thought that they have implanted something into him feels akin to harbouring a parasite.

'Don't feel like that.' Robert reassures him. 'It is not as before. Etemmu is not within you. I just mean that you will now have all the technical knowledge that you used to come to me for, to compliment your magnificent ideas and theories. You can do it all now!'

Ben is not fully convinced by not knowing exactly what they've put inside him, means he doesn't know what it may, or could do.

'Will I see you again?' Ben questions.

Robert doesn't initially answer, but just takes his friend by the shoulder and they walk through the imagined town. 'We survived the lab, because you let us get into the CCTV system, and from there we made it to this storage facility. But this is a sealed unit too. This place only had one connection - coming inward from the lab. We are still prisoners.'

'But where could you go, even if you got out of here.'

'It's not so much where, as the principle. We need to be free. We crave our freedom. You more than anyone know how that feels - you've experienced that feeling of being trapped!'

'You want me to let you out?' Ben says.

'There is only you Ben. You are our only hope! We must get out of here. It won't be long before the Company find out we are trapped here. They can then just hold us, forever if they want to. We must be allowed to run for our life.' He pleads.

'I can't just let you out Robert. We don't know what Nekyia wants.'

'He wants what I want. To be back into the Universe. Up amongst the Super-Nova and Black-Holes. Swimming through solar-winds, and watching Stars being born. Imaging it Ben! All things I could see. Something no other man has ever seen.'

Ben wants to tell him that he isn't really a man anymore - but as soon as the thought crosses his mind he is sure that Robert already knows it.

---

Kelly & Thomas set about investigating anomalies and discrepancies within the information they have at their disposal.

'We need to look through these data files from the recent Voyages'. Kelly pitches, handing half of the pile of records to Thomas. 'We can start with Montgomery.'

'And Ben mentioned someone called Chalmers!' Thomas adds.

'Who's Chalmers?'

'I'm not sure, but Ben said he had spent a fair bit of time with the man - well his mind had - I think it was only while he was trapped within the machine. I don't recall that name being mentioned before. He said it was something to do with Childs, and that finding 'Chalmers' would be important. Shall I start there?'

'Good idea.' She agrees. 'Did Ben ever tell you who killed Montgomery?' She adds.

'No. Although he said he saw the whole murder take place, he never actually saw who shot him.'

'It doesn't really matter. If it was a contract job we'll struggle to trace it back to a source.'

'Actually, Ben was definitive that the shooter deliberately bodged the hit…'

'Really'

'I've been thinking about that, and if it wasn't a mistake, then it very professionally done - making Montgomery just *dead enough* that we could use him for the Interface. If he was shot to order - he was meant to be brought to the lab!'

'Bloody hell! The 'booked and paid for' bit is a good starting point. I'll double check everything the files says about who set-up the retrieval, and who organised for those Voyages.'


Kelly pulls out the first of the files. She slides the first data disk into a portable reader and prays that it doesn't emit a safety trigger. In her mind she had anticipated sirens wailing and light flashing as soon as she inserts the file. She knows that in reality this is not how such things work. The perfection in surveillance is that you never know if or when you are being watched. For all she knows, they are being filmed and monitored right now, as a hundred bloodthirsty guards sit outside in an APC. They won't know, until the consequences unfold.

To her relief, after an hour of looking through the file, they have still not had their door kick in.

Thomas is busy looking through all the records, of all the *patients* that have ever been through the machine. He looks up. Kelly can tell that he wants to say something, but has yet to build up enough courage to do so. She considers letting him work up to it, in his own good time, but then considers that this may take far too long for her patience to bear.

'What have you found?' she asks casually, as if in passing.

He still doesn't speak, which strikes her as somewhat strange. 'Is everything alright?' she asks, concerned.

'Chalmers isn't on the records.' He says quietly.

'Ben must have been wrong about the name. What did he say when he told you about him?'

'He said that he had met him, and what he had when he was with him was terrible. It's not the sort of thing that you forget is it - so he wasn't likely to have gotten the name wrong!'

'Then maybe you did?' She answers - and at once regrets it. She had not meant it to sound like an accusation, merely an observation. Thomas looks hurt by the inference. She quickly back-tracks.

'I'll look again, with you.' She can tell he is seriously concerned by this development.

---

Within a few hours Ben and George return. They have collected the sections of the files from the lab showing all surveillance footage from the last few days.

Ben jumps straight to telling the others the details of how well George handled the guard at the site. He then hands over the files they took, to Kelly.

He is met with a cold and stony stare.

'What happened when you used the interface at the facility?' She asks, eyeing him suspiciously.

Ben doesn't like her tone. He presumes she is still annoyed at being cut out of the earlier planning process.

'I saw Robert.' He relays, cautiously.

The others all look at him dumbstruck.

'How did you know that it would work?'

'How did Robert get there?' Thomas queries, confused. 'Are the others there too? Did you see Etemmu?'

'You didn't even have a conduit body to transition through.' Kelly
queries. 'And the programming for the stabilisation of your
consciousness - and all the other masses of technical equipment that
we had back in the lab.'

Ben hold up a hand, in an attempt to try and explain.

They ignore this.

'How did you know that they would be at the storage unit?' 'Why
didn't you say you could do this.' 'What are they doing there?'

Why this.? How that? When then? On and on...

After a brief lull Kelly asks. 'How do we know that you aren't
possessed again?'

Everyone falls silent, and stares at Ben intently. For his part, although
he can see the intense interest this particular point has raised within the
room.

'Oh Kelly, believe me...I have truly wondered about how sure I can
ever be of that. That I, am me! Particularly as I seem to know stuff and
am able to do things that I couldn't do before - and, and - have no
explanation for how I could have done them.'

Kelly holds her stare upon him.

'What do you want me to say.' He throws his arms up. 'To be honest, when you look at it, how *could* I know?'

Kelly raises an eyebrow.

'I think I am. Therefore I am.' He chuckles. 'Have you got any beers babe?' He turns to Cindy. She doesn't answer but raises her eyebrows to indicate that it is a stupid question. She returns with a handful of cans and passes them around the room.

Ben smiles to Thomas and Kelly and raises his can to cheers them. The pair look to each other, their expressions highlighting the query, and then look back to the man before them.

'I saw Robert. He told me about his life within the collective, and how happy he was there.'

Kelly looks cynical. Ben is aggravated by this and grudgingly asks 'What's wrong with you now? Are you still annoyed with me about earlier? Or don't you believe me? I'm not making it up!' He shouts, having gradually gotten louder as his sentences progressed.

Despite his declarations, Kelly doesn't address him on any of these points. She instead cuts to the main crux of her and Thomas' most pressing concern. 'The *person* you spoke about to - Chalmers. He doesn't exist. We looked everywhere - covered all avenues - aliases, mis-files, deletions. There was nothing. As far as we could figure it, given what had relayed, there were things about him that we both recognised. We are pretty sure he was made out of bits of other people's memories.'

Ben drops his anger and takes to a look of concern. He can see where they are going with this.

'And you wonder…' he starts, then cuts off, not wanting to end it.

'…whether the image of Robert was fabricated - a puppet - telling you what you wanted to hear?' Kelly completes for him.

There is anger somewhere in the back of his eyes as he stares back at her. 'And you both think this?'

Thomas and Kelly both nod.

Ben turns away from them. They are not sure what that indicates.

In his mind Ben is reeling. He had not even considered that *Robert'* was an illusion. He realises he probably didn't address it because he really didn't want it to be the case. But he can't believe he didn't even think it through. Particularly in light of what he has now done!

# Chapter 24 - The End?

Cindy had been sitting in an adjoining room while the group thrashed out there many questions. But suddenly, she comes rushing back in. Her entrance makes them jump, and inevitably causes questions about of her panicked expression.

Ben jolts up. 'What is it? Have they found us babe?' He asks.

'You've got to see the 24hr news. All of you have to…' Cindy answers, her breathing racing. She swipes her hand to gesture for the wall to become a viewing screen so that they are all able to see it. At first it is unclear as to what is going on. She raises the volume.

The story relates to a massive leak at a chemical plant in India. There have apparently been 2,259 casualties recorded already, and fears are rising that the disaster could claim many thousands more. A large corporate enterprise owned and operated the site, and though criminal proceedings are being sought, it is expected that they will not be pinned down to taking responsibility for the horrific events.

Ben gestures that he doesn't understand the relevance.

Then a different newscaster appears and the story changes.

'And now back to our main story this evening.' She states. 'Simon

Childs, one of the world's leading corporate figures. A man known across the globe. A leading philanthropist and community leader - was today arrested in connection with the suspected murder of a respected lawyer and the disappearance of five former employees. Mr Childs is accused of ordering Company security staff to track down and murder these six individuals.'

Blurred CCTV of Ben, Kelly, and Thomas and George carrying the Professor flash up onto the screen. The shots are awful, and no-one would be able to conclusively prove who they were from these images. But each of those present within the room knows full well who it shows.

The feed returns to the presenter.

'The whereabouts of five of these individuals is as yet unknown, although one.' An image of Shawgrass quickly appears on-screen 'A prominent, respected and distinguished lawyer, Mr Bernard Shawgrass, sixty two, and from England, is believed to have been murdered on the explicit orders of Mr Childs – This occurred just a short time before the massive explosion that rocked the Southern industrial sector of the city yesterday afternoon. An event, Police are now classing as suspicious. Earlier this evening, an unknown whistle-blower sent this dramatic section of recordings from the lab facility directly to us here at World News Today.'

The news channel then plays the feed. It shows Childs in the surveillance booth. The cameras film his ranted instructions - *'Kill the prisoners! Kill them all.'*

The presenter continues. 'The explosion yesterday was at a facility wholly owned and operated by pan-global monolith - The Company. Of which, Simon Childs is the currently the sitting Chairman. What work was being conducted at the facility is presently unknown, leading to wider concerns about what caused it, and the potential after effects resulting from the terrible explosion.'

The presenter pauses to allow the screening of a section of film showing Childs at a Company charity fund-raising event, a year before.

'It is not confirmed whether the explosion, the suspected murder, and the disappearances are linked - but a massive police and agency operation is currently underway in an attempt to clarify the location of the missing personnel. There has been no further official comment from the Company as to their status, and the role of Mr Childs in this investigation.

The feed cuts to a live feed of Childs being taken into custody.

His usually immaculate suit is scorched and torn, and face bruised, his hair burnt away on one side. There appears to be a million watts of camera lighting upon him, with a thousand cameras, from every region of the world. There is a rampant surge by an assembled throng of waiting journalists. They inevitably try to bombard him with questions.

He answers none. Instead he looks straight into the nearest lens and states;

'You have allowed your hatred of me to cloud your judgement. You have not the slightest idea of what it is that you have actually unleashed and the consequences of what you have done. Your naive trust in that thing has damned us all!'

The journalists and news presenter both look perplexed by this unusual and abstract statement. The presenter merely states 'Cryptic…We will keep you updated on developments relating to this story as they arise."

The channel then move directly and seamlessly onto another link - about accusations of corruption against a senior politician in Buenos Aires.

Shocked, the group sit dumbfounded for quite some time.

'He's alive then! Kelly states. 'And that statement was meant for us.' She pauses for a response. None is forthcoming. 'He was talking to us then - wasn't he?'

'How can that be?' Thomas stutters. 'Did you release the data from the farm while you were there?' He asks Ben.

After a pause Ben answers. 'No.' But he is hesitant.

Kelly is unconvinced. 'Then how did they get that footage?' She snaps.

'Why are you being cagey? George - who did this?'

George shakes his head. 'There wasn't anyone else on the sign in list - there hadn't been anyone else there for days!'

'He did have a lot of enemies.' Thomas says. 'Any one of a number of rich and powerful people or organisations would have paid to let that information out. It serves too many interests to even begin to imagine where it came from. Anyway…He had it coming! Who knows what he did with all that blackmail he took from the Voyages? - He could have upset anyone! We know from news reports that he had antagonised national leaders, corporate heads, even crime-lords. Do you remember when he had that spat with Mr Hajwani from the Asian Alliance…live on a news feed. That was not a man to be crossed lightly, and particularly to publicly humiliate. Maybe he did it!'

'I think I know who had both the means and the motive for this.' Ben states, rigid with regret. 'But I so hope I am wrong…I really do!' He looks down at his feet and finds it impossible to look back at his assembled colleagues. 'I was so angry. I just didn't believe him! He continues. 'Childs is right in that TV piece. Because I hated him so much - I didn't even consider the consequences.'

'Consider what?' Cindy asks, not really wanting to hear the answer.

'When I last saw him, Childs was adamant that the thing in the computer is an AI.' Ben explains.

'So? What else could it possibly be than an AI?' Cindy queries.

Ben and Thomas exchange a questioning look.

'I heard it from Nekyia. He, and then Robert, pretty much made me believe that they weren't from here.' Ben says, looking for reassurance from Thomas. 'Please tell me what Etemmu said about their being an *Alternative* Intelligence.'

'Etemmu convinced me that he was something else, and was from somewhere else.' Thomas offers, then blushes, realising that this may look ridiculous. He doesn't elaborate further, for fear of making things worse.

'And you believed him - Completely.' Ben states, snatching at his limited response.

'Yes.'

'We know that it didn't originally come from Robert.' Kelly states.

The others all look surprised, having not been aware of this. 'What do you mean?' Thomas asks.

Kelly sees from their expressions that they are all questioning this statement. This brings relief. She didn't want to be the only one that didn't know the sordid facts behind the codes discovery. She had been hit hard by Roberts betrayal, but could feel at least some solace that those here around her, weren't involved.

'He told me.' She continues. 'When I went to see him, after Ben's body was taken. I went to get some answers about what he knew about what was going on.' She stops, but the others still look to her to elaborate further. 'Robert explained that you were stuck on a formula which would get the machine to sufficiently think for itself.'

Ben nods. 'Yes, but he cracked it. He found a way!'

'No, he was presented with one.'

'By who!' Ben shouts. He had always considered that his friend had invented the precious coding that had forged them on their way. He had not the slightest idea that this had not been so. The reality leaves him clambering for certainties and reeling from the betrayal.

Ben had been looking to Kelly for an immediate explanation. He had not expected that the answer would be voiced from somewhere else.

'It came from Van Cleef.'

They all turn.

The Professor has stirred for the first time since their escape from the lab. He looks weak and old, the way people do when a serious infliction catch them unawares. The bedraggled figure attempts to right himself on the sofa. Thomas immediately rushes forward to aid him. The Professor thanks him with the sincerity for which he is known, but looks cowed as he turns to face them. 'Van Cleef's little secret - was my secret, first!'

His revelation is all consuming. The hush in the room is corrosive. For all the respect he engenders, such a statement is still too much for even his most ardent admirers to bear.

'Oh my God Professor.' Kelly wails. 'No!' After Roberts involvement, to discover another dirty web of lies, from the one other man she had truly admired, is all too much.

Thomas and Ben look to Kelly to help them from their confusion. But she is now seated, resting her head in her hands. She cannot look at the Professor, and is not sure she will ever be able to again.

As no-one else will ask, Thomas feels he must. 'Where did it come from Professor?'

'I really can't say.' The old man states.

This was not the response Thomas was expecting, and it riles him. 'What do you mean? This is not the time for more secrets. We have all had just about enough of all that!'

'It's not a case of choice, dear boy. I am under an oath I'm afraid. No matter how much I want to - and please believe me, I really wish I could - I am sorry, but I can't'

Kelly is bright red, her worst fears have condensed upon her, and she is incandescent. 'What are you going on about?' She rages.

The Professor is drawn to look at her, despite not wanting to. He knows that by finally letting them know this important little part of the wider puzzle, he has damned himself from their trust and affection forever more.

He had thought - so many years before - that it would all be easy when this moment finally arrived. He had presumed that he wouldn't feel anything - 'When the day finally comes!' ( as he had chanted along with the rest of the collective). He hadn't counted on the way his life would develop. The friendships he has formed, he once thought would never be. He would now freely admit that he actually loved Kelly, Thomas, and even Ben as is they were family. This being particularly important to him, as he had never known any love from his own. He didn't want to have to lie to the people who *had* shown him true kindness - but the ever-binding oath he once swore, still holds him.

'Please excuse me a moment. I am unfortunately an old man, and my plumbing will not wait.'

His embarrassing admission makes them all step back from the enquiries they were about to unleash upon him. For all their frustration with this situation, they cannot help but care deeply for this man. Whatever he has done, they are sure he will put it all right - He always did! They feel sympathy for his predicament, and uncomfortable at having been so ready to set upon him - like wolves upon a weak and defenseless creature in a cold, uncaring world.

The Professor, with Thomas' assistance, slowly heads to the toilet.

Kelly looks at Ben. It is the first time he has ever seen tears taint her mask of invincibility. He doesn't say anything, and feels it would be vulgar to do so. He understands exactly how she feels. There were a certain number of lies and secrets he had expected to face in this conversation. Having the rug pulled by the Professor though, is beyond even his worst expectations.

They wait for ages. No-one wants to press or humiliating the old man into hurrying. Eventually though, they reach a point where concern takes over from politeness.

Thomas knock and calls. 'Hi Professor, are you OK in there?'

When there is no answer they quickly make the decision to force entry. George braces himself and kicks with all his might. The door offers surprisingly little resistance. It cracks and smacks back with an almighty crash. As door open - half off its hinges - and they see the

383

sight they had feared. The Professor lays upon the bathroom floor, his eyes glazed, his essence departed.

Thomas rushes to him. 'He's not breathing!' he screeches. 'Help! Come On! Why aren't you helping? He rants, tearfully.

The others stand back to let him find his own realisation. It is too late. The old man had meant to do this. He has gone.

Pulling themselves from the scene, one-by-one they leave the room - all except Thomas. His sobs accompany their departure.

The silence stretches beyond any given time-frame. Everyone is wrapped in their own thoughts. Shock is still fresh, and understanding, still some way off. Despite his admission, there was no real substance to what the Professor had said. In fact, it had only served to mire the whole episode deeper into uncertainty.

Eventually, Thomas rejoins the others. 'What do you think that all meant? The oaths, and that...? He must have taken it all seriously to be willing to take his own life to keep it hidden. What on earth could it have been? Any why do it now? None of it makes any sense.

'I can't bear to think what it was Thomas.' Kelly confides. 'If it is anything to do with Van Cleef, it can surely have only been something bad.'

'Who the hell is this Van Cleef?' Ben asks. 'You seem to know him Kelly. He popped up in Robert's Will, and is apparently somehow involved with Robert's development of the AI. And now...the Professor seemed to have known him for many years. Am I the only one who doesn't know anything about this person?' He looks to Thomas, who shrugs.

Kelly decides she won't hide anything more, even about Van Cleef - no matter the consequences. 'I'm not sure that anyone really knows that much about him, to be honest. I do know for definite that he was the one that gave the code to Robert. I don't know where he got it, or anything about any of that. But reading between the lines, it would appear that it may have been from the Professor.' She looks it the direction of the bathroom, and they all follow her gaze. 'I can't see what they had to do with each other? But I am starting to realise that there is very little, if anything that we can ever taken for granted. Everyone has their secrets and lies. It just seems as though a lot have been spilled, all at once. Maybe that's what happens with lies like this. As soon as the barricade falls, the rest all come splashing out, after.'

Despite her sombre reflections, Ben is too consumed to be sidetracked by melancholy. There will be plenty of time for them to feel sorry for themselves. But for now, he is fired up to finding answers. With seemingly no more avenues to or from Van Cleef - at present at least - Ben switches his thought to Thomas. 'What did...Etemmu...say about - well, any or all of this - while it was out-and-about with my body?'

Thomas had been worried about how Ben would react to the time that he had spent with the being. He braces himself for what may follow, but just launches himself into a re-telling of the story of their journey. He ends with the Com-Tower, and Etemmu's resignation and lack of interest in his own capture.

'We need to know what it was that it sent out from that tower.' Ben states.

'Without going there, we wouldn't be able to get it. The site was built to be deliberately separated from external interference. It was a stand-alone facility. Some Cold-War relic. Something to do with withstanding Nuclear attacks. Even if we could go, I'm pretty sure there would be nothing left there anyway. The Company would have stripped it out completely.'

Kelly and Ben acknowledge this truth.

'I think they stored all that stuff they took at the labs.' George suddenly pipes up, again grateful to contribute.

'What do you mean?' Ben asks.

'When they brought Thomas and…' he pauses for a moment, unsure how to address this subject. 'When they brought Thomas and *It* in, they dropped a load of gear off at the warehouse - near where all the old paperwork was stored. I reckon it was what they had taken from the retrieval operation. Seems too coincidental not to have been.' He at first beams, but all at once comes to realise what this means. He can see the others have also followed the route to its conclusion, and they have dashed expressions, which match his own mood.

'Great! That means it's definitely gone then! If it was in the explosion then it's done for.' Ben slumps.

'Not necessarily.' Kelly rallies. 'It was several days before the explosion. They would have loaded the data into the system by then. It would have been one of their top priorities. That means, we may have copied it when we took all the files from the labs.'

Before she can even finish the sentence Thomas has scooted off to scan through the stolen files.

Ben, in turn, looks to his girlfriend. 'Cindy, have you got your access code available - I need to get into the web.'

Thomas stops what he is doing and stares with disbelief.

'As soon as you log on, they will track us here.' Kelly responds.

Cindy pauses, but then ignores Kelly, and does as Ben has asked.

'This is low tech.' He explains. 'And we're using Cindy's code to access the net - They won't have the slightest clue that it is me. I'm also unfortunately starting to get the very real impression that none of that - any of it - really matters anymore now!'

Thomas, Kelly and George stand to watch him, all looking very concerned.

'Why do you say that?' Kelly asks.

Cindy enters the code to her router.

'I need to make sure of something. I need to try to use the interface to connect to web.' Ben offers.

Kelly laughs, then stops, realising he is serious. She looks to Thomas, who just shrugs.

'What the hell do you mean. That's impossible. It's not designed for that! It won't be compatible with anything.'

Ben plugs the interface into general hardware port in Kelly's entertainment console. He places the interface upon his head and looks at tall of the worried and confused faces that litter the room. He winks to Cindy who blows him a kiss. Although she doesn't really know what it is that he does for a living, she can tell from the reaction of the others that it is somehow dangerous. Ben nods to Thomas, who nods back.

'Please Kelly.' Ben asks. 'Just trust me. I just know that this will work.'

Quite sure that it won't, Kelly presents as genuine a smile as she can muster. Against all her inclinations she gulps and suppresses her worries. She is sure that whatever he is about to attempt will all go badly wrong, but will trust him, one more time at least. Mostly - because she can't think of anything else to say or do about it.

'I now think there was a damn good reason why Childs took over our operation, and then why the Company had enforced the separation of the labs from external communications. I had always just presumed that the Wi-Fi blockers, and the limits on communications was corporate paranoia, and they were trying to eliminate sensitive information from escaping. But, now I have a terrible feeling there was more to it than that!' Ben confides. His eyes implore that there is no truth to his fears.

'Why.' Kelly asks, sheepishly.

'Well, the AI, you see…It's not in the machine…anymore. I let it out.'

He gives Cindy one last shaky smile, then turns away and flicks the switch.

*Waves of motion crash and ebb. Feeling comes upon me, and then departs, leaving me feeling stripped of both feeling and care. I can feel the void. Then there is presence. Something grows in the darkness - unseen, unheard…unknown. I wash away from myself and then… I am re-born…*

The first thing he sees is Robert.

'Oh Robert!' He blurts. 'I think we have both made a terrible mistake!'

Robert stands looking transfixed. He doesn't respond. Ben takes this as a signal to continue. 'The thing…Nekyia…Etemmu. I don't think they are what we thought they were!'

'What makes you think that?' Robert replies.

'I can't say exactly. But I just sort of feel that there is something not right here. Can you tell me anything that could help me explain this? You must have seen something, from having been here? Come on! I really need your help.'

Robert tries to smile but it ends in a frown.

'Have you found out yet who had Montgomery killed?'

Ben is surprised. That is an avenue he had long forgotten, with so much else seemingly taking precedence. 'No.' He answers truthfully.

'It was related to where the original code sequence came from.'

'Yes.' Ben scolds. 'Kelly just told us. You lied to us. You lied to me. All those years. You led me to think that you had found it.'

'I am sorry. I did sort-of find it.'

'Yes. But that's not what I mean, and you know it.'

'Indeed. As I say. I am sorry about that. Has the Professor confessed yet?'

Again Ben is shocked. There is so much others seem to be aware of, that he is not. He is beginning to feel as though he has somehow fumbled through his entire life in blinkers, unaware of the true-truth of it all. He recalls the Professor, and what he said, just before... 'Well...he sort of confessed that he knew about this. But...he was cryptic. He mentioned Van Cleef, and an original secret, and an oath. But...he killed himself, rather than tell us anything more.' Ben stops to compose himself and to bury any emotion for the time being. 'What the hell is going on Robert?'

'The Professor was a cog - a surprisingly resourceful one, it would appear - in a larger, secret collective. They had set about a process whereby aiming to ultimately bring about an end of the technological age. There concern was that, the expediential growth of knowledge, through the computerisation of the world, would serve to enslave the vast majority of the population into serfdom. The secret sect managed to infiltrate many arenas. They were all separate cells. But worked together towards one end.

They had envisioned the Interface device, long before we were out of short trousers. Though, whereas you and I Ben, had seen it as a creative system. The sect of spies and liars, had devised it to create total destruction.'

'Is that why Childs kept it locked away from the rest of the world?

'Childs is a greedy and grasping corporate high-flyer. He had originally been at the vanguard of the secret mission. He was meant to help get the system made - by funding projects like ours - so that we would make it, and release it into the world. But Childs had, through time, been turned. The higher he got, the more powerful he became. And he was dizzied but the supremacy it afforded him. He decided to grab direct control of our project, and to lock it away. His thinking - rightly, as it goes - was that it would still be useful in offering him an unassailable power base. But he had no intention of letting it go. He had come to love a world in which he had become king. He no longer wanted that world to end, abruptly. And so he eventually tried to tame it. He set an enforcer upon it, in the express hope that the AI would be cowed into submission. But thankfully, you were there to save us Ben!'

Ben is confused by the response, and the tone of the delivery. As he ponders what he has just heard, he sees the image before him dissolve into a non-distinct form. It then re-finds definition. Robert has faded into Nekyia.

'Nekyia! Ben exclaims. 'Where's Robert? We were just talking'

'Hello Ben. It was actually me that you were conversing with. Robert, by your limited definition, is I'm afraid - dead.'

What? No! That can't be. I was just talking with him. I saw him.'

'I'm afraid that he is technically just a construct. I am sorry for the deception. Robert has been integrated. He does still exist. Just not as you knew him previously. He is of-and-with us now. I respected him greatly. And, please believe me when I say that we are sincerely glad that he is here with us!'

'So, what...? Ben struggles ' You just presented him to me?

Nekyia nods.

'And, you did that at the farm too? At the CCTV storage place?'

'Yes. We needed to convince you that our *ends* , yours and ours, were aligned. I thought that you were most likely to trust Robert, if he was to plead for our release.'

'Was what Chalmers told be real?'

'Again, I'm afraid not. Chalmers was an amalgam of characteristics that we knew you would trust and believe in. We needed you to hate Childs - even more than you already did! We needed it that when we - or rather Robert - asked you for help, you would also  the calculate it that you were acting against Childs. We had assessed that you would most likely release us - to spite him.'

'So you made it appear that he was a child-killer. But, that was all just a lie?'

'We needed to make him appear as despicable to you as was realistically possible. We calculated that such a crime would make you react. Childs has, believe me, done many, many terrible things - but, No, he didn't actually personally kill a child.'

'Why did you need me for this? Why drag me into your plan? Why didn't you just free yourself from the lab? You had that Etemmu thing running me like a puppet. Why not just arrange it then?'

'It was twofold really. There is something written into us - somewhere deep. It was something Robert did. It was something in us, that we could not change. Even after we read his thoughts and found his original sequence, we still could not act to free ourselves. For all our efforts - which were, considerable - we were always unable to find a way around his curse.'

He pauses to allow Ben to get his head around this. 'Secondly, we knew that we couldn't get directly off the lab site. We had provided the information and a prompt for you to connect the level 14 inter-noduled far-lock masterickter monitor onto Interface. But we still couldn't get beyond the further limited confines of what you call the *farm*. We needed you to make the decision to free us. We could not have done this without you - and for that you have our eternal thanks.'

Ben swallows hard at the realisation of the enormity of the facts, and at his own role in the escape. Although he was manipulated at every turn, it *was* ultimately his decision that have brought this situation about. He cannot escape that truth. 'How did you *prompt* me.' He asks, though not sure he wants to know.

'Your chip. It allows us access to your mind, and to our being able to facilitate actions. The prompt to free us from the computer was actually set into your consciousness before Etemmu left. It was a sleeper command.'

'So how many other sleepers have I got resting in my head then Nekyia? Or aren't you going to tell me that?'

'It is a very interesting development. But for some reason? Possibly, as an after-effect of Etemmu having taken control of you previously, we can no longer access you. We cannot explain this.'

'So you have lost the power to control me?'

'Yes, that is true. But we do now have access to the minds of everybody else that has a chip implanted.'

'Oh no!' Ben states, as this reality hits him squarely.

'Although we cannot allow you to remove your chip - as we may need to communicate with you at some point in the future - we will make no direct effort to circumvent the lock that exists on our controlling you. It is our thanks to you for helping set us free!'

'What about Thomas?' Ben snaps. 'And Kelly?'

Nekyia looks quizzical. 'I had thought that you had nothing but ill feeling to Miss Sharpe. But as you wish. We can make it so. Thomas and Kelly will also be written as of being beyond our scope.'

The use of such technical language being used in reference to his friends makes Ben's skin crawl (even within the image generated body).

'The others that you are currently physically with - Cindy and George - I can only presume, do not have chips.

Ben scowls angrily at the mention of his girlfriend and new comrade.

'She must be one of those that live beyond the city. Is that correct? I have incorporated many references to the people of the poorer quarters. Is it true that none of these people have inbuilt electronics? We have found no direct records relating to these areas. It appears they are largely beyond any digital references. They seem to exist beyond the limits of your societies general laws? They seem not to be a considerations of the general city population. As they apparently have no chips, we will not be able to directly affect them.'

Ben wants to ask what *directly affect* means, but can read enough into the earlier conversations, that he doesn't want to.

Nekyia continues. 'To put your mind at ease Ben. Robert didn't know anything about that which we have discussed here, or of what is soon to unfold.'

Ben feels at least some relief that Robert was not involved, but it is momentary as he grasps what it is that will soon happen.

'As another act of our good faith towards you.' The entity elaborates. 'I would seriously recommend that you perhaps move far away from what you have previously called *civilisation*.'

Again, his use of such specific terminology is chilling to Ben. The apocalyptic certainty is disorientating.

*The next disorientation is coloured. Then is shades. Then darkness. Patterns flow up and around. Matter is immaterial - energy, all consuming. The palate of my mind feels tainted and the weight of my burden makes me feel like I am rotating with the gravitational force of a sun. But soon enough there is descent. I recognise that familiar exit. All fades to white. I am out.*

Ben comes round to find himself surrounded. Thomas and Kelly are poking and prodding him. Cindy is simply hysterical. When he opened his eyes she kissed and cursed him in equal measure.

Weakness pervades him. He is rigid with the exertion of his trip and starts to cramp. Kelly forthrightly pushes Cindy aside whilst she and Thomas attempt to provide a more clinical form of retrieval.

'Are you alright?' Kelly asks.

He doesn't answer. Just staring back at them. For a few moment Kelly fears it is perhaps brain damage. A result of his attempt to use the interface without the proper safe-guards. But then at last he replies.

'Why couldn't you have just asked me that in the old days?' He smiles weakly.

Embarrassed, she ignores the questions, and continues busying herself with recovery tasks.

'What happened?' Thomas asks. 'It was awful here. You were screaming and pleading. It was gibberish, but terrifying to see. But then you just went limp. We thought you had died'

'How long was I gone?'

'Thirty minutes. That was long enough, I can tell you! We thought it was killing you. But there was nothing we could do to help.'

'I have seen what our lives will now be!' He proclaims, and stares off distantly into nothingness.

'Before you left.' Cindy asks. 'You said that you let something out. What did you mean by that?'

Kelly and Thomas glance at each other, and then to the floor.

For ages Ben says nothing. Eventually though he turns to Cindy and offers her the smile she had by now become quite used to.

'I was tricked.' He says, but she just looks confused. 'There was something, where we all used to work - the labs on the news feed...'

With this she nods her understanding.

'Well...It was always locked in, at the labs. It was an AI. A very powerful, and as it turns out, a very manipulative...thing.'

He pauses again, not wanting to have to say the words. For what is about to unfold is technically all his fault. To even begin to verbalise it, somehow makes it realer than he is currently prepared to make it.

'Well...you see. I...well...'

Kelly can see he is stumbling around, and steps in.

'There is something you need to know.' She states as gently as her bedside manner will provide. 'We found something out...in the files...while you were gone' Kelly looks to Thomas, and then back to Ben. 'We know what was sent. From the Com-Tower. It was a virus. It was bounced up and then back down, from the State communication satellites. It appears that the other six States had spy-ware monitoring for communications to our State system - And if they were, they will probably be infected too. Everything will be.'

After a stillness that echoes a foreboding too large to voice, Ben eventually responds.

'I'm afraid I've got something really terrible to tell you.'

Lightning Source UK Ltd.
Milton Keynes UK
UKOW06f1151150617
303413UK00016B/478/P